Yomping Outside

To Margaret

Yomping Outside

Enjoy

[signature]

By David Zelder

First Published in Great Britain in 2011 By Quizás Books, Lincoln
Further Info: www.davidzelder.co.uk

This novel is a work of fiction. Characters, names and events are products of the author's imagination. With the exception of historical figures in the public domain, any similarity to actual events, locales, or persons, living or dead, is purely coincidental.

A CIP Catalogue of this book is available from the British Library.

ISBN 978-0-9569732-0-7

Cover Design by Avalon Graphics

www.avalongraphics.org

Prepared and printed in Great Britain by CPI Group (UK) Ltd, Croydon, CR0 4YY

I dedicate this work to my lovely wife Pauline.
She has been my inspiration and my rock
for the past 20 years.

Author's Note

Since 1664 the Royal Marines have been providing a highly effective flexible fighting force as a vital part of Britain's armed forces. Initially named the Duke of Albany's Maritime Regiment of Foot, they now continue in the traditions of the Second World War Commandos and provide highly skilled amphibious troops, expert in expeditionary and manoeuvre warfare, and capable of generating strategic effect in a multitude of theatres around the globe.

Whether it was in the D-Day landings, the Malayan Emergency, Korea, Suez, Cyprus, Northern Ireland, the Balkans or leading the recapture of the Falkland Islands, the Corps has never been far from the front line, proud of their reputation for being first in and last out.

This remarkable organisation sustains the commando ethos, preserving the very highest standards in all it does, and instilling the commando qualities of unselfishness, cheerfulness under adversity, determination and courage in all its members – no surprise then that this small corps provides around 40% of the United Kingdom's Special Forces.

Service in Afghanistan and Iraq has brought particular challenges. The Royal Marines have *pro rata* sustained two and a half times as many battlefield fatalities and injuries in Helmand province than any other organisation in defence, principally because they have been committed to operations in Afghanistan and more consistently than any other.

As a result of this the Trustees of the Royal Marines Charitable Trust Fund (RMCTF) are running a fund raising campaign to raise £6,000,000 by the Corp's 350th anniversary in 2014. This is to ensure that the RMCTF can support its beneficiaries long term and particularly as those with service limiting injuries transition to life outside the Royal Marines. The RMCTF has among the widest purposes of any service charity, supporting as it does serving and retired Royal Marines and their dependants.

That is why the author is supporting the RMCTF with £1 from each copy of this novel sold going to that worthwhile charity.

Thank you for buying this novel and for helping to achieve the target.

For additional information and to make further donations please go to:-

www.rmctf.org.uk

CHAPTER 1

What to do outside

It was gone 11.15 on a Wednesday night so the Liverpool streets were relatively quiet, apart from the siren incessantly blaring on its way to some incident or other and the gentle pitter-patter of rain drops on the pavement.

Being October, the moon's weak glow, softly diffused through the clouds, combined with the rain to create a canopy above me which now assumed the colour of frosted steel.

Already one or two shops had started to put Christmas displays in their windows. As I padded softly past the garish signs screaming out their yuletide bargains, I wondered what the hell I'd be doing at Christmas.

I'd been on the outside for six months now and really needed to decide what I wanted to do with the rest of my life. I was almost thirty eight years old, quite a good looking guy, with neatly cropped dark red hair, a level of fitness and a body that, although covered in battle scars, most Premiership footballers would die for. I'd a bunch of money in the bank but no identifiable future and no woman in my life.

I smiled to myself as I saw the armed forces recruitment office opposite The Liverpool Hotel on James Street. The adverts in its window were offering a life of excitement, a good career, first class training and excellent rates of pay. I thought back to the time when I first walked through the door of a similar office in Bristol nineteen years ago as an impressionable, and completely lost, eighteen year old.

I'd been pulled off the rugby pitch where I was playing in a County trial game to be told by the police that my parents had both died in an accident on the M4 motorway. After the funeral and the inquest I realised how desperately alone I was. As an only child, living in a small but neat terraced house in the Bristol suburbs I'd been planning to go to Liverpool John Moores University to study for a BSc in Sport Science but then my world had collapsed around me.

What to do next had troubled me for some weeks after the funeral. I couldn't face my friends; I'd no close relatives and spent hours walking the streets in Bristol, trying to clear my head. With no-one to advise me I'd suddenly lost the desire to go to University.

What I needed was something in my life that would be all consuming and enable me to assuage the guilt I felt about losing my parents.

I felt responsible for their deaths as they were on the way to watch me take part in the trials when the accident happened. I was thought to be a good player and my parents were proud of me. There was even a chance I might've been good enough to have joined Bristol or Bath as a professional, after university.

One Thursday afternoon I crossed the road from Bristol University and was wandering aimlessly down Colston Avenue when I saw a giant photo of some guys playing rugby in the window of the forces recruitment office. Next to it was an even larger photo of a landing craft delivering its cargo of thirty five Green Berets on to some foreign beach in full combat mode.

At that moment I thought to myself that I'd have nothing to lose, playing rugby and maybe seeing some action around the world, whilst also getting paid for it.

Almost subconsciously I walked inside and, after chatting with a pushy careers adviser, I completed the short questionnaire and then booked an appointment for the four part written test. After successfully passing that part, and then sailing through the interview, all that remained was the fitness test. This required me to run 2.4 km in less than twelve minutes and twenty seconds, which for a man with my sporting background and fitness training, was a doddle.

After receiving my join-up papers I began to look forward to starting my new life, training to be a Royal Marine. I was successful in passing the Potential Royal Marines Course and very shortly was on my way to Commando Training Centre Royal Marines (CTCRM) at Lympstone in Devon, with a steely and dogged determination to forge a career for myself.

I'd managed to sell my parents' Bristol home complete with all its furniture for a tidy six figure sum and, for the first time in my life had a healthy bank balance and a future career to look forward to.

The next nine months were tough and very challenging and I learned a great deal about myself as I moved inexorably towards my goal of being awarded the coveted Green Beret.

I began to realise that most of my friends on the outside were very shallow and, as is often the case nowadays, very materialistic. The friendships which I forged during my nine months' training at CTCRM were very different. We looked out for each other, we worked closely together, and in the many armed conflicts in which we subsequently became involved, we were totally dependent on each other just to stay alive. You don't get that on Civvy Street, where more often than not it's every man for himself and stuff the rest.

Now here I was on James Street in Liverpool passing another recruitment office, nineteen years older, wiser, much fitter and satisfied with my career as a Royal Marine, but what the hell was I going to do now?

I'd come to Liverpool for a break and to see where I might have been living for over three years if I'd actually gone to University. What was I going to do with the rest of my life? I'd come here also to clear my head and give myself some thinking time.

I quickly left the recruitment window behind and decided to walk on in the direction of the waterfront by the great River Mersey before going back to my hotel.

As I walked slowly and easily towards the Cunard Building I reached the bottom end of Water Street, and stopped to look up in awe at the Royal Liver Building. The huge clocks showed it was 11.30 as the rain continued to beat down on the copper statues of Liver Birds that stood proudly on top of the two towers. The bodies of both birds had turned duck egg green in the near one hundred years that they'd proudly guarded the entrance to the mighty ferry terminal.

As I admired the beauty of the building with its hundreds of windows, I thought wryly to myself that there must be plenty of profit in the insurance industry to afford such an imposing headquarters.

I was woken from my reverie by the sound of a high revving car engine and the tortured squealing of tyres coming down St Nicholas Place at a fair rate of knots. The car slewed to a halt about 100 metres in front of me and its two front doors swung open violently, almost before the BMW convertible had come to a stop. My years of training and many tours involving active armed combat, plus my natural instincts, warned me this was trouble.

The two men who jumped out of the front seats had their backs to me as I moved closer, keeping in the shadows. One of them opened the car's rear nearside door and shouted a few harsh words in a guttural Eastern European tongue and heaved something out of the back of the car on to the softly lit road.

I peered through the gloom, straining my eyes to penetrate the swirling mist that was only just dimly lit by the muted autumn moon. Eventually I was just able to make out that they'd dumped a slightly built young woman who was now on her knees, sobbing loudly on the road. One of them immediately smashed the girl in the face with his clenched fist, causing her to fall screaming to the ground. They then both started kicking her and shouting obscenities in phrases I recognised from my time in Kosovo. The thugs were obviously Serbians.

I could see that each time the girl tried to get up the two scum-bags knocked her back down. Even in the poor light I noticed blood starting to trickle down her face.

I covered the last couple of metres to their car in an instant and quickly pushed my hand hard on the horn. The noise had the desired effect and the two thugs stopped attacking the girl and looked in my direction. As I shouted for them to leave her alone I stood by the driver's door. The first man ran at me screaming insults and threats, with his head down in an angry and violent charge.

You learn in the Royal Marines that surprise is the first element of attack so I waited until the man was level with the front wheel then I slammed the car door open as hard as I could. The attacker had no chance and collapsed unconscious with a broken nose and his face covered in blood. One down, one to go, so far so good.

The second assailant was now almost upon me and as he launched his attack he flashed an eight inch knife.

"Stupid bastard", I muttered, that was his first mistake. My size ten shoe, followed by twelve stone of muscle, hit his wrist on the underside and the knife went flying over the bonnet of the car. He then reached into his pocket to pull his gun out, and that was his second mistake. A second kick fractured his knee cap and he collapsed in a crumpled heap screaming in pain.

I hadn't spent eighteen years in the best armed service in the world without learning how to look after myself far better than most men can. I kicked away the knife and in an instant scooped down to pick the gun up off the pavement and threw it on the back seat of their car, before knocking the second man out cold to stop him screaming. I then relieved both men of their mobile phones, I didn't want them calling in their mates.

I quickly picked up the girl and put her in the front seat of the car and drove off into the night. No point in leaving these two rat bags the means of chasing after me.

The girl was fully conscious but in great pain. As I drove carefully down Strand Street I was thinking I had to get away from the city centre and then dispose of the car, as its owners would doubtless be looking for it. I headed for my own car parked near the budget hotel by Sefton Park where I'd spent the last week.

Driving quietly and purposefully, trying not to draw any attention to the vehicle, I looked across at the girl. She was slim and quite pretty with long black hair, dark brown eyes and skin that was slightly sallow. I asked her softly if she spoke English. She nodded so I told her to put on her safety belt.

She then thanked me in an accent that was quite pronounced and I figured might be from one of the Balkan States. I asked her what her name was and where she was from. She looked nervously across at me, and told me her name was Elena Borovic and she was from Montenegro.

I told her not to worry and said she was safe now. I drove carefully past Queens Dock and glanced at her. She smiled through the pain and nodded at me.

I cursed as I heard a siren and saw the blue flashing lights in the rear view mirror, the road was clear ahead of me and my heart began to pound as the noise got louder. Then I smiled in relief as the vehicle overtook me and turned out to be an ambulance. A couple of hundred yards on, it turned left towards Toxteth, so I carried on in the now pouring rain, formulating in my mind what I should do next.

Turning down towards the recreation ground I eventually reached Ullet Road and stopped some way short of Croxteth Drive where my brand new Seat Ibiza Sport Rider was parked. My training had taught me not to lead any possible pursuer directly to my own position.

I was considered to be smart as well as tough, which were perfect attributes for a long and distinguished career as a Royal Marine Commando. While driving from The Liver Building, I had worked out that the BMW was a liability, with a gun on the back seat, my prints all over the car and with Serbian blood all over the driver's door, though some of that would have been washed off by the rain. So I had to get rid of it and cover my tracks.

As I parked up I looked across at Elena whose face was now puffed up from the beating and covered in blood. She was wearing a pale citrus smock top with tight black jeans and black high heeled shoes. I thought at least she's wearing typical clobber for a divs, not likely to arouse any suspicion and the blood from her face hadn't got on to her clothes yet.

I got out of the car and looked round in all directions. As it was now past midnight and the rain was coming down hard, the street was deserted, thank God.

I jumped back into the driver's seat and softly explained to Elena that I was just going round the corner to fetch her a hooded coat from my own car. I told her to stay put and not to make a sound, whispering that I'd be back in a minute then we could get away from Liverpool in my car and I could move her to somewhere safe.

She gave me a painful smile and nodded in agreement, so I slipped out of the BMW again and moved swiftly and silently to where my car was parked. I was back with Elena in a couple of minutes with my hooded jacket, not noticing as I opened the driver's door that the gun was no longer on the back seat.

"Right, young lady, let's have a look at you. Is there anything broken, do you think?"

"No, I think I've some cuts on my face and bruises on my ribs and back. I'll be OK, though. What's your name and why are you doing this?"

"Nathan Sawyer and I thought you needed a bit of help," I said playfully. She smiled ruefully, wincing at the pain from her face and holding her upper body gingerly.

"OK we're going to get in to my car now, which is just round the corner. Are you OK to walk?"

"Yes, I think so."

"Right, Elena, put my coat on and pull the hood over your face, just in case anybody is looking out of their window and thinks I've beaten you up!!"

Again she smiled and heaved her bruised body into my well worn green wax jacket and pulled the hood right over her bloodied face. I smiled back at her reassuringly and locked the BMW, then we hurried in silence to my car; I de-activated the central locking and held the passenger door open for her to slide in.

"Just wait a couple of minutes, my hotel is just round the corner, I'll get a few things then we can be away and get you to safety. If anyone comes near you, use the horn. I'll lock the doors, so don't worry."

In a flash I let myself into my hotel using the night key then hurried quietly up to my room. There was nobody around to bother me. Fortunately the only other residents usually went to bed early so, after a hard day cooking and cleaning up, the owners did likewise.

I quickly packed my things, took a clean face flannel from the towel rail and soaked it under the cold water tap, dropping it into the toilet bag at the top of my holdall. Locking the room behind me I moved like a ghost down the back stairs towards the bar. Taking a bottle of Scotch and a bottle of brandy off the shelf I slipped them into my bag, along with a box of matches then put my room keys on the counter and wrote a brief note.

"Room fifteen, had to leave early, keys are here along with £40 for a bottle of whisky and of brandy, thanks."

I figured that would be alright with the pleasant young couple who owned the place. I'd paid them in advance for the room a week ago. Closing the front door, I looked around outside and listened intently before moving off, thankful that all I could hear was the rain splashing down relentlessly on the deserted pavements.

I walked round the block towards the convertible. After checking that I was not being watched I quickly opened the back door and emptied the two spirits bottles inside, saving a few ounces for the bonnet. Half a dozen matches later it was well alight so I ran back hard to my car.

I unlocked the door and slid in beside Elena, telling her to quickly take my bag as I started up the engine. As I drove away I was able to see the orange glow from the BMW in the rear mirror. What I didn't know until months later was the person who was looking out from behind their bedroom curtains near where I'd parked could also see what was going on.

As we crossed Smithdown Road I heard the explosion as the petrol tank blew. I thought to myself that they couldn't trace it back to me now, smiled grimly and wondered what the hell I had got myself into. The girl looked across to me as she realised what I'd done.

"You don't take any chances, do you?" she whispered hoarsely with a touch of admiration in her voice.

"Years of training. If you look in the top of my bag, there's a clean, wet face flannel. You could do with getting the blood off your face. I'll concentrate on getting us out of Liverpool safely and without attracting any attention."

"OK, but where can we go?"

"Don't worry, we'll get on to the motorway in five minutes and then we'll be safe, I've a cottage in the Lake District, we can go there and lay low for a few days."

I figured her attackers wouldn't be too happy that I'd snatched her away from them, so I needed to put mileage between myself and the city of Liverpool in short order.

A couple of minutes later I joined the M62 at Junction 5 and headed eastwards, cursing the spray that the lorries were throwing up in front of me. Fortunately after just a few more miles the rain eased off and we soon reached the junction with the M6 where we turned off and sped off northwards towards Preston, en route to my cottage in The Lake District.

CHAPTER 2

Elena's story

The cold wet flannel had been put to good use and Elena had managed to get most of the dried blood off her face. After a while I stopped briefly at Charnock Richard Motorway Services to grab two cups of steaming hot coffee and a can of ice cold cola.

"Elena, wrap this coke can in the flannel then hold it against the swellings on your face. It'll take the pain away and reduce the inflammation, and here's some nice warm coffee to calm your nerves."

Weals of burgundy, tinged with violet, were beginning to appear under her eyes and on her cheeks, so hopefully my improvised ice pack would help control the damage, which looked to me like it was only superficial. Fingers crossed, then.

As we continued our journey and put some miles between us and our slight altercation in Liverpool, I gently persuaded Elena to tell me why the two scran bags had been attacking her.

She spent the next hour tearfully telling me her story. As each trauma came out in graphic detail she would stop and compose herself, slowly sipping her coffee as she struggled with her emotions.

Quite often the memories were too much and she would have to pause before continuing. At one point, when she broke down completely, I reached over and squeezed her arm gently and smiled at her, reassuring her she was safe now.

She told me she was born in 1986 near Podgorica, the capital of Montenegro, an only child, born to kind and loving parents, both professional people, who each earned a reasonable living as a lawyer and accountant.

Following the disintegration of Yugoslavia in the early nineteen nineties and the subsequent violent conflict that ensued, the UN imposed sanctions on Montenegro and Serbia. The hardship that followed throughout all the troubled Balkan States persuaded Milo Borovic to move his family to Croatia in 1992 to escape both the economic problems they were experiencing in Montenegro and the violent excesses being meted out to non-Serbs.

The family settled in the beautiful old coastal city of Dubrovnik with Elena gaining a place in a good State primary school where she quickly made many friends and became proficient in speaking both Croatian and English.

She proved to be a first class pupil over the next twelve years with her favourite subjects being history, literature and English Language. She worked hard and enjoyed a happy and settled home life, as far as was possible in a region being torn apart by genocide, treachery and ethnic cleansing on a level that was unheard of in Europe since the Second World War.

Her parents tried hard to keep her mind away from the fact she was living through such unsettling times by giving her a stable and loving home environment that helped settle her down to a new life in her adopted country.

Elena adapted quickly and had an aptitude for absorbing knowledge that gave her a great head start in life.

Elena's father, Milo, continued working as a lawyer, having taken a partnership in a small commercial law firm in Dubrovnik. His wife, Darinka, with the blessing of her husband, had become involved with the Montenegrin freedom movement in her native land.

She was an articulate and passionate activist who knew how to communicate and she habitually hit the headlines in the press on both sides of the nationalist debate. Usually her speeches and rallies drew wide audiences, much to the extreme annoyance of the nationalist Serbs.

Her efforts intensified after the proposal by the President and Prime Minister that Serbia and Montenegro should recognise each other as an independent nation. This was strongly opposed by the Serbs. They saw it as a violation of the Accord signed between them in March 2002 and which then led to the 'State Union' of Serbia and Montenegro being formed in February 2003.

Darinka was a proud Montenegrin and tirelessly campaigned for independence from Serbia, organising rallies, marches and giving speeches on a regular basis.

She frequently drove from the family apartment they rented in Dubrovnik and across the border back to her homeland. Milo insisted she should never travel alone, fearing for her safety as a high profile champion of the Montenegrin cause. Quite often he would accompany his delightful wife to the marches and rallies.

When he wasn't able to do so he had a couple of young male Croatian friends, who were happy to do the honours as their families had suffered terribly at the hands of the Serbs during the break up of Yugoslavia.

In February 2006 Darinka set off on a three day drive from Dubrovnik to Montenegro. She was to give a keynote address to nationalist supporters in the city of Cetinje 30 km south west of the present capital of Montenegro, Podgorica. Until 1945 Cetinje had itself been the Montenegrin capital.

For this trip she had as her travelling companion Vjekoslav Vuletić a thirty year old who worked as a builder in Dubrovnik and whose father was murdered in Srebrenica and whose mother perished in the Serbian siege of Sarajevo, the family having moved to Serbia to find work in the early nineteen eighties.

By European standards Cetinje is a small town, with a population of under 20,000, but for Montenegrins it's the cultural and spiritual centre of the country. Darinka had chosen the location for her rally carefully, the courtyard in front of the National Museum of Montenegro.

This beautiful red brick building was the former Palace of King Nicholas I who ruled the country until 1918 and it formed part of the 'beating heart' of this proud nation.

The three day drive to Cetinje was uneventful for Darinka and Vjekoslav as they took their overnight stops with supporters of the Montenegrin independence cause.

The Karst Plain on which Cetinje stands was lit by the weak golden hue of the late winter sun which helped swell the attendance at the rally to a respectable twelve hundred or so.

As the sun's rays glimmered through the bare branches of the majestic deciduous trees in the Museum's square, Darinka gave a rousing and passionate speech.

Elena's mother's standpoint was widely, but quietly, echoed throughout her homeland, that Montenegro's independence from Serbia should be ratified without further delay.

She implored her audience to vote for independence in the May 2006 referendum and begged them to persuade their friends, relatives and everyone they knew to do the same.

As the crowd roared their approval, Darinka warmed to her cause, but kept casting worried glances at the half a dozen dark suited men at the rear of the courtyard, hiding behind cheap dark glasses and gazing impassively at the proceedings. After around twenty minutes they left, so she relaxed a little and carried on rallying her supporters for a further half an hour.

Leaving the square with cheers ringing in her ears, she was joined by her young travelling companion who had been watching her excitedly from the side of the beautiful quadrangle. After a simple but satisfying meal with the rally's organisers, the two of them set off on the journey back to Dubrovnik.

Elena went on to say, amid deep sobbing, that her mother was destined never to return to Dubrovnik. The Montenegrin Police found her bullet riddled vehicle about 10 km from Cetinje, in the shadow of Mount Lovćen.

The bodies of Darinka Borovic and Vjekoslav Vuletić lay at grotesque angles inside the vehicle, the bursts of automatic weapons having killed them both instantly.

The police were unable to find the culprits, as the only clues at the scene were a broken pair of cheap sunglasses lying beside Darinka's car and black tyre marks on the road at right angles to the direction of travel, indicating an ambush. It would seem that the assassins' vehicle had pulled across the road in front of Darinka's car, forcing them to stop. Then the Serbian gunmen had opened fire, and fled into the night.

In 2004 Elena had won a place at Croatia's top University, Zagreb, where she entered the Law Faculty and, to the delight of her father was awarded her Law Degree in August 2007. She had to take an enforced break of two weeks when her mother was murdered and then returned to Croatia where she made a vow to herself that she would carry on with her studies in her mother's memory.

Milo had decided that he wanted to go back to Montenegro to try and carry on the good work for which his sadly missed Darinka, in the name of their country, had made the ultimate sacrifice.

Eventually he moved to the ancient port of Kotor on the Adriatic Coast during Elena's last year as an undergraduate and picked up his career as a lawyer again. After a few months he also started putting together the strands of a Montenegrin charity to help families who'd been struggling in the conflict that had beset the Balkans since the early nineties.

Mr Borovic proudly attended his daughter's graduation in Zagreb and after a celebratory lunch together he left her so she could spend a couple of days with her graduate friends. He headed off back to Kotor with mixed emotions. Immensely satisfied and proud that Elena followed him in studying Law, but, in equal measure he was filled with huge melancholy that Darinka was not there with him to witness their daughter's academic success.

Two days later, Elena set off in the hire car her father had organised for her to drive from Zagreb to Belgrade. She'd booked a flight to take her to Tivat airport which was only 5 km from Kotor, where her father lived. She was joined on her journey as far as Belgrade by her University room mate, Lucija Babić, an attractive Croatian girl who'd managed to fix herself up with a job in the Legal Department in the Town Hall in Belgrade.

They shared the driving to Belgrade Airport where Lucija's parents were to collect her and then Elena was to catch her flight to Tivat. After a tiring journey, they drove into the car park to return the rental car. They were in plenty of time for Elena's flight to Tivat so made their way through the car park to the coffee shop in Terminal One where they'd arranged to meet Mr and Mrs Babić.

As they reached the edge of the car park and stepped on to the pedestrian crossing a large car with blacked out windows pulled in front of them. Two men jumped out and bundled the startled girls into the back of the car. The men picked up the suitcases the two travellers had dropped, quickly slung them in the boot and then drove away from the airport, tyres screeching.

One of the abductors leaned over into the back of the car and shouted at them in Serbian to stop screaming. Both girls tried to open the doors but the kidnappers had put the child locks on, so there was no escape. As the car got clear of the airport and on to the main road it pulled into a lay-by.

The Serbs leaned over into the rear seats and grabbed Elena and Lucija roughly by their throats. One of them had a handgun which he waved menacingly at the girls causing them to recoil even more in abject terror. Then his companion, foaming at the mouth, pulled a chloroform pad from his pocket and held it first over the nose of the Croatian girl, then that of Elena.

The unfortunate girls never saw their kidnappers again. When they regained consciousness they found they were lying on filthy mattresses in the back of a large truck, which appeared to be travelling at a rapid pace, judging by the way they were being thrown about.

As they looked around, with terror in their hearts and straining their eyes in the dark interior, they could see they were with ten other girls of about the same age. As they began to question their fellow travellers, it transpired they all had suffered a similar fate and had no idea why they were there or what lay in store.

Elena went on to tell me her unwilling travelling companions were a mixture of ethnic backgrounds, but all from Eastern Europe, Bosnians, Croatians and Macedonians, plus Elena as the sole Montenegrin. They were all under twenty five and were slim and attractive. By the absence of any Serbs amongst the captive girls, Elena and Lucija took the view that their abductors were Serbian nationals.

They found their suitcases in the corner of the truck, stacked with a few others but their mobile phones had been taken away. Not all the girls had suitcases, so presumably some of the young prisoners had been snatched while going about their daily business.

The journey seemed to take a number of days and the truck regularly stopped for fuel. A couple of times each day their captors would open one of the rear doors. One of them would stand there on guard with a semi-automatic gun pointing at the young women and his companion would throw in water bottles and simple food such as bread, cheese and salami. The bewildered captives had to make do with a portable caravan toilet in the corner of the truck during their nightmare journey. Their captors emptied this occasionally.

Quite a few times over the next few days the truck would stop at what Elena surmised to be border crossings and they could hear muffled conversations. As the prisoners caught odd snatches of the discussions they deduced that money was changing hands at frontiers, so that the truck wouldn't be searched.

Whoever had set up this kidnap had obviously planned it well and had clearly done it before.

Eventually, their rolling prison stopped for around an hour and there was much shouting and clanking of machinery outside.

In due course the lorry moved forward for a few minutes, but very slowly as if it was manoeuvring into a tight space, then the sharp hiss of its air brakes signalled it had halted.

The girls all looked at each other with fear and apprehension wondering what fate held in store for them now. The truck stayed locked and after another hour it then began gently swaying and the girls guessed they were now on board a boat.

They were on the ocean for several more days before the ship docked and the driver took his human cargo back on the road again. Elena told me, in a voice choking with emotion, that they'd no idea where they were, where they were heading, or why they'd been kidnapped.

Within the next forty eight hours they were to find out.

After the truck left the ship, the next day and a half followed a very similar pattern of travelling by road and occasionally stopping for fuel; with the exception that there didn't seem to be any border crossings, so Elena guessed they must have been travelling in just one country.

Eventually their nightmare journey drew to a close and the doors were flung open at the rear. Elena, Lucija and their fellow captives blinked uncomfortably as their eyes were violently assaulted by the amber street lights that flooded in, a complete contrast to the virtual darkness they had all suffered since their capture.

Their arrival was in the middle of the night and they were herded out of the truck in a rough and very brusque manner by four men speaking in, what to Elena and Lucija especially, was a strange English accent, to the other girls it was just a foreign language, although some of them did understand a little English.

As they gazed around and their eyes became accustomed to the garish street lights, they found they were in a deserted back street with several oldish but grandiose-looking three storey buildings around them.

They were pushed through a rear entrance into a long corridor which was resplendent with a deep pile burgundy carpet. As they huddled together in fear, they saw they were in luxurious surroundings but were quickly ushered up the magnificent staircase and each of them put into a room, just like a quality hotel suite.

As she was pushed through the door of the room Elena was told, in English, to get showered and changed.

She nervously looked round her and was amazed to see it was expensively furnished. There was a three seater taupe sofa in soft leather along with matching armchairs, a large flat screen HD TV on the wall and a walnut veneered coffee table inlaid with mahogany marquetry work. She opened the double doors of the cream wardrobe which was trimmed with antiqued gold beading and was filled with a sumptuous array of brand new quality clothes.

The truffle coloured curtains were closed and were fashioned from deep pile velvet with gold tassels and matching tie backs. Elena pulled one of them back to look out of the window. Her heart missed a beat when she saw steel bars had been fitted across the inside of the window in what, although she didn't know it at the time, was to be her prison for the next year or so.

She could see out of the window that the building looked on to a non-descript street and was part of a crescent of similar looking buildings.

Mentally and physically tired, Elena felt disgustingly filthy after many days cooped up in a truck with only the barest and most rudimentary sanitary facilities. So, opening the bathroom door she quickly stripped off, ready to go into the shower.

She was unaware that her every move was being watched on the CCTV pinhole camera hidden behind the ornately framed print on the wall behind the sofa. It was of the painting 'Nevermore' by the French Post-Impressionist artist Paul Gauguin. The print turned out to be hauntingly prophetic. The young Polynesian girl lying naked on the sofa appeared to be wondering about the mystery of her life. Behind her is a raven, perched by the window, possibly symbolising the 'bird of death' from the poem 'The Raven' by Edgar Allan Poe.

There was a further camera behind the mirror in the bathroom, which was now transmitting live pictures to the evil mixture of Serbians, Albanians and Englishmen who were her captors.

The CCTV pictures of the young Montenegrin showed her standing forlornly under the gold plated power shower, sobbing her heart out and arching her firm and beautiful body to get the stiffness out of her joints after the nightmare journey from Belgrade.

As she lathered herself with the delicately fragrant shower gel, Elena watched the bubbles disappearing down the plughole, lost in thought and with her mind on trying to figure out where this weird and frightening situation was going to take her.

She dried her painful body slowly and went back into the bedroom, wrapped in the soft fleecy robe which was hanging behind the bathroom door. She'd just sunk on to the edge of the bed, wondering what to do next when the door opened and one of the four men who'd met them at the truck came in and brusquely told her to get dressed and come downstairs.

As we reached this point in Elena's story, I glanced across at her as we moved on swiftly up the M6 Motorway. We were now approaching the Service Area at Burton-in-Kendal and she started sobbing again but quickly regained her composure as if telling me her story had been cathartic and was helping to exorcise her demons.

I touched her lightly on her forearm and whispered some words of comfort. She smiled in response and was about to take up her story again but I figured that it was time for a little sustenance so I pulled into the services.

As I picked up a burger, fries and coffee each I told Elena not to worry about her face as there were few people around. Nevertheless we went into a quiet corner to avoid any nosey parker staring at her.

She picked up her story where she'd left off and went on to tell me that she dried her hair and picked some clothes out of the wardrobe then nervously went downstairs.

At the bottom of the winding staircase, brightly lit by imposing crystal chandeliers, Elena was met by one of the men with strange English accents and led into a large and extremely grand dining room. It had the appearance of some of the quality restaurants she enjoyed in Belgrade when her parents had visited her at university and taken her out for a special treat.

Like the staircase, this room was resplendent with sparkling crystal chandeliers and the same deep pile burgundy carpet as the hall.

She was shown to a large dining table where most of her reluctant travelling companions were already seated, including her room mate from University, Lucija Babić. They were all clad in the fashionable clothes that each had found in their room.

It was the first time they had seen each other cleaned up and in clear light. There was no-one else in the room apart from the girls.

While they waited for the last of them to come down stairs, the young women anxiously asked each other if they knew where they were or why they were there. None of them was able to shed any light on their situation as they sat there in trepidation, vainly praying some glimmer of hope.

Having finished our supper, we went back to the car and set off on the M6 once more.

As soon as we were on our way Elena started her story again.

Once all the late comers were seated, the double doors to the dining room were closed and, over the next hour and a half, the girls were treated to a sumptuous feast, including fine wines, meticulously served by a deferential maître d'hôtel supported efficiently by a brigade of four waiters in immaculate uniforms.

Most of the girls were on their second cups of strong black coffee when the maître d'hôtel clapped his hands and his brigade cleared away everything but the coffee cups from the table where the girls had enjoyed their first proper meal for a long, long time. Their forced merriment was soon to be replaced with sheer terror and an overwhelming feeling of shame.

The double doors were opened and in walked a man in his late thirties, flanked by two large men in cheap grey shiny suits, wearing dark glasses, even though it was the middle of the night. They all took up a position standing at the head of the table and turned to face the girls.

Elena scanned the faces of the three men. She shuddered as her gaze fell on the face of the man on the right. The left side of his face, from the frame of his shades down to his chin had a wide mulberry coloured scar which gave him a fearsome and intimidating look that struck fear into her young heart.

She knew from living through over a decade of conflict in the Balkans that this was not the result of an accident but this was the scar of a man who'd been slashed with a large blade. The fellow with the scar caught her gaze and scowled at her, causing her heart to beat even faster with apprehension.

The man in the centre was smartly dressed in a grey pin stripe suit, immaculate white shirt and perfectly knotted red silk tie with white polka-dots but he exuded evil from his small piercing steely grey eyes. He sported gold cufflinks and an expensive watch on his wrist. The image was spoiled by a flamboyant pony tail of wavy black hair tied back, giving him a sinister appearance.

Elena looked at Lucija who was seated next to her and raised her eyebrows at her friend as if to ask what was going on. Lucija shrugged helplessly and looked back towards the three men.

After looking round the table at the girls, the man smiled as he spoke for the first time. Elena looked at him and although he was smiling she saw that his eyes were cold and unsmiling, it was just like, she mused, looking into the eyes of a red snapper on a fishmonger's slab. Over the coming months she was to learn that his heart was as cold as his eyes. Yes, Michael Grogan was not a man for young ladies to mess with.

"Good evening ladies, welcome to England and the exciting city of Liverpool. I'm Michael Grogan and I regret the unconventional way in which we had to bring you here and hope we can make that up to you. This is our brand new executive centre, the Board Room, where our prestigious clients can come to relax, away from the pressures of business, politics and their nagging wives."

He paused at the end of each sentence while Scarface translated into Serbian for the benefit of those whose English was sketchy. As soon as he started speaking in that tongue, Elena and Lucija looked at each other knowingly and with a hint of terror in their eyes.

"As you've just seen we can provide them with the finest food and wine. On the other side of the staircase we have a fully equipped casino with tables for roulette, black-jack and poker, plus a lounge area and comfortable bar. Down the corridor there are a fully equipped gymnasium, treatment room, swimming pool and hot tubs.

Your jobs, ladies, will be to entertain our clients. Some of you will be trained as croupiers, some as masseuses and all of you will be hostesses for the guests. They may be the chairman of a public company, a Cabinet Minister, the Chief Executive of a County Council or The Chief of Police.

Whoever they are they'll be paying us a large amount of money for the services they use, so we expect you to keep them happy and make their stay here as enjoyable as possible so they'll come back and visit us on a regular basis."

It was now beginning to dawn on Elena and the others that their bad dream was to get worse. In listening carefully to her story on this wet October night I was way ahead of her. I'd already sussed out that no matter how luxurious the premises, how important the clients or how expensive the services, Elena and her companions had been kidnapped in order to perform as sex slaves.

To make matters worse, I'd seen active service in Bosnia in 1995 as part of the Rapid Reaction Force during the armed conflict and, sadly, I knew what Serbs were capable of doing to women.

"We have put CDs of English language courses in your rooms and we expect you to learn our language as quickly as possible. Each of you has seen your room, which is where you'll now live and where you're expected to stay until your services are needed.

We'll provide your food and laundry services, the clothes in the room are for you to keep. If the clothes are the wrong size, let us know and we'll change them.

In return we expect your full cooperation and we remind you that our prime concern is to entertain our clients, in the bar, in the restaurant, the gym or pool or the casino. If our guests want you to entertain them in your room, then we expect you to do that as well. No exceptions."

This last statement produced a chorus of gasps around the table as the girls' worst fears were now realised. They were about to be thrust unwillingly into the nightmare scene of high class prostitution.

"My boys will now relieve you of your passports. Please be aware that you will **not** leave this building and if you make any attempt to do so you'll be severely punished. Go and get a night's sleep now and we'll see you again in the morning."

Scarface collected passports or ID papers from those who had them; many didn't as they'd been kidnapped in their own country. They then trooped out of the dining room looking fearfully at each other with many of them already in tears. Elena looked at Lucija as they walked together towards the double doors to exit the dining room.

Her young friend's face was cadaverous, her skin ashen grey, her sunken eyes were streaked with blood and surrounded by slate coloured rings and Elena could see she looked on the point of collapse.

"Don't worry Lucija, we'll find a way to get out of here," But she knew in her heart that they were trapped, at least for the moment. As she reached the bottom of the stairs she saw that the double front doors in solid oak had a security key pad and were covered by a CCTV camera.

She told me she hardly slept that night, despite having had virtually no sleep for over a week and having taken a few glasses of red wine with her meal. She undressed slowly and got into the large four poster bed and sobbed desolately long into what was left of the night.

She must have eventually dropped off to sleep as she was woken by the door opening and one of the waiters coming in with her breakfast. As he put the tray on the coffee table he told her she was expected downstairs at 9.30 a.m.

Elena glanced at the ornate clock on the wall to the right of the bed and she saw it was already 8.45. After showering and getting dressed she poured herself a coffee and had a nibble at some toast. She'd never enjoyed large breakfasts and at this moment was too wound up to eat anything substantial.

As the girls went downstairs they were shown by one of the Englishmen into a room that resembled a board room. In due course they were to learn that the strange English accents was because the men were scousers and their strong Liverpool accents differed from the type of English the girls had learned at school.

They all waited with foreboding until the two Serbs arrived with their boss. Then Grogan spent a couple of hours getting as much information as he could on each of the girls.

He made copious notes, and asked searching questions, wanting to know the basics such as name, nationality and age. But he also was interested in their background, which of them was good at sport, who had worked in hotels, bars or even casinos, and so on.

He then started allocating main duties to each of them based on what he'd managed to extract from his fearful audience.

Because both Elena and Lucija spoke good English they were told that they'd be trained to work in the casino.

Elena went on with her story and her voice trembled as she related the traumas she and her fellow captives had experienced. Within a week of their arrival at their evil but luxurious prison, one of her fellow captives had committed suicide. Many of them were regularly beaten up until they learned to follow their vile captors' instructions.

Elena and Lucija started working in the casino and proved themselves to be first class croupiers. They struggled for a long time to be polite to the clients as they viewed them merely as iniquitous extensions of their jailers. Their masters dealt with discipline in a brutal fashion dishing out frequent beatings and there were periods where food and drink was denied them in a crude attempt to impose their will on the unfortunate girls.

Eventually the two friends had to knuckle down and they began to put on an act of pretence to welcome the clients and they were eventually quite skilled at being able to show them fake affection.

Even though the centre had just opened it soon became popular and was well frequented by many regular clients and all of them seemed to be in elevated positions, either in public life or industry. Presumably they were the type of people who could afford the fees that Grogan was charging.

Most of them were reluctant to talk too much about themselves, presumably as they knew that they should not be in that den of iniquity and didn't want to risk any chance of press exposure, or their families finding out. That was unlikely, though, as none of the girls was allowed outside to tell the world what went on behind that imposing but malevolent façade.

What the clients did not know, however, was that their visits were videoed by the proprietors as a possible future insurance.

Elena only briefly dwelt on the times she had to entertain clients in her bedroom. The girls played games in their heads, not seeing them as a council leader with bad breath, a plc Chairman with a huge belly or a police chief who was cold and whose sexual staying power was minimal.

If any of the girls showed the slightest resistance to providing sexual favours to the clients they were given a severe beating. Usually they were hit on the body so as not to spoil the look of their face and thus put off any of the clients from admiring them.

Always the policy was to persuade the clients to continue to put their hands in their pockets. There appeared to be about ten men on shifts in the brothel in addition to the catering staff. It was open from 10.30 in the morning until midnight, except on Sundays when it was closed. Two of the men alternated at being on reception to let clients in and out and take payment from them.

The front doors had a CCTV on the outside and visitors had to buzz the video intercom to gain admittance. Once the visitor had been identified the man on reception would walk forward to the large front doors and let them in.

Elena noticed that as each client was leaving, they would pay in cash at the front desk for whatever services they'd used. After they'd paid, the man on reception would then open the doors for them and usually collected a handsome tip as they bade goodnight to their guest who then presumably slunk quietly back to his wife and family.

The casino was the last part of the complex to close each evening so Elena would often be walking past the reception area as the last guests were leaving – that is unless she had been forced to provide sexual favours in her room. She saw that the front door was the only possible way to escape from her prison. Her room was barred at all the windows, the rear door, where they had originally entered on that first night, was as heavy as the front door and was permanently locked. The route through to the kitchen was permanently guarded by one of the ten heavies and all the inside windows, as far as the girls were able to determine, had the same steel bars as in their bedrooms.

Over her months of captivity, Elena watched the front door procedure carefully, as far as she could without making it obvious what she was doing. At last, on this very wet October night, she was walking slowly along the corridor towards reception and heard one of the Liverpudlians saying goodnight to a regular guest.

After the man had paid for his night of lewd entertainment and perversion with notes taken from a large wad of £20's, the door was opened for him and he stepped part way through it. He then stopped, turned back and told the receptionist he'd forgotten his coat. There was a small cloaks area between reception and the casino, about twenty metres away from the reception desk.

As both men walked past Elena she smiled at them and her heart skipped a beat as she spotted that the door was not fully closed. She glanced over her shoulder and saw the men were talking with their backs to her, so in a flash she bolted out of the door and ran for her life down the street.

She took off her high heeled shoes and ran as fast as she could. She had no idea where she was or where to go to as this was the first time she'd left the building since arriving there in August, and it was now October the following year. The rain was starting to come down and she ran from the side street where the brothel was situated and into a main street then just blindly carried on with her flight. Unfortunately she only managed to get about half a mile before the two Serbians caught her and threw her in the back of the BMW convertible.

As they drove off towards the area around Albert dock, Elena put her shoes on again and sat back in her seat breathing heavily.

The milder mannered Serbian was driving and after a minute the other man turned round and started screaming abuse at Elena which seemed to throw a switch in the mind of the young Montenegrin.

As he turned back to face the front, the car pulled past where I was walking and Elena took off one of her high heels and hit him hard several times on the back of his head with the spiked heel.

That is when the car screeched to a halt and the two furious villains threw her out and started beating her. Big mistake.

CHAPTER 3

Safe House

Whilst Elena appeared to be coming to the end of her story, I was keeping a close eye on the road signs and eventually we turned off the M6 at Junction 40 on to the A66. We headed towards Borrowdale through the dark autumn night and rain, now reduced to a mist-like drizzle. Our destination was a pretty hamlet south of Derwent Water where my rented cottage clung to a steep hillside in splendid isolation.

That'd been my ideal location to sort my head out and plan my future after I completed my service in The Corps.

I spent the last half hour of the journey giving Elena some idea of my background. When I was in my last few weeks in the Royal Marines, I wasn't sure what I wanted to do on the outside.

I phoned one of my contacts Sandy Parker to ask his advice. He was my Captain in The Corps until he retired in 2003 and wasn't a bad bloke for a Rupert.

Captain Parker served with distinction in the Falklands conflict in 1982 as a Lieutenant and we did tours together in Bosnia and Sierra Leone when he wore the three pips of a Captain with the great honour that is expected of all Commandos. His final mission was in March 2003 and was part of the Operation to clear The Al Faw Peninsula in Iraq and seize key Iraqi oil infrastructures.

During our service in The Balkans, when we came under heavy fire near Srebrenica, Sandy was shot in the chest as he led our troop up an incline to take out a Serbian gun position.

The enemy gunners had seen he was down so they started firing fiercely in his direction to finish him off. I was his second in command on this sortie so I ordered the rest of the platoon to provide blanket fire against the enemy gun position. This gave me the opportunity to go forward and lift The Boss on to my back and run back out of range of the incessant automatic fire that was now buzzing around our ears.

We then radioed for the medics who were there with us in less than four minutes. While waiting for them to arrive I took out my emergency pack and was able to staunch the flow of blood that was staining his camouflage battle dress deep crimson. I remember saying to him something like,

"Would you stop fucking bleeding sir, you're making a mess of my battle tunic."

He smiled grimly. *How better to endure than with humour?* This is one of the individual commando spirit characteristics in The Marine Corps. The rest are courage, unity, determination, adaptability, unselfishness, humility, cheerfulness, professional standards and fortitude. Individual commando spirit plus collective group values make us the best fighting team in the world.

The bullet had missed his heart by a couple of inches and resulted in his hospitalisation for three weeks then a period of recuperation lasting a couple of months back in the UK. I also sustained a flesh wound in my shoulder as I was picking him up, so it gave me double pleasure to find out later that my platoon had wiped out the Serbian gun position thus allowing us to progress and take control of the area.

So, I was quite close to Captain Parker, and when I was preparing myself to leave the service, I phoned him for advice on what to do on the 'Outside' which is what we commandos call life after leaving the Corps.

He advised I should take six months minimum to decide what I wanted to do with the next twenty years of my life; this would give me time to wind down and make an informed decision on my immediate future.

He went on to tell me with a chuckle in his voice that he'd just the place where I could do that, his cottage in the Lake District which is where Elena and I were heading now. Trust a bloody Rupert to come up with a piece of advice that earned him some money!

I'd been living at Fellside Cottage now for over two months and had been using my new found freedom to take in the wonderful scenery in the midst of which my temporary but very comfortable abode nestled.

I enjoyed a wonderful and rewarding career as a Royal Marine Commando and made some life long friends, but eighteen years of blood and bullets is enough.

I rested for the first couple of weeks then started yomping around Grasmoor, Honister Pass and Rosthwaite. This helped maintain my fitness levels and enabled me to breathe in the wonderful fresh Lakeland air which was laden with myriad fragrances of wild flowers and pine trees.

I also made a couple of road trips, driving up to Carlisle where I bought some clothes that were more suited to life in Civvy Street than my present wardrobe and then ventured over the Border into Scotland.

I explored the delightful Border town of Dumfries and drove along the soothing coast road that bordered the Solway Firth, desperately needing to wind down after having lived on a knife edge since I was eighteen.

The cottage was situated high on a hillside with no other building within two miles. Captain Parker had used it as a holiday home when his two kids were younger but now they were teenagers they wanted livelier holiday destinations so he was happy to rent it out.

As I swung the car through the gap in the stone wall that bordered the winding country road, the headlights picked out "Fellside Cottage" on the slate name plaque. There was then a mile long tarmac path up to the house with two cattle grids between the road and the cottage as this area was long established sheep country.

The stone built house with its neat blue slate roof had a rose covered trellis either side of the front door leading into a cosy lounge with a warm terracotta coloured brick inglenook fireplace and cottage suite; a new flat screen TV sat in the corner with a DVD player.

The dining kitchen looked over the back yard where I usually parked my car and there was a guest cloakroom tucked away in one of its corners, behind the freezer.

The natural wood stairs led up to a landing which had a stained glass chapel window looking back down towards the road.

There were three double bedrooms, the one I was using being on the front, also looking down the driveway.

The bedrooms were not huge as each of them had an ensuite bathroom taking up part of the space but were all blessed with a comfortable bed and a welcoming armchair, built in wardrobe and dressing table with a padded stool in front of it.

Sandy had clearly spared no expense in making this a great second home for him and his family.

The grounds on either side of the drive were short cropped grass and there was a neat and easily managed garden all the way round the house.

Behind the yard there was a range of outbuildings and then the land began to rise steeply. After a hundred yards or so there was a thickly wooded area of about ten acres with a peat brown stream babbling its way through the fresh smelling pine trees.

As we pulled off the road my car headlights shone on to the chapel window, I stopped the car in the gateway and unlocked the post box to take out my week's mail.

I turned to Elena and smiled.

"This is where I live; you'll be safe here."

I hoped that was going to be true but knew that this situation was far from over. Michael Grogan, along with the Serbs and his other henchmen would be looking for swift revenge and would certainly be fearful that their operation was now at risk of exposure to the law enforcement agencies.

I unlocked the back door then switched on the lights and touched Elena lightly on the arm.

"Don't worry, I'll look after you. Tomorrow we'll start to plan our next course of action. In the meantime, I'll show you around. Fancy a coffee?" She nodded with a smile on her face and looked round the kitchen.

The swelling on her face was going down but some bruises were beginning to appear on her cheek bones. I was especially concerned as to whether there was any serious injury to her body so I asked her to let me have a look. As she coyly lifted up her top, I gently felt all round her ribs and was pleased that although they were sore, the pain was subsiding, so it was most likely that there was nothing broken and, hopefully, no serious damage.

I took her up into the bedroom at the rear of the house and she smiled at the three foot high black haired gorilla that was sitting on the easy chair, I had bought this cuddly toy from a street trader in Sierra Leone along with the red headed orang-utan that was lurking on the chair in my bedroom.

I gave her one of my soft fabric shirts to use as a night dress and a new terry towelling dressing gown in sea blue that I'd bought in Carlisle before I made my trip to Liverpool.

"Get a good night's sleep Elena and I'll see you in the morning. Do you need anything else at the moment?"

"No, I'm fine, thank you. You're a good man Nathan Sawyer. I'm sure those Serbs would have killed me if you hadn't come along when you did. I owe you my life; for sure they would have finished me off. Nobody walks out on Michael Grogan. Thank you, thank you, a million times. Good night."

She gave me a quick peck on the cheek and ran into her room with tears in her eyes.

"OK, good girl, I'll see you in a few hours."

My words floated unheard in the air behind her as she ran away in her confusion.

I checked the lock on the glass panelled front door then quickly went through my mail. Usual crap, bills, bank statements, charity begging letters (how the hell did they get my address?) and a few catalogues and holiday brochures, finally a number of replies from recruiters telling me to send them my CV, but nothing important.

I poured myself a Scotch and gazed into its amber glow whilst reflecting on the evening so far. I mused that I wouldn't have done anything differently, so was at ease with myself. My concern was what to do next. I had the ideas going round in my head when I came to the bottom of the glass. Now I figured it was time for bed and tomorrow we'd put the plans into action.

I turned the lights off except on the landing, in order to give Elena some security if she needed to move about the house. I undressed quickly and, as usual, immediately went to sleep as soon as my head hit the pillow.

CHAPTER 4

Practicalities

I woke up with a start in the morning, hearing the noise of someone moving about downstairs. Quickly jumping out of bed, I pulled on my dressing gown but soon smiled with relief when I opened the bedroom door and the delicious smell of bacon, eggs, toast and ground coffee wafted up and hit my nostrils.

As I padded down the stained wooden stairs I shouted a greeting and Elena popped her head around the kitchen door and a smile broke out on her pale but very pretty face.

"Good morning, Mr Sawyer," she said cheekily "now its time for me to look after you. I hope this breakfast will be OK for you. I managed to find everything I needed in the fridge."

I told her that was fine, thinking to myself how cute she looked wearing my shirt with her long black hair tumbling over the collar. Her long slim legs certainly looked better in the shirt than mine did.

As we tucked into our breakfast she told me she had slept quite well for the first time in over a year. She went on to say since the rain had stopped she could see out of the windows and witness how beautiful this part of the Lake District is.

It was so different peering through a window that did not have steel bars across it. For the first time since leaving Belgrade Airport she'd heard birds singing and had even watched a fox scurrying past, stopping for a moment to look up at her, curious as to who she was and then carrying on up the pathway and over the hill.

As I ate my bacon and eggs I was turning over in my mind my thoughts from last night so I told Elena of my plans for the next couple of days and asked for her views.

First she needed clothes, toiletries and other such items. Second I had an urgent need to do some shopping for groceries, food and stuff like that, as for the first time since I had left The Service there were now two mouths to feed.

Third I wanted to work out a plan of how I could get the other girls out of their Merseyside prison. Elena looked at me nervously when I told her of item number three on my list.

As if to vocalise her fears, she then began telling me how vicious Grogan and his cronies were, and described in more detail than she had been able to do the previous night some of the atrocities they had committed during her enforced stay under their control.

She recalled how one of the girls, a pretty red haired Bosnian named Mejra was especially reluctant to follow the orders of her captors. Her room was just down the corridor from Elena's and often Mejra would creep into her fellow captive's room after the clients had gone home to try and get some comforting words from the Montenegrin.

After their captivity had been going on for some months, Elena was just dropping off to sleep when she heard a commotion in the corridor that ran past her room. Recent experience had taught her not to try and observe what was going on and certainly not to interfere otherwise she would get a severe beating at the very least.

By listening at the door of her room, she sadly realised that some of the captors had gone into Mejra's room and were giving her a very savage punishment beating.

After some minutes had passed there was silence for a short while, then she heard the heavy footsteps of the men going past her door, panting very roughly and swearing at each other in Serbian.

She was able to catch what one of them said and she understood enough of their language to translate,

"You bring the car round to the back. We can put her in the boot."

Elena's blood ran cold and over the next couple of days her fears were confirmed as they never saw Mejra again. Missing, presumed dead.

Michael Grogan frequently picked out one of the girls and took them up to his own special bedroom where he'd take out his sexual gratification on them, using force if they showed any reluctance to comply with his demands.

Quite often he'd get one of his goons to bring one of the captives up to his office for a chat. Usually it was to give them a warning by means of a good slapping if there had been any cases of them refusing to toe the line.

Occasionally the summons was to tell them that a particular client had been pleased with their services and had expressed a desire to see that girl again for special favours. Twice Elena had been taken to Grogan's office after a particular client had taken advantage of her. The man turned out to be a high-ranking police officer.

Grogan referred to him as Chief Superintendent Rowley, so Elena stored that information at the back of her mind in case she was ever able to use it.

Rowley had indicated to the brothel owner that he was pleased with her so had asked Grogan to make sure that she was there for him on each of his visits to the vice den.

On her first summons to his office, Elena was listening to the Englishman and glancing nervously round the office while he was fiddling in his bureau, looking for some paperwork or other.

She saw a rack of video tapes in the corner by his leather topped desk and wondered to herself what purpose they served.

As Grogan pulled the large drawer open in his desk, she noticed that it contained a number of passports, but when he saw her looking at the drawer he slammed it shut and gave her a hard slap across her face, screaming at her,

"Keep your eyes to the front you nosey bitch!"

When she was summoned to his office for the second time she had just taken a seat in front of his desk when Grogan took a phone call on his mobile which then went on for some time and clearly was causing him some problems.

As he paced up and down his large and opulently furnished office, engrossed in the phone conversation, Elena looked surreptitiously around the room.

When his back was turned for some time she was able to focus on the rack of video tapes. Each had a handwritten label on the spine with the name of a client. This made her stomach turn as she realised that Grogan's men were videoing the activities of their clients, probably in order to blackmail them if necessary. Obviously the girls were most likely featured in the videos as well.

Elena looked across the table at me with nervous apprehension in her eyes, so I tried to allay her fears by talking about the shopping I was planning to do today and giving her a couple of quick examples of some of the rescue work we had done liberating captives in various conflicts around the world.

"I'm not superman, Elena, but as a Royal Marine you are trained to survive and make sure your comrades survive too. I'm quite sure Captain Parker can help us put together a strategy to bring down this evil man."

That calmed her down somewhat and we cleared the dishes away before going back upstairs to get showered and dressed for our shopping expedition.

I decided that we'd drive up to Carlisle where I knew it should be easy to get Elena fitted out with a good selection of clothes.

I gave her one of my wax jackets as a top coat. Apart from that she had no choice but to wear the same clothes she was wearing when I rescued her, the only ones she had, of course.

She had done a good job covering up the superficial injuries to her face with whatever make up she had in her handbag. So at first glance no-one was likely to become suspicious or even give us a second look. So far so good, Mr Sawyer, I thought to myself.

We reached Cumbria's largest city by mid-morning and managed to find a space at the multi-storey car park in the Lanes shopping centre so that we had only to take a short walk to the main shopping area on English Street.

We started off at M&S. Both of us were a little embarrassed as we filled the shopping basket with a suitable selection of lacy and sexy looking bras and knickers, plus a couple of nighties and a dressing gown but at least this very brave and clearly intelligent young woman was seeing life on the outside again, for the first time in over twelve months.

After I had paid for the items we went to find a coffee bar and enjoyed a latte and cappuccino respectively.

As we took the weight off our aching feet and cupped our hands round our drinks Elena was at great pains to tell me that I should keep a record of everything I was spending so that she could pay me back in due course. I smiled back at her and admired her honest spirit; I said there would be a large amount of interest charged if she didn't pay immediately. That put a smile back on her face.

We then walked round to Debenhams and after an hour and a half had managed to get Elena a selection of street clothes and some country apparel that were suitable for living temporarily in the Lake District.

To start with, the purchases were not easy as Elena was obviously experiencing the vagaries of UK shopping for the first time. Once she got the hang of the sizing she was able to look through the racks to find items that were suitable for her.

We picked up some slacks and jeans, a couple of skirts and jumpers, a pair of nice winter dresses, some warmer blouses and a mixture of shoes, including flat shoes for walking and some fashionable high heels, then a pair of boots as winter was approaching.

At BHS we bought a waterproof anorak and a three quarter length woollen top-coat in a stylish poppy red colour which looked great with Elena's long black hair tumbling over its collar.

As the day wore on, Elena began to relax more and her personality began to return and show through from the understandably sombre and frightened state she was in when I snatched her away from the thugs in Liverpool.

Her sense of humour, which had probably been suppressed since she'd been kidnapped at Belgrade Airport, was beginning to return.

When she was trying on some of the clothes, she would come out of the fitting rooms and prance about and pose like a model and then giggle when I gave a nod of approval.

I was beginning to like this girl and becoming increasingly determined to rescue her friends and bring Grogan to justice along with all the other scum who worked for him.

Over a nice pub lunch in Yates' Wine Lodge we reviewed our purchases and agreed that the only other items needed for the moment were toiletries so we spent an interesting half an hour in Boots.

There we chose a selection of fragrances and body lotions, then finished off with toothpaste and toothbrush, soap, shower gel, shampoo, talcum powder and tissues and finally sanitary towels.

God knows what my fellow Green Berets would have thought of my stumbling around giving advice on whether to buy Tampax or Boots own label!! My mouth seemed like I was chewing cotton wool, I was so embarrassed, so I decided to let Elena make her own mind up on that one.

By mid afternoon we were all done in Carlisle now so headed off back South on the M6 with the back seat of my car laden with plastic bags full of our purchases. We stopped off in Penrith on the way back and parked at Morrisons supermarket on Brunswick Road.

Despite not knowing each other's tastes in food, we managed to get a trolley full with a mixture of fresh and packaged produce that would last us around a week including a couple of bottles of wine. So around £70 later we set off back to Fellside Cottage.

When we got back to my place it was around 6.00 p.m., Elena went upstairs and tried all her purchases on again before cutting off the price tags and hanging up all her new outfits while I unpacked the food and looked at what we might have for our evening meal.

I put the early evening news on the TV and stopped packing the food away when it came to the North West local news to listen out for any mention of the events of last night. Sure enough there was a report that two men, believed to be Serbians, had been attacked in the car park near the Liver Building.

They told the police when they'd stopped for a smoke they were set upon by a gang of six youths who beat them senseless and stole their car. The police report also went on to say that one man had a broken nose and fractured cheekbone, the other had a smashed kneecap.

They were currently under armed police guard in hospital as further police checks had revealed that they were illegal immigrants, possibly part of a gang of people smugglers and would be deported as soon as they were discharged from hospital. Good news, really, and I smiled to myself as I heard the newscaster say they'd described me as a gang of six youths!!

After half an hour Elena came back downstairs wearing a pair of skin tight black slacks and a lilac coloured blouse, with a smile on her face looking just like a perfectly fashioned little china doll.

She looked radiant and happy and her smile widened when I told her what I'd heard on the news. Her face was a little swollen from her beating, and her ribs still ached somewhat, but she was mending quite well.

I guess if I'd been a couple of minutes later in coming to her aid, I'd have had to take her to hospital. As it was, it was her assailants who were now guests of Her Majesty's Government and The NHS.

For the next three days we followed a pattern of rising around 8.00 a.m. and after a light breakfast we dressed in warm outdoor gear and explored the surrounding area, taking a packed lunch with us each time.

I pushed Elena quite hard in an attempt to increase her strength and stamina and she struggled to maintain the pace so I eased off a little on the first day. But by mid afternoon on the second day there was some colour in her cheeks and her breathing was less laboured.

We walked through wooded valleys and up hillsides where the autumn hues were providing a wonderful backdrop for our yomping. There were bracken covered inclines, moss covered banks by streams with their fast flowing brown waters and pine woods smelling sweet as the damp autumn air moistened their needles.

Over the three days, we walked round the shores of Derwent Water and Bassenthwaite Lake and marvelled at the birds of prey searching for thermals to take them aloft before plunging down on some unsuspecting mammal.

On the third day, we stopped for our packed lunch on a pile of black rocks rising out of the grassy hillside like the gigantic, but eerily silent, pipes of a cathedral organ.

The waters of a small lake were only twenty feet or so away from where we were sitting and after a few minutes a pair of ducks came noisily to the water's edge.

The mallard hung back, nervously, but the brown female told us in no uncertain terms, with her incessant quacking and darting backwards and forwards, that she fancied joining us for some morsels. I tore a couple of pieces of bread from one of my sandwiches and tossed them into the water where the duck quickly swallowed them both.

Elena clapped her tiny hands together in delight, the sudden noise causing the two ducks to retreat a few feet. But when they came back she started throwing bread in their direction, making sure that the beautifully coloured mallard got his share.

Within minutes we were surrounded by pigeons, more ducks and a pair of chaffinches, the male's reddish pink breast less colourful than it would be in its spring and early summer pomp.

Very quickly Elena realised that if she held her arms out with crumbs on her hand that some of the birds would feed out of her hand, not seeing humans as a threat to them. She squealed with delight when this happened and I felt a few butterflies in my stomach as I witnessed her enjoying the real life on the outside. Simple joys that she had missed for so long.

After three days on a fairly strict regime, Elena was already looking a lot fitter with a nice pink colour in her face and was moving much more easily as the soreness in her ribs began to ebb away.

As we walked back to Fellside Cottage we were laughing and joking that if she was a man I would soon have her fit enough to join a crack regiment. Our joy was soon shattered when we switched on the late local TV news.

CHAPTER 5

Retribution attempts

When we got back to base I asked Elena if she wanted to go bird watching again on the following day as I knew a spot where we could see magnificent birds of prey, including buzzards, kestrels and red kite and, if we were really lucky, we might spot the magnificent golden eagle which roamed the airways above the fell, just north of my cottage.

She smiled as she nodded her assent and then told me she'd cook me a meal tonight so that I could put my feet up in front of the TV for the next hour and a half.

In fact I said I would be making a phone call while she was in the kitchen, so I took my mobile up to my bedroom, where I first made a call to international directory enquiries.

After I'd written down on a piece of paper the number I wanted, I secreted it in my wallet. Then I called Captain Parker and brought him up to speed with my latest operation. He listened intently and in silence to what I had to say.

"Just like the old days", he quipped drily. "Give me a quiet half hour to think, and then call me back, Nathan."

Sandy now ran a large security company based in Leeds, employing mainly ex Royal Marines, Paratroopers and SAS personnel. More like a private army, in fact.

Like the Americans, our own armed services supplemented the complement of regular service personnel with bought in mercenaries on a needs basis. They were also used by the police when special skills and combat experience would provide back-up to our law enforcement guys.

When I called back, I briefed him on what I'd learned from Elena over the time she'd been in my care. I also gave him some ideas on the manpower that I believed Grogan had on site at any one time, the approximate locality of the brothel and the layout she'd described to me.

"As yet, Sandy, I don't know the exact location of the place, but Elena knew that they answered the phone 'welcome to The Board Room' so it should be easy to trace".

"OK, I'll give some thought on how we could put together an operation to rescue the other girls and bring Grogan and his evil henchmen to book."

Parker brought our conversation to a close by telling me he'd sleep on it and I should call him in the morning, and as his final advice he told me to make sure that I continue to sleep in my own bed. Bloody Ruperts, even on the outside they still wanted to tell you what to do!!

I put my mobile on charge then padded downstairs in my moccasin slippers, my nose again sensing a delicious aroma coming from the kitchen. I shouted to Elena to see if she needed any help. She suggested I could open some wine as the meal would soon be ready.

Ten minutes later we sat down to a delicious beef goulash served on a bed of long grain rice.

50

After polishing off the last of the meal, I cupped my glass in my hand and as I stared into its rich red contents I told Elena more about Sandy Parker and his private army.

They provided a wide range of undercover security, rescue and combat services at home and, increasingly, overseas.

I'd kept in touch with him regularly, a man for whom I had enormous respect, which intensified after I saved him in Bosnia. He'd given me some insight into several of the operations his team had been involved in. This included providing body guards for visiting foreign politicians (or as he put it, baby sitting egotistical and power-hungry arseholes).

What he really enjoyed, though, was the active ops, such as reconnaissance in Afghanistan and Iraq or slipping over the South African Border to pull Brits and other whites out of Zimbabwe after their farms had been seized by local thugs. I suggested to her with a smile, then, that a couple of Serbs and a few scouse gangsters were hardly likely to trouble his team. Nevertheless, she looked at me, still with a degree of anxiety in those limpid and sparkling dark brown eyes, resembling occasionally the bottomless brown pools where we'd fed the ducks.

As we debated what ideas Parker might come back with tomorrow I was getting excited about the prospect of some action again.

"Elena do you know the address of The Board Room, or even its phone number?"

She smiled and nipped upstairs for a minute then came back with a personalised pen printed with a logo, the name and an 0151 phone number, so I said I'd phone later in the week and check the address, pretending to be a prospective client.

I also told her that early in the morning she should try and draw me the building layout, in as much detail as she was able to remember.

Elena tensed at this point as clearly the memory of the place had been pushed to the back of her mind over the past few days and it pained her to bring it to the front again. So I changed the subject and asked her how her new wardrobe suited her.

She blushed and said she felt like it was her birthday and how could she ever thank me; I grinned and replied that she just had done with that meal she had cooked for us both.

With a cafetière of Blue Mountain coffee between us on the coffee table in the lounge I put the ten o'clock news on the TV and we watched with detached interest the usual gloom and doom on the national news.

When the BBC Regional News came on, I felt sick in my stomach.

The lead story showed a young couple who'd been savagely beaten in Liverpool. Their faces were in a terrible mess and the camera also showed the wounds on their arms where they'd been deliberately burned with cigarettes. Despite the injuries to their faces, I saw to my horror that it was the couple who owned the hotel where I had been staying for the week before I encountered Elena.

The Police Inspector who was being interviewed by the TV reporter said they were looking for two heavily built men with local Liverpool accents who'd gone into the hotel and asked to see the managers.

The thugs then forced them back into their own office and secured them both in chairs with strapping tape before starting their torture of the two terrified hoteliers.

It turned out that the yobs wanted to know the address of the hotel's resident who drove a black two door Seat Ibiza.

"That would be me", I fumed to myself as I listened to the newscast.

Clearly the young couple had refused to give that information out for a long time. The report went on to say that eventually the two assailants found the hotel register that I'd signed when I checked in. So I figured to myself that we'd soon be receiving a visit, now Grogan's men almost certainly knew where I lived.

As the TV news finished I switched off the TV and turned to Elena, with barely suppressed anger in my voice.

"Well, pretty lady we now have a real problem, but not as big a problem as Michael Grogan has. Those poor people were the owners of the hotel I stayed in and that's my car they were looking for. Someone connected to Grogan must have seen us when I set their car on fire and worked out that one of us had been staying at that hotel.

They will certainly come looking for us so we need to be prepared and be ready to move out as it won't be safe to stay here any longer".

Elena looked at me intently and that look of fear had come back into her eyes.

"So what do we do now Nathan?"

I told her that as the story had been on the news tonight the Grogan henchmen would want to deal with us before we could alert the police.

I therefore decided that we must make preparations for a strategic withdrawal at first light, but in the meantime we should anticipate an invasion of some sort.

My training had taught me many things. Whilst all men who had the honour to wear the Green Beret with the coveted Globe and Laurel cap badge could look after themselves very, very well, we all knew we should always ensure we controlled the situation. Therefore we made sure we didn't hand the initiative to our adversaries but should avoid conflict whenever possible.

Gaining, then keeping control, wins battles, wins wars. I had to gain control for both our sakes.

So I told Elena my plan. If we had no visitors during the night, we would leave in the morning after I'd spoken to Parker and we'd temporarily relocate ourselves to somewhere near his offices in the Leeds area.

Tonight we would pack a case for a week's stay away, ready for an early start in the morning, but we should hide the cases away in the wardrobe in case of inquisitive intruders. We must sleep fully dressed and on top of the bed clothes, ready for a quick get away. I'd spent almost twenty years sleeping ready for action in combat zones, so was well schooled in advising my companion on what to do.

I told her I'd leave the front door unlocked and if we did have visitors we'd slip quietly out of the back door and secrete ourselves in the pine woods 300 metres up the hill, immediately behind the cottage.

I got out a pair of night vision glasses which I'd bought at an army surplus store on leaving The Service. I also pulled out of my 'armoury' a large rubber-bodied torch, which if you held it at the end where the light was and swung it hard over your wrist in a semi-circular motion, it made a great weapon. If you were hit on the head with one of those, you stayed hit!!

"Elena you should wear warm clothes and your walking shoes, with anorak to hand and be ready for action."

She was, understandably very nervous; I had in my own mind that firearms were likely to be involved so we needed to anticipate the most extreme form of retribution being taken out against us.

Therefore, after the suitcases were packed away out of sight, I put us both to bed to enable any potential assassin to do his worst. Or rather that is what it was supposed to look like.

I looked at the clock on the radio alarm as I started dozing off; it was just coming up to midnight. I'd switched on the small table lamp on the pie crust table on the landing. Although its soft ivory glow was relatively subdued, it would enable any unwelcome visitors sufficient light to find their way upstairs and into the bedrooms.

Three hours passed and that's exactly what they did.

I heard the vehicle's engine long before its head-lights pierced the autumnal darkness surrounding my cottage. The stained glass chapel window was lit up, casting a diffused rainbow coloured light on the landing carpet.

Clearly our visitors were stupid as well as aggressive. There was no building within two miles of where we were, so the clack, clack, clack of a powerful diesel engine carried for miles in the still night air. I jumped off the bed while the vehicle was still around a mile away, rearranged the crumpled bed covers to look authentic, picked up my night vision glasses, my torch and threw on my dark green hooded wax jacket.

I went into Elena's room and woke her, put my hand over her mouth, and silently organised her. We slipped out of the back door quickly and ghost-like then headed off up the hill, with me holding her hand to help her over the relatively rough terrain.

We'd reached the brow of the hill by the time the vehicle arrived at the gap in the wall that was the start of the long drive up to the cottage.

I turned round and through the mist that hung over the fell like a wet blanket saw them switch off the car headlamps in the gateway then get out and noisily slam the doors; nice to give your victims a bit of warning then. Idiots. If I was still in Iraq, they'd be in my cross hairs by now and in the next two seconds consigned to history.

I gently guided Elena into the pine woods and found a spot where we could have a full view of the cottage and the drive leading up to it.

I suggested she kneel down and recover from the fairly strenuous dash up the hill and hopefully her heavy breathing would die down before there was a chance of the visitors hearing us.

I focussed the binoculars and picked out two men walking up the drive. The powerful glasses revealed they were in street clothes, so obviously clandestine operations were not their usual modus operandae, rank amateurs, in fact.

They were also very clearly unfit since they stopped for a rest at least twice on their way up the drive. It took the two intruders around fifteen minutes to cover the mile or so length of the drive.

I whispered to Elena that there were two of them as they were almost at the front door she should keep perfectly still so their activities would not be disturbed.

Quite unexpectedly she reached out for my hand and gave it a squeeze and as the moonlight lit up her pretty and eye-catching luminous face I could see a mischievous half smile appear on her lips and she put her finger to her lips in a shushing sign, nodding in assent as she did it.

As we waited in the shallow dip in the pine woods a barn owl suddenly gave out its blood curdling shriek as its wings beat silently in the clearing to the side of the wood. The sudden rent of the stillness gave Elena a huge fright and she only just managed to keep herself quiet. I was looking through the binoculars at the time, so quickly turned to her and whispered,

"Bird out hunting, don't worry".

Fortunately by this time the two men had reached the front door so any slight noise from our direction was masked by the building. Unfortunately they were now out of sight so I again signalled to Elena to keep still and listen.

Sure enough about ninety seconds later I heard three gun shots. Then, less than a minute later, three more shots pierced the still air and set a number of birds off in flights of panic. Almost immediately the front door slammed shut and two more birds took off, but they were of the human kind this time.

As I refocused the night glasses on to the drive I was able to see in the green image that the intruders had started running down the drive.

They gave up after a hundred yards as they realised there was no-one in pursuit, and they must also have sensed they weren't fit enough to run for over a mile.

Fifteen minutes later they reached the end of the drive, stopped for a breather, lit a couple of cigarettes and stood by their vehicle until they'd smoked them, then threw the butts on the ground.

They climbed inside their Land Rover 4x4 and backed out on to the country road then roared off very noisily into the night, making absolutely no attempt to slip away surreptitiously. I watched their lights closely as they arced round the bends on the winding country road to the left of Fellside Cottage until eventually they were out of sight. I told Elena that we should wait for the engine sound to be out of earshot, and then wait for at least five more minutes before we made any move.

I cocked my head and listened carefully; I was happy that the only sound now disturbing the cool night air was the sporadic yelping of a fox and the spine-chilling scream of a male pheasant protecting its territory.

"Right Elena, let's go and inspect the damage".

We moved out of the pinewoods and as we started to move back down the hill the moon came out from behind a huge cloud just as the majestic barn owl flew a few feet over our heads. Its ghostly white appearance seemed wholly appropriate on this eerie night in the English Lake District.

We went back into the cottage through the rear door, after I had quickly checked the tyres on my car, just in case they had been slashed. They all looked ok, thank goodness. As we went upstairs I asked Elena not to touch anything for the moment, nor to put on the lights, just in case we were being watched.

I pulled on a pair of gloves and we first went into Elena's bedroom. I switched on my torch, and there in her bed, just showing out of the bedclothes, and face down, was the long black shiny hair of my gorilla, and as I pulled back the bedclothes we could see that it now had three bullet holes in its head.

In my room a similar fate had befallen my reddish haired orang-utan. So the pair of decoys had done their job, and, thankfully, the two would-be assassins were too stupid to check fully.

All they were interested in, apparently, was a woman with long black hair and a red haired man who were to be their targets at Fellside Cottage. Luckily Michael Grogan had chosen his most moronic thugs to carry out our assassination. I was dealing with a vicious bunch, but they were first class idiots, so it shouldn't be too hard to outwit them.

Elena looked at the two apes and then at me, then leaned forward and gave me a peck on the cheek, whispering hoarsely as the fear suddenly grabbed her in the back of her throat,

"That's twice in one week that you've saved my life Mr Sawyer!!"

I was touched and a little taken aback, so I broke the ice by reminding Elena not to touch anything in the bedrooms so that any areas where our visitors had made contact with their hands would have a nice set of fingerprints.

I opened both wardrobes using my gloved hands and lugged out the suitcases, and heaved them downstairs. After picking up my mobile phone and charger, I also put my 'armoury bag' on the back seat.

Not knowing exactly how we were going to proceed until I'd spoken to Captain Parker, I wanted to have some of my support gear with me, just in case.

I checked with Elena whether she'd everything we needed. She nodded her assent, so we locked up and killed the light on the landing.

I put my young companion into the car then pushed the vehicle round to the front of the cottage and on to the drive, then coasted down the drive with no lights on, just in case our visitors were not as stupid as they appeared and may have crept back.

I braked to a halt around a hundred metres before the entrance, then silently got out and walked to the road, my rubber soled footwear making no noise on the tarmac surface. I stopped as I reached the road and listened and looked in all directions. Not a sound to be heard and as the moon had again disappeared behind a cloud I could clearly see that there were no lights showing anywhere in the vicinity.

So it was safe to set off and leave our two murdered alter egos behind.

Checking that Elena was OK, I then fired up the engine. Before setting off I got back out and, still wearing my leather gloves carefully picked up the two cigarette stubs and placed them in a small plastic bag in my coat pocket. They would provide great DNA evidence in due course.

I left the country roads after a short while, then on to the A591 road to Kendal followed by the A65 towards

Skipton and Leeds as we now needed to meet Sandy Parker face to face and agree between us the next steps and the rescue plans.

I also needed to find somewhere safe for Elena, even though both of us were now 'dead' in Grogan's eyes. That is a fact that I did not wish to disabuse him of. So, Yorkshire, here we come.

CHAPTER 6

Captain Parker

We stopped for breakfast at a Little Chef on the roundabout where we were to join the road to Keighley. I managed to find a quiet corner table where I could phone Sandy Parker without being overheard.

We both ordered a traditional English breakfast and coffee, and as soon as the server had taken our order I phoned Parker, knowing he was always in his office by 7.00 a.m.

I started off by relating the events of last night, beginning with what I'd heard on the news about the unfortunate hotel owners.

"Nathan, I think it's important that Grogan's gang really believe you are both actually dead so as to lull him into a false sense of security.

My older brother is the Chief Constable for a Northern County and has previously been head of the vice squad in Liverpool, so has a vested interest in getting scum like Grogan behind bars.

I think I can persuade him to issue a press release announcing the two murders and send in a team of SOCOS to the cottage."

I told him I'd picked up two cigarette butts dropped by the pathetic hit squad.

"OK I've noted that, we can discuss the rest later. I'll sort out a suitable hotel for the pair of you so you should drive over to my office once you've finished your scran".

As our breakfast arrived, I started telling Elena of the plan. If Grogan thought we actually were dead, then he'd probably relax for a while. This would give us the opportunity to put into play the wider plan, rescuing the other girls and putting the whole sordid and evil team behind bars.

She seemed OK with this but selflessly expressed her sorrow that she was the only one to have escaped so far and that she felt so worried about the safety of her friend Lucija Babić.

As we left the restaurant I quickly checked out we weren't being watched by anyone, and then drove off in the direction of Keighley. We passed through Bingley and the outskirts of Bradford before hitting the Leeds Ring Road and the morning rush hour, so it was a good hour before I was able to park up in the multi-storey car park at The Light, right in the heart of this fine city.

The square where Sandy's office was situated was surrounded by high quality and exclusive Georgian fronted offices, mainly barristers' chambers and a couple of property companies, but also the offices of a man who had served with distinction in the Royal Marines and now quietly ran his private army from this beautiful location.

The brass doorplate on the building gave nothing away, merely bearing the engraving in neat black letters 'Trans Continental Solutions Ltd'. The casual observer would've thought it was an IT company, and I'd learned from him that the door was never opened to anyone who didn't have an appointment.

The CCTV camera above the black panelled door quietly swivelled in our direction as I pressed the shining solid brass buzzer set into the hardwood door frame.

"Sawyer for Captain Parker", I answered into the intercom as I heard an educated female voice enquire if she could help me.

Five minutes later we were standing in an impressive wood panelled board room alongside a huge and highly polished table. I stood stiffly next to one of the chairs with my companion by my side.

Almost immediately Sandy Parker entered the room, a tall dark haired man with the bearing and presence of an officer, wearing a neat dark blue suit and a maroon and white striped tie.

"Good morning sir" I proffered as I stood to attention.

"No need for that Nathan, we're on the outside now, stand easy man." He shook my hand warmly and we both smiled with the genuine affection we had for each other.

He quickly turned to Elena and smiled warmly, speaking softly to her, "Ćao, Elena, dobro jutro. Šta biste da pijete." *Hello, Elena, good morning. What would you like to drink?*

"Kafa, molim." *Coffee, please.* Your use of the Serbian language is very good, Captain Parker".

He replied in that kind of English that you expect of an officer and a gentleman, "It's not bad, but I *am* sorry that I cannot yet appreciate the subtle differences in the Montenegrin version, so please forgive me."

She smiled as Sandy poured us both a strong coffee and he motioned for us to take a seat in the regency style chairs that were neatly set around the table.

"OK, first things first, I've booked you both into this hotel. It's owned by a recently retired Major from 29 Commando Regiment Royal Artillery, so he's on our side, and has been fully briefed."

He handed me the hotel brochure which I quickly glanced at. It had twenty five bedrooms and was overlooking Roundhay Park on the north side of Leeds.

"Next, here's your obituary" he joked, passing me a copy of the police press release that was going out to the media in the North West in time for the evening news bulletins and first editions on the news stands.

I read it out to Elena:

The Police have announced there has been a fatal double shooting in The Lake District. The bodies of a man and a woman were discovered in two separate bedrooms by a cleaner in a cottage near Derwent Water. The pair each had three bullet holes to the head, which has all the hallmarks of execution style killings. Neither has been identified, but the woman appears to be in her early twenties and of Eastern European appearance, the man in his late thirties and with red hair. Anyone who can provide any information or recently was in contact with the deceased should contact their local police station.

Elena looked at me and then at Captain Parker and took in a deep breath.

"What can I do now to help get the other girls freed and put those wicked men behind bars for a long time? They've killed one of my friends, beaten and abused all of us and you should know that most of us were absolutely pure before we were taken prisoner."

Her lips trembled, her body shook and then she started sobbing, so I put my hand on her shoulder and smiled at her in an attempt to console her. Sandy looked at me with a furrowed brow. The young Montenegrin soon recovered her composure and apologised for her behaviour.

Captain Parker turned to her and smiled reassuringly, "Please, don't concern yourself my dear. You've had a terrible ordeal and both Nathan and myself are going to put together a plan which should ensure that the people who did this spend a long time in prison. Nathan, give me the cigarette stubs, I'll get them couriered to the police."

I handed him the plastic bag then turned towards Elena and spoke quietly to her.

"What you need to do now for Captain Parker is to draw a plan of The Board Room as far as you can remember. Also give him details of everyone who works there, in which room they're typically employed plus the whereabouts of the guards, especially those who guard the place after closing time.

I'll leave you for a while now as I need to make a couple of phone calls, one of which will be to find the address of that infernal place. I suggest you also tell The Captain about the policeman who visited the place, so we can deal with him as well. Is that OK?"

She nodded and I then turned and asked our host to show me another office where I could use the phone.

He took me upstairs into a single-person office fully fitted out with a desk, chairs and filing cabinets. I told him of my planned phone calls.

"Good, come back down when you've finished. Let's make sure we plan and execute this properly, in the way that the Corps would have done."

"Right, but we must have three stages in the plan. The rescues, the arrests and then, when those are complete, we must close down their whole operation, not just here in the UK, but back in eastern Europe as well."

"Agreed", he said briskly and then he was gone.

As I heard him going down the stairs I sat down at the desk and looked on to Park Square, gazing at the neat but fading flower beds which were now giving way to autumn colours and hues.

I needed to get clear in my mind what I should achieve in these two phone calls. So I composed myself and focused on my objectives. Firstly I took out of my pocket the pen Elena had given me bearing the logo and phone number of her former jail.

I phoned the number shown on the pen, putting on my best English accent. Giving a false double-barrelled surname I told the guy who answered the phone that a friend had recommended The Board Room as a place where top executives could relax and enjoy themselves.

I asked about membership and where they were located and, after I'd been given some facts about the facilities, I finished by saying I would pop in, pay the £1000 joining fee and pick up my membership card.

I wrote down the address and the details he gave me. I also told him I was a senior civil servant so needed absolute discretion, which he assured me would be the case. My flesh was still crawling at the unctuous voice when I eventually put the phone down.

I then opened up the computer on the desk in front of me, logged on to the internet and spent twenty minutes or so checking out some information on the search engine. Once I was satisfied I had the required details, I turned my attention to the telephone once more. I took a very deep breath and moved on.

This call was more difficult, and I was on the phone for thirty minutes. I took out the piece of paper where I'd written down the number obtained from directories while Elena was preparing the meal after our Carlisle trip. I wasn't looking forward to making the call but I was the best placed person to do it so I steeled myself and connected to an outside line again.

As the call clicked through it rang out no more than five or six times before it was answered and a male voice said "Zdravo", *hello*.

"Zdravo, dobro jutro, govorite li engleski, molim?"
Hello, good morning, do you speak English, please?

"Yes I do, how can I help you?"

"I would like to speak with Mr Milo Borovic, please."

"I am Borovic, who is this?"

"Good morning Mr Borovic, my name is Nathan Sawyer, I'm calling you from England. I recently retired after serving eighteen years in the Royal Marines spending part of my time helping your cause against the Serbians.

Can I ask you, sir; are you the father of Elena Borovic?" There was a startled gasp at the other end before he answered.

"I was, but my daughter is dead, why do you ask, what do you want?"

"Mr Borovic, your daughter is alive and well here in England with me." I could hear Milo had started sobbing at the end of the phone, so I waited a moment for him to regain control of his emotions.

"Last week I was coming to the end of a week's holiday in the city of Liverpool and late at night I was taking a walk when a car stopped and two Serbian men got out and started beating up a young lady very badly. I stopped them, knocked them both unconscious and put the lady in their car and drove her off to safety. That lady told me her name was Elena Borovic. I picked up my car then drove her to my house and during our long journey she told me her story."

"Mr Sawyer, if what you say is true I thank you more than you can imagine. You can't begin to understand how I've missed my beautiful daughter and how difficult it's been, not knowing what happened to her. But I must ask, how do I know that you are genuine and that this isn't some horrible joke?"

"I fully understand, Mr Borovic; your daughter was born in 1986 near to the Montenegrin city of Podgorica, her mother's name was Darinka. Your poor wife was murdered along with her minder Vjekoslav Vuletić by the Serbs on the way back from a nationalist rally in Cetinje. Elena eventually went to The University of Zagreb where she earned a degree in Law, your own subject."

"Ok, I'm sorry to have doubted you, Mr Sawyer but this has come as such a huge shock to me after over a year of not knowing what had happened to her."

"No problem but I must warn you, I'm afraid she's had a terrible time but I repeat she's safe now. She and a group of other girls, including her friend Lucija Babić were kidnapped and forced to work, I'm sorry to say, as sex slaves in Liverpool."

"Oh, my God, my poor little baby. What can I do now, can I speak to her?"

"Not at the moment, but I would like to engage the help of your organisation. Today, Elena and I have driven over to Leeds to meet my former Captain in The Royal Marines, whom I served under in Sarajevo, Sierra Leone and many other places.

He retired from the Corps a few years before I did and currently runs a high level private security firm working for the British Government. Right now, we are devising a suitable plan to rescue the other girls and put in prison the gang behind this terrible business.

As well as reuniting you with Elena, I need your help to repatriate the other girls and return them safely to their own families. There are about ten of them, from Bosnia, Croatia and Macedonia.

There aren't convenient flights from Podgorica or Tivat but on Wednesdays there is a flight just along the coast from you, leaving Dubrovnik flying direct to Manchester. It's flight number TOM 3526 and departs at 12.20, arrives in Manchester at 14.30. Today is Monday; could you make the flight this week on Wednesday?"

"Yes of course. I'd do *anything* to see Elena again," there was a genuine passion in his voice.

"Good, I'll meet you at Manchester airport and drive you back to Leeds and to our hotel, where you can be reunited with Elena.

I won't tell her you are on your way. She can have a nice surprise when you show up.

Then, over the next few days we can put the finishing touches to the plan to free the other girls and get them back to the hotel where we'll be staying in Leeds.

Believe me Mr Borovic, these men are very dangerous and the Serbs who work with them will think nothing of using the guns they have, so we need to plan very carefully.

The good thing is that in The Royal Marines we handled situations like this every day, so we know what we're dealing with. Are you happy with that?"

"I understand, Mr Sawyer. Is there anything you need me to do before I set off for England?"

"It would be a good idea for you to contact the parents of Lucija Babić. Unfortunately I don't know who the other girls are but at least Mr and Mrs Babić should know that we're trying to liberate their daughter and she's still alive."

He agreed to do that and I confirmed the flight details and filled him in on some more details of Elena's story, so he knew what to expect when he was reunited with her.

After I put the phone down, I spent a few moments collecting my thoughts. I was happy the call was over and I'd been able to give the poor man some good news after all he'd suffered in the last few years. I then gathered up my notes and went back downstairs.

When I walked back into the meeting room I saw there were lots of papers laid on the table with building layouts roughly sketched out on them.

"Everything OK, Nathan?"

"Couldn't be better, all went well. How are you two getting on?"

"We're making good progress, but I think we should stop for some lunch at this juncture. My secretary has been to the sandwich shop in the corner of the square and she'll be coming back shortly so let's clear this stuff off the table and relax for an hour or so."

"OK, Boss why don't we get ten minutes of fresh air first?"

"Good idea, let's do just that. Elena, if you wish to freshen yourself up first, the ladies is down the corridor to the right." He pointedly held the door open for her, so I think she got the message he needed to speak with me.

She smiled and left me alone with Sandy. I quickly told him that her father would be here on Wednesday and I was to pick him up at Manchester Airport and he'd agreed to help us with the language issues and help organise the repatriation for the girls.

Sandy was happy that we should keep this from Elena and said he'd keep her busy while I travelled across the M62. She came back into the room at that point so the three of us put on our coats and headed out of the front door into the city centre oasis that is Park Square.

Sandy was a perfect guide and pointed out some of the famous barristers' chambers on the square and regaled Elena with some of the renowned cases they'd tried or defended. He also told her about the TV series about a team of lawyers that was filmed there in the mid nineteen nineties. As Elena had qualified with a degree in the profession, she listened intently with genuine interest.

After a fifteen minute stroll enjoying the pleasant but weak October sunshine we retired to Sandy's office for some welcome sustenance and a warm drink.

As we tucked into our refreshments, Sandy asked Elena about her time at Zagreb University in an attempt to keep her mind away from her terrible ordeal.

She told him that she'd enjoyed her time there and her deep immersion in her studies had been very cathartic in helping her come to terms with the tragic murder of her mother. He enquired what her plans would have been once she had graduated, had she not been kidnapped.

She'd wanted to specialise in international law. Over the past fifteen years there had been many conflicts in Europe which had given rise to huge increases in refugees, fleeing for their lives, and a great rise in the number of economic migrants seeking a better life elsewhere.

In addition, the spread of various less savoury characters from some Eastern European States had been the root cause of higher levels of organised crime of which she had been a victim.

This she felt, provided great opportunities to provide personal assistance and a legal support system for the victims of both armed conflict and organised crime.

"That seems a good plan, Elena. Maybe when we've sorted out this present crisis we can look at that in more detail."

She looked at him with those deep brown eyes and gave him a brief smile, then looked across the table at me with a look I had not seen before in the time I had spent with this bruised and delicate young lady. It seemed to me that it was a mixture of restrained joy, but still with a hint of fear. After all, she had been through a terrible experience and was here in the care of relative strangers in a foreign land.

I was going to have to work on building her confidence and resolved to do just that.

Parker went on to tell her of some of the work he'd done since he left the Royal Marine Corps. He first described the various body guard duties he'd organised for his team to carry out.

Elena's interest increased substantially when he recalled how his organisation had carried out various overseas rescues and other dangerous missions. They'd brought over a dozen people safely out of Zimbabwe just before the recent elections had caused the violence against Brits to escalate.

A squad had parachuted into the war zone in Iraq and helped the British Army successfully extract four troopers who had been captured by insurgents.

Another detachment had been secreted into Bosnia and Serbia and picked up four key war criminals who now awaited trial in The Hague.

Sandy then changed the subject to our present situation. He had spoken to his brother who was Chief Constable of a NW Police Force. They discussed the fact that, with at least one senior Liverpool Police Officer frequenting the high class brothel, there was a concern he would alert Michael Grogan about the trouble that lay ahead for him. In addition we should find out how many other bent local officers there were who might help out Grogan.

Having finished our lunch Sandy took us back upstairs to another room, which had a sign on the door 'Operations Room.'

He brought with him his notes and the drawings he'd made during his discussions with Elena. As we went in I wasn't surprised at the layout, pretty much on military lines.

The room was equipped with a huge white board on one wall, and an LCD projector fixed on the ceiling. There were flip charts either side of a group of small meeting tables that were laid out in an open U fashion. Around the table six office armchairs were neatly placed in position. CD and video players and a laptop were all ready for use.

Elena and I sat on either side of the room, facing each other, while Sandy stationed himself at the front and picked up a couple of felt tip pens. He laid out the rough sketches he'd made from the description Elena had given him and started transposing them into larger and more detailed plans. Before drawing each section, he checked it out with her for accuracy and was anxious to increase the detail as much as possible.

Once he was reasonably happy the layout had been accurately portrayed he then started plotting locations of the personnel.

We spent the next hour or so discussing some of the logistics and tactics we could employ in the rescue mission. Sandy thought that it was likely that the best time for the operation was around 1.00 to 2.00 a.m. when it was almost certain that there'd be the minimum of staff on the premises.

Elena believed that there were no more than two men on duty during the night. My former Captain suggested that we should have a team of six men to carry out the exercise and take two ten seater-mini buses with us to bring back the girls with our team.

At that point he sat down and said that was as far as we should go for today and we should reconvene in the morning. He suggested I should take Elena to the hotel and get in some R&R and we'd take up the planning again tomorrow.

As a security measure the hotel owner had agreed not to have any other guests staying there whilst we were residents.

The only other person who wasn't on the hotel staff was one of Sandy's team who would stand guard during the hours of darkness. He would have an ID card, Sandy showed me his own card so I knew what to expect, and said he would get two made for Elena and I in the morning.

We took our leave of the great man and walked back to the multi-storey car park in The Light. After paying a small fortune at the ticket machine I set the sat-nav and we were soon on our way to the hotel in Roundhay. I turned to Elena as we drove out on to Great George Street, "Are you OK?"

"Yes, fine thanks but a bit tired."

"So what do you think of Captain Parker?"

"He's a good man, just like you Nathan Sawyer. Now I understand why the Serbians became very nervous and hated it so much when the Royal Marines were brought into the conflict."

I could see her radiant smile in the reflection of the traffic lights outside St John's Shopping Centre as we hit a red and waited for the pedestrians to cross. A few butterflies jumped about in my stomach at that moment. "Get a grip on yourself, Sawyer, you've only just met the girl" I thought to myself.

CHAPTER 7

Planning the Operation

As I pulled up on the gravel in front of the imposing red sandstone building with turrets on each corner I could see that this place wouldn't be easy to sneak into unnoticed.

It was built on a mound, and after we turned off the road, there was a 200 metre drive covered with crunchy gravel leading up to the front of the hotel.

There were no trees around the immediate area of the building, no shrubs to hide in and the whole area was covered by CCTV cameras. The noise we made on the gravel plus the TV monitor had obviously announced our arrival as the front door opened as soon as my car stopped.

As I got out, I turned round and saw the large steel gates shutting automatically at the bottom of the drive. Security was obviously being taken seriously.

A tall lean man came down the half a dozen stone steps with his hand held out in greeting and a warm smile on his face.

"Nathan, how good to meet you. I'm Adam Stones. Welcome."

He spoke in crisp clipped tones and shook my hand with a firm warm grip and met my gaze, eye ball to eye ball. Good start. Seemed like he was a man to be trusted.

He looked like a retired Rupert for sure, was even dressed like one; cavalry twill trousers and green sweater with brown leather patches on the elbows!! He then turned to Elena and smiled as he spoke softly to her,

"Miss Borovic, welcome to my hotel. You'll be safe here and I hope you find the accommodation is suitable for you."

She thanked him and then we took our cases from the car and followed Adam into his hotel. It was a building in pristine condition, craftsman fashioned from sandstone and built in the 19th century with mullion glass windows. We followed our host upstairs as he showed us to our rooms, which were opposite each other on the first floor. He told us we were expected downstairs for dinner at 19.30, if that was OK. We agreed so he left us with our room keys, our cases and a warm feeling of welcome and safety.

I let Elena into her room and recommended she make herself comfortable and have a sleep after a long and stressful day. She nodded and gave me one of her sweet smiles. She volunteered that we could go down for a drink half an hour before dinner.

"Good idea I'll give you a knock." She gave me a little wave as she closed her room door quietly.

I stepped into a nice double room with smart and comfortable furnishings and put the case up on the bed and moved over to the window.

As I gazed out the electric gates at the bottom of the drive were just closing. I looked to see who had arrived, remembering they had shut behind me when we drove in. A small red car was just disappearing round the back of the hotel.

As the gates clanged shut, a set of orange floodlights came on and bathed the extensive and pleasant grounds in their warm glow. It was now becoming clear that Adam's services were used regularly to provide a 'safe house' for whatever project Captain Parker was currently overseeing.

I sat and reflected on the events of the last couple of weeks and started making some detailed notes for discussion with Sandy in the morning. I figured we'd done pretty well so far but had a long way to go to complete this exercise. My main concern, which I would put on the agenda for tomorrow was, not the rescue, which should be easy for a small team from the Corps or the SAS, but how to bring Michael Grogan and his team to justice.

After an hour of deliberation I checked the time and decided to shower and change.

On the dot at 19.00 I knocked lightly on Elena's door. She asked me in as she wasn't quite ready. As I sat myself on her armchair I could see that her room was identical to mine except for the dominant colours which were pink whilst they were blue in mine.

Elena looked lovely in a red flared mini skirt that showed off her great legs to good effect. Her outfit was completed by a gold silken blouse. It looked like our shopping trip to Carlisle had worked well. She finished putting in her earrings, then applied her lipstick and turned to me with her hands on her hips and asked if she looked OK.

"Just perfect young lady, let's head off downstairs and I'll buy you a drink."

We walked down into the lounge where there was a small bar in the corner, complete with a barman waiting to serve us.

He proudly wore several campaign medals on his white jacket and displayed a confident but respectful demeanour as he served our order, a Jack Daniels and lemonade on ice for me, a fresh orange juice for Elena.

We'd just taken our seats on the leather chesterfield sofa when another man came in.

"Mr Sawyer?" he enquired. I nodded affirmation and stood up, positioning myself in front of Elena, just in case.

He showed me his ID card which was from Sandy Parker's company, Trans Continental Solutions Ltd and told us he was our added security, rejoicing in the name of Terry Davies. He gave me a heavy handshake and told me that he had spent ten years in the SAS and each night that we were in the hotel he would be here until 8.00 a.m. I surmised it was him who'd arrived in the small red car earlier.

As our eyes met we both smiled as there was always friendly rivalry between The Royal Marine Corps and The Special Air Service, but now was not the time to bring that up.

"Great to see we're in good hands then, Terry. Anything we need to watch out for?"

"At the moment, we're not aware of any issues, but, given the events of the past two weeks I'm here as an extra precaution, and, hopefully neither of you will need to use my services."

He smiled at Elena and as he reached forward to shake her hand, I could see he'd a gun under his jacket on the left side. Sandy was obviously not taking any precautions, which was good to see. As he turned back to me he gave me an electronic device, clad in small black case, with a button on the top.

"Press the button if you need to and that sends in the SAS in 20 seconds," he said with a wink and then he was gone.

When we sat down at the dinner table I made sure I kept Elena off the subject of her ordeal. We would have a long session with Sandy the next day so she needed some time with more pleasant thoughts running through her pretty head. Although I had seen some terrible things in my time in the services, it was usually man on man, except in Sarajevo where the Serbs had randomly killed women and children, but the traumas Elena had been through were something quite different.

So, to keep her mind off her recent past, I spent some time telling her about the city of Leeds, where we were currently holed up. How it was the third largest city in the UK after London and Birmingham and had a large financial and legal infrastructure. Like most UK cities it had to reinvent itself as the Far East had taken away its stranglehold on its traditional industries, which, in the case of Leeds was textile manufacture.

"So, why were you in Liverpool when you found me? Were you with a girlfriend or on your own?"

"No, I was on my own and I don't have a girlfriend. It's a little difficult to establish long term relationships when you spend so much time overseas on active combat duties and may be killed at any moment.

Before I joined The Royal Marines I'd always planned to go to Liverpool John Moores University to study Sports Science, but when my parents were killed I was completely on my own at eighteen. I had no family left and no longer had the heart to go to university.

I therefore decided to join up and make my career in the Corps instead of going into higher education. When I left the service, Sandy offered to rent his cottage to me at a good rate to help me to decide what I wanted to do with the rest of my life.

I booked a week in Liverpool to see the city where I'd have spent at least three years of my life if I had gone on to University there. I thought that after almost twenty years I'd finished active service, but then you turned up and screwed that up for me."

"So, have you decided what you're going to do yet?"

"No, before I met you, I hadn't really formulated any plans but right now I just want to keep my head free so I can concentrate on getting all your fellow captives out safely, and Grogan and his team behind bars. Once we've achieved that, then I may be able to think more clearly about where my future lies."

During dinner, I learned Elena was good at sport at school and kept on competing as an Undergraduate, representing Zagreb University at both tennis and sprinting, showing immense prowess in the 200 metres. She showed some disappointment that my rugby potential had been curtailed by the accident to my parents but was pleased to hear I still kept an interest in sport of all kinds.

"Although I'd spent all my adult life fighting other peoples' battles around the world, I still managed to read plenty and enjoy good literature and now look forward to being able to start going to the theatre and concerts when I have someone to go with."

She blushed and then smiled, suggesting we have an early night ready for what would be another traumatic day for her in the morning. I said I'd go for a walk around outside before going to bed so I suggested to Elena she should turn in. She smiled in agreement and left me in an instant.

I let Terry Davies know I'd be wandering around outside and set off to get my first bit of exercise for a couple of days. In the Corps we had to keep fit to stay alive and old habits die hard for me.

The autumn air was chilly but clear so I enjoyed a slow stroll through the extensive grounds of the hotel, kicking the fallen gold and brown leaves underfoot. Whilst there were no trees immediately round the hotel, round its boundary there were various conifers and some beech and chestnut trees.

My head was clear so I put my brain to use to think of how to steer Sandy in the right direction in the morning.

I was also thinking of how he would keep Elena busy whilst I headed off to Manchester to collect her father on Wednesday. Eventually I crunched back through the leaves to the hotel's front door.

Terry Davies must have been watching the CCTV since he opened the door as soon as I reached the steps. He told me he'd be stationed inside the front door and would tour the grounds every hour; I nodded at him and smiled my thanks then went upstairs to bed.

The next morning, we again parked in The Light and as we walked through its shopping centre I could see Elena's eyes light up as it was much more up market than the shopping areas we had visited on our trip to Carlisle when we were kitting her out. I steered her round to Park Square, and the office where Parker's PA let us in with a smile.

"He's waiting for you in the ops room."

We joined Sandy who greeted us warmly and enquired whether the hotel arrangements were satisfactory. I concurred and ventured he must use the place regularly.

"Yes, in the last few months I've had a renegade foreign President holed up there, then a British Cabinet Minister who needed to be kept away from the press for a couple of weeks. Finally two Crown Prosecution key witnesses we were protecting until they were needed at the trial of some drug smugglers we brought to justice. Never had any trouble, absolutely safe and Stones knows what to expect and gets well paid for it."

"Yes, that's a good point, as well as paying for the hotel, there will be a large cost for the rescue, Sandy. Where's the money coming from to pay for all of it?"

"Don't worry about that. What we're doing is providing a service to the Police, so I've been given a special budget from the Home Office that covers such eventualities. Although we have to account for all our costs, covering legitimate expenses for the operation won't be a problem."

I then realised what a powerful man my former Commander had become and maybe I should let him take the lead in this exercise. He started off by putting his agenda for the day up on the screen.

Plans for Wednesday
How to isolate Chief Superintendent Rowley
Infiltrating the premises to do a full recce
Transport
Choosing the team
Assault on the premises
Arrests
Witness protection
Repatriation

1. Plans for Wednesday

"Firstly the plans for tomorrow morning. Elena, Nathan has some private business to attend to tomorrow, so won't be back until late afternoon."

She looked at me anxiously but I told her not to worry, I should be back in the office at around 17.00.

"He'll bring you here in the morning, then, after that, I've arranged for my wife and eldest daughter to come into the office and take you into York by train for the day.

It's one of our oldest cities, with a beautiful centre, magnificent 1000 year old Minster and an ancient river running through its centre; it'll give you chance to relax and if you have time, you may even round off the day with afternoon tea at Betty's world famous tea rooms. A bodyguard will also be with you all day until you return to the hotel. Is that OK?"

"Sounds wonderful Captain Parker, thank you. I've read about York and the Wars of the Roses and seen pictures of The Cathedral."

"OK, but when you get there, don't refer to it as a Cathedral. They're very touchy about their Minster," he chuckled.

2. How to isolate Chief Superintendent Rowley

"Second, we need to take Chief Superintendent Rowley out of the picture. I realise this must be painful for you Elena but what did you learn about the man's work, if anything?"

"Not very much, on one occasion Michael Grogan sent for me to discuss Rowley. He told me the man was a very important client, for two reasons, so I 'should be nice to him' or I'd be in trouble.

I was informed Rowley was head of the vice squad in the city and therefore I assumed he was being bribed to keep the police away from The Board Room. Also Grogan said

Rowley was able to bring many high spending clients into the place."

I frowned and looked first at Parker then at Elena.

"I now have two deep concerns. Firstly Grogan tried to have us both assassinated by his gunmen at the cottage. Secondly he clearly was the man behind the torture of the two unfortunate owners of the hotel where I was staying.

I *had* signed the hotel register and entered my name and car registration number but I most certainly had *not* written my address. Therefore, for Grogan to know where to send his goons, he must have traced my address through my car registration number."

"Which means access to the police computer presumably, Nathan?"

"Yeah and I would put money on the fact that Rowley has a team around him who are as corrupt as he is. So it looks like he must have provided Grogan with the address from DVLA records or wherever they get their data from.

Since we both joined you yesterday I've been concerned about how they traced me. Someone close to Grogan must have seen me when I put Elena in my car in Liverpool and when I set fire to the BMW.

I guess we bought some leeway, maybe a couple of days, by issuing the press release saying we were dead, but I believe we now have to rethink our position.

If the gunmen go back to Fellside Cottage they'll see that my car is no longer there and possibly draw the conclusion that we're both still alive. They may even have persuaded those members of the police that they had in their back pockets to issue a call to search for my car."

Sandy thought for a brief moment: "OK, I agree. As he's head of vice, who is a regular customer of an expensive brothel and Grogan seems to be untouchable, I suspect that many of Rowley's team are also on Grogan's payroll.

My brother chairs a clandestine Home Office committee on police corruption. I'll ask him to arrange with his opposite number in Merseyside to second Rowley to some unimportant team based in the south east of England, out of harms way. Once the operation is underway, we'll have him arrested. We must also get your car back to Fellside Cottage today Nathan so give me your keys and I'll arrange it and get you something else to drive. Make sense?"

As we both nodded in agreement he picked up the phone and asked his secretary to come in for my car keys and parking ticket.

3.   Infiltrating the premises to do a full recce

"Whilst the information that you have given us, Elena, is fantastic, we need a risk assessment and first hand survey of the premises. If we're to undertake to extract around ten hostages with the minimum danger to them and the task force, we **must** know the premises intimately.

We should also have observed first hand the behaviour, the habits and the demeanour of the staff on the site. With all due respect to the information you've given us, my dear, we need to look at the building with a military eye and weigh up the risks. Any ideas, Nathan?"

"Yes, I thought this through after dinner last night as I walked round the hotel grounds. I suggest we get one of the team to actually become a member of The Board Room and visit the premises regularly as a customer. As a client he would not arouse suspicion as he moved around the building."

"OK, I think that's a capital idea. I'll sort one of my team out for that. Right, let's have some coffee and biscuits before we move on."

At that juncture Elena excused herself, which gave Sandy and I a couple of minutes on our own. I said that on that my return from Manchester Airport, I would go straight to the hotel with Milo Borovic and give Sandy a call with our ETA.

"OK, no problem, I'll have my wife drop Elena back here from the station then I'll drive her back to Roundhay. I never let my family go near the hotel when there is an operation underway."

"OK, copy that Captain," I was feeling almost happy to be back on active combat planning again.

4. Transport

When Elena returned we broke for coffee then moved on to the next item on the agenda. Sandy figured we would need a couple of ten seater mini-buses; we would have a team of six on hand and Sandy plus myself and possibly an interpreter, if needed. In addition there was the small matter of around ten freed hostages. So we needed to be able to seat everyone on the return journey back to Leeds.

Sandy and I would travel in a separate command vehicle with whatever equipment we needed. The vehicles would all be unmarked and dark in colour so as not to attract attention when they moved into place on the mission.

"All our vehicles in the fleet are deliberately unobtrusive, though not camouflaged. I figure that was about the total vehicles we would be likely to need."

5.   Choosing the Team

"I suggest that given the violence displayed towards Elena and all her fellow captives, and then the cold blooded intent of the gunmen who turned up at the cottage, we were looking at opposition who would stop at nothing to achieve their own ends.

Although clearly very dangerous they seemed not too skilled in planning operations or keeping themselves hidden. It should, in theory, therefore, be possible to outwit these thugs.

It was essential the six we put into the team should be battle hardened, fully experienced in unarmed combat and preferably have proven experience in extracting hostages from dangerous situations."

Parker responded positively and agreed to put such a team together. He finished by saying we would sort out an interpreter after tomorrow and suggested we take a lunch break.

6. *Assault on the Premises*

Sandy started us off again after a good cold buffet his secretary put together.

"Elena what are the arrangements after the premises close for the night?"

"As far as I am aware, all the section heads (bar, casino, gym, etc) took their cash takings up to Grogan's office and handed them in to the duty manager or Grogan himself if he was on the premises.

The two night guards would arrive about half an hour before closing. After cashing up, a check was made that no clients were left on the premises; then the girls were sent up to their rooms. The staff went home for the night, just leaving two security men on duty.

One guard was stationed on the reception desk during the night, watching the CCTV. The other stayed in the office, so presumably they changed round part way through the evening."

"Does Michael Grogan's office have CCTV monitors, as well as the reception desk?"

"Yes I saw them on his wall when I was in his office. There are also hidden cameras in each girl's room and they videoed us with clients; I saw his library of video tapes on a rack near his desk," she said this with a tremble in her voice.

I came in at that point, "We could use the video tapes as evidence, then, especially to convict Chief Superintendent Rowley."

"Yes we can. I think our first task on the night is to get in without arousing suspicion or without using too much force. Any ideas?"

"When I escaped I could see that door security was usually observed quite strictly. If you're going to have one of your men become a member, he would be the best bet to get back in. Maybe he could return after closing time, ring the front door buzzer and say he'd lost his wallet inside the club earlier in the evening. What do you think, Nathan?"

"Good idea, then as the night guard opens the door, our man knocks him out and lets the team in."

Sandy countered, "We would have to be quick to get upstairs and neutralise the second man before he could raise the alarm. OK let's fill in the detail later and move on."

7. Arrests

"We not only have to plan the entry and rescue very carefully, but we have to ensure that all the miscreants are taken into custody on the same night.

I need to discuss this with the police. My own view is that we should have an armed police special ops team, from outside Liverpool, on standby in the environs of the target zone.

After we've entered and secured the premises, and liberated the girls we should bring in the police hit squad. They should pick up whoever is on the premises at the time, and then wait inside for the remainder to arrive for duty and arrest them immediately."

"OK, the police will need secure vehicles to put everyone in once they're arrested. I think if the cops are armed, it would be better if the reprobates were all taken out at once. If they are taken out one at a time there is a chance the alarm could be raised if a staff member spots them as they arrive for work."

8. Witness Protection

We discussed this briefly as it was quite easy to agree on a course of action.

The Crown Prosecution Service would need the evidence of the girls in order to get a maximum convictions and sentences.

Clearly Grogan was still going to have criminal friends on the outside and may well attempt to intimidate the witnesses.

Therefore we concurred that the best course of action was for them to be hidden away in the hotel in Leeds with a team of armed guards protecting them round the clock until the trial date. We'd need to reassure the girls that they were now safe, and we'd be helping them get back to their homes and families, in due course.

9. Repatriation

Given that Elena didn't know we were going to be joined by her father, we skated over this item in short order. We merely agreed that we'd set up a team to get the girls safely home when the trials were complete. We had to engage Social Services, the Immigration Service and any other Government Agencies that were appropriate.

Sandy closed by saying he'd draw up a formal plan and set up a meeting with the police to agree the protocol and detailed planning.

So, at that point we bid him goodnight, left his offices and headed off back to our hotel.

CHAPTER 8

Milo Borovic

The replacement vehicle Sandy had provided for me was a suitably anonymous Ford Mondeo in a steel grey colour. We made our way back safely to Roundhay and I used the twenty minute journey to get Elena's views on how she thought the planning was going, given her fairly detailed inside knowledge of the layout of The Board Room.

She seemed reasonably happy, but at the same time clearly very nervous as we were both acutely aware of how vicious our adversaries were.

"Another thing I remember Nathan is maybe as often as two nights per month, I heard a lot of noise just along the corridor from my room.

We weren't allowed outside our rooms, but from the noises I could make out, it sounded like bulky material was being moved from upstairs.

Then on the occasions I'd been in Grogan's office, there were Turkish/English phrase books on his desk, along with an A-Z of Istanbul."

I made a mental note to let Sandy have this information, wondering to myself whether Grogan was merely a pawn and the real 'Mr Big' actually resided alongside the Sea of Marmara.

Rested and showered, I joined Elena in the bar at 19.30 where we both had a couple of soft drinks whilst making our choices from the menu.

Dinner was going to be difficult for me as Elena may innocently enquire what my plans were for Wednesday. So I took the plunge and did my tourist guide job for Yorkshire, and York in particular, trying hard to keep her mind occupied.

She seemed quite interested in the background information I was able to give her on the County and was certainly excited about visiting a real medieval city in the heart of Britain.

As we were taking our coffee in the lounge, I suggested that she might like to take a relaxing holiday when this nightmare was over. Somewhere with winter sunshine and a laid back attitude where she could recharge her batteries and get some colour back into her cheeks.

Her skin was like bone china and still had a pallid look after over a year spent indoors, apart from the few days with me in The Lake District.

She smiled in assent, "Where would you suggest, Nathan?"

"There are many islands in Europe which are warm all year round, such as Madeira or The Canary Isles. Cyprus also has lots of winter sunshine, but is an island divided by politics."

"Maybe you could show me what they're like, then."

I looked into her bright brown eyes long and hard, before answering. I saw genuine affection in there. I'd have been unhappy if she made that comment out of sheer gratitude.

I put out my hand and squeezed hers, "We've a lot to do yet, and we must keep you safe, but that would be something nice to think about, and a good thought on which to end the day."

We both stood up, looking at each other slightly self-consciously, her words hanging heavily between us and then made our way in awkward silence upstairs to our own rooms.

I put a collar and tie on the next morning, feeling the need to present a professional image for Mr Borovic.

Elena was animated over breakfast and during the car journey to Sandy's office. She was obviously excited about the prospect of a conducted tour of one of our most beautiful cities.

Mrs Parker was awaiting our arrival at her husband's offices along with her daughter Natasha. They were both striking and attractive ladies, each with carefully coiffured natural long blonde hair and sporting smart casual clothes, understated but coolly elegant.

Elena looked lovely herself, her shiny black locks tumbling over her red coat, under which she wore a cream high neck sweater. Black cords caressed her slim legs and black ankle boots completed her outfit. She greeted her guides with enthusiasm and anticipatory pleasure.

I acknowledged them warmly and then checked out their assigned bodyguard, who introduced himself as Sergeant Barry King, twelve years as a Para. That'll do for me, I thought to myself, he should be able to look after them OK.

They set off almost immediately to catch the train to York, which was good as it gave me a fair bit of one-to-one time with Sandy before setting off to collect Milo from Manchester Airport.

We poured ourselves a coffee each and then sat down to discuss tactics. I told him of the comments Elena had made last night about Istanbul. He was very interested in the possible connection with Turkey and how she'd heard noises that suggested someone was moving large items after hours.

"The two facts are probably connected, Nathan. Turkey has a growing reputation for being heavily involved in the illegal trafficking of women for the sex trade.

By the mid nineties, over 500,000 women were being trafficked annually into The EU from various eastern European countries and parts of Asia.

The Home Office estimates that 4,000 trafficked women are being forced into prostitution in The UK alone at any one time. Istanbul seems to be one of the main sources of supply of these poor unfortunate ladies.

I wonder whether Grogan may well be involved in drug smuggling as well. Clearly if these suppositions are true we could possibly be taking on a large international network.

If the Liverpool operation is protected by corrupt police men we need to tread carefully and keep this in house. The alternative is to put some police untouchables in our squad.

If we choose the wrong cops to work with they are likely to alert their paymasters which would put us all in danger and could screw up the whole operation."

"I agree. Obviously you need to confer with your brother. My view is we should run it in house, possibly supported by some guys from MI6 who know how to handle themselves and would be able to take down the overseas operation as well."

"Roger that. How are things going with Elena? She must have been really traumatised when you rescued her."

"She was, boss, but I gave her some retail therapy and lots of yomping in the fresh air in the Lake District, plus I tried hard to make her feel safe.

She's certainly much happier than when I rescued her, although the attempted assassination in the cottage spooked her quite a lot.

She couldn't believe how easily the goons found us, but she's quite happy now considering the terrible experience she's gone through and gets a little stronger each day.

I think when she sees her father tonight she'll begin to believe that she's one step nearer to getting back to normality, although it could be many years before the nightmare is completely pushed to the back of her mind."

"OK Nathan is she still unaware of her father's intended arrival?"

"Correct, I worked hard last night to keep her mind off the fact that I'd be AWOL today."

"One tricky thing we'll have to watch is her father may well want to take her home straight away. Indeed, the families of the other girls may want them back immediately and to hell with our trial."

"That did cross my mind, but as far as I can tell, all of them have suffered much and Elena believes once their families know they're safe, they'll do what they can to help us get Grogan and his gang behind bars.

The overseas element is another kettle of fish. Presumably MI6 would be able to work with their foreign counterparts to pick up the alien members of the hierarchy?"

"In theory, yes, but we're dealing with some suspect nations. As we know from our time in the Corps, some of the overseas police may well have been bought as well. Don't forget that the girls were brought to Liverpool in a truck and, for part of the journey, by sea, which suggests that it was all too easy to get past border guards and customs officers."

"Shit, yes, I'd forgotten about that. Maybe some summary justice is called for in the case of the gang members based in Europe."

"An interesting thought, which may well be our only way forward, but the repercussions of a hit squad taking out a number of foreign individuals may be difficult to cover up. Not impossible, though, as you may recall it was done several times in the Balkans crisis.

But that was war, where the rules of engagement are somewhat different to crime fighting. Maybe my brother and I should speak with the Home Secretary and the Foreign Secretary. First things, first, let's get the rescue over and the UK arrests made, then consider what's to be the next part of the operation."

We talked in some more detail about the first phase and when to kick it off. The first thing to do was to get someone on the inside.

Parker also told me there were no signs of anyone having been back to Fellside Cottage when they took my car back there, so hopefully Elena and I were still dead as far as Grogan was concerned.

The SOCO squad had got some good fingerprints and handprints from the front door and the bed heads at Fellside Cottage so would need to take mine and Elena's to eliminate them. They had also recovered six bullets and shells.

I took my leave of Sandy and headed for Manchester. The journey across the M62 was uneventful so I was soon parked up in the short term car park and I remembered to take with me the placard that Sandy's secretary had given me with Milo's name on it.

I called in at the gents before going to arrivals and had a quick look at myself in the bank of mirrors there. My face looked back at me from beneath a reddish brown crop of straight, neatly cut hair (old habits die hard), with just a dozen or so grey hairs beginning to appear and with a nose that was slightly crooked from an altercation with the butt of a rifle when on ops in Sierra Leone.

The guy who was holding the other end of the rifle was immediately put on his back for his trouble, nursing a broken arm and relieved of his weapon!!

So this was what Elena's father would see, a man in his late thirties, lean, suntanned, muscles well toned, medium height and not bad looking, or so I had been told in my past during a couple of close encounters of the female kind!!

I straightened my tie and went back out into the arrivals hall, feeling somewhat nervous about this meeting, for some reason.

After a coffee to settle my nerves I walked towards the barriers in the arrivals hall where several flights were disgorging their passengers. I held my board up with the name of Elena's father clearly visible.

The crowd started to thin out and then there were a few stragglers just ahead of the cabin crew. I scanned their faces and then a smartly dressed man in his late forties smiled and waved at me.

As I looked in his direction with a smile, I saw he was around six feet tall with neat black hair and a face that was slightly drawn, which was not surprising after what he'd gone through in the last two years.

He wheeled his luggage trolley towards me and held his hand out "Mr Sawyer?"

"Yes indeed, Mr Borovic, welcome to England. Elena's fine. She doesn't know you are coming, so Captain Parker's wife and daughter have taken her out for the day to York, one of our most beautiful tourist cities.

We've been staying at a hotel which is run by a former British Army officer and is used by our government to provide secure accommodation for diplomats and foreign nationals who are in danger.

Security measures are high and you'll be staying there so I'll drive you to Leeds right now."

He told me the trip had been OK but he'd been totally pre-occupied since we spoke on the phone a couple of days ago. He was fearful of how her terrible experience had affected his daughter and how Elena was bearing up after her ordeal.

I took the luggage trolley off him and walked across the arrivals hall to the car park pay station with Milo carrying his small carry-on case following me at a brisk pace. We were soon sitting in the car and on our way back to Leeds.

"Mr Sawyer…"

"Please call me Nathan."

"OK, Nathan, thank you, I'm Milo. Can you tell me as much as you can about what has happened to Elena and how you came to find her?"

His English was very good, with only the slightest hint of an accent.

As we pulled away on to the M56 then the M60 I told him of my background and my time in the Royal Marines, including our operations in Bosnia and Kosovo.

As a 'local', as it were, from that region he was most interested in this aspect of my career as the conflict in Bosnia had, of course had a terrible impact on his family.

I also gave him the full low down on Sandy Parker's private army and their high standing with the British Security Service, and the Foreign Office. He relaxed a little after listening intently as my story unfolded.

As I told Milo about my chance encounter with Elena he kept interjecting with probing questions. Obviously it pained him to hear of the dreadful ordeal that his daughter had experienced, along with her fellow captives, but he wanted to get clear in his mind what we were up against.

He was especially interested in hearing that Serbians, and possibly Turks were the main perpetrators of this particular activity in the murky world of people smuggling and the sex slave industry.

After I'd given him chapter and verse he enquired what the next steps were.

"Well, we're planning to rescue the other girls and have the gang members arrested and brought to trial. Captain Parker's team is full of ex military personnel who're fully experienced in hostage rescue and close combat.

We'd hope we can persuade the girls to testify against the villains who have held them for the last twelve months or more. We will, of course, wish to reunite them all with their families and enlist the aid of the UK Government to facilitate their repatriation."

"I am eternally grateful for what you've done for Elena and I can assure you that my organisation will be at your disposal to help with your task.

We're not soldiers, you understand, but we do help refugees and individuals affected by the Balkans war.

In addition, we have many high level contacts in the Governments in that part of the world, especially Montenegro of course, plus Croatia, Macedonia, Bosnia and Kosovo, with limited contact with Serbia.

We can bring language skills, local legal knowledge and have a good relationship with Interpol. Since you and I spoke on the phone I've made contact with their department which is responsible for stamping out the illegal trafficking of girls for the sex trade."

This was music to my ears and I told him so. Clearly Parker's team were likely to have good support after we'd liberated the girls.

Exactly four hours after Milo's plane landed I was buzzing the intercom at the hotel gates. I left his luggage in the car and then deposited Milo in the lounge, in the far corner away from the door and went swiftly upstairs to Elena's room.

She answered my tap on the door almost immediately and gave me a radiant smile. She let me in and started to tell me enthusiastically what a great day she had 'doing the tourist thing' in York.

They'd seen much and the visit ended up at Betty's Tea Rooms for what she said was a wonderful afternoon tea which would require her to go on a diet for a month. She also told me how much she'd enjoyed the company of her gracious hosts.

"Great, I'm glad you enjoyed it, now come down to the lounge and we can talk about my day."

I didn't give her the opportunity to reply and walked ahead of her downstairs and across the hall into the lounge. As we crossed the room into the alcove Elena followed me then gave out an almighty scream, burst into tears and ran across the room.

Her father stood up and took her in his arms with tears flowing down his cheeks.

They stood locked together for several minutes, not speaking, just sobbing in each other's arms.

The relief and the joy were immense and despite my years in the armed forces I too was greatly moved by the scene in front of me.

I left them to it.

CHAPTER 9

Next Steps

I'd decided to leave Elena and her father alone for the rest of the evening. They clearly needed to do some private catching up.

After she'd recovered her composure and broken free from Milo's protective embrace she rushed over to me and threw her arms around my neck and gave me a huge kiss which took my breath away,

"Nathan, you found my papa for me, thank you, thank you. How did you manage that?"

"Just call it intuition. There weren't likely to be many lawyers called Borovic in Kotor, so it was quite easy, really. Now, listen to me, I'm going to leave you and your Dad on your own to catch up, so let's bring in his luggage, you settle him into his room, then the two of you should have a nice quiet dinner together. Is that OK?"

"Fine but what will you do?"

"I'll eat out and see you both in the morning. We'll all three go together to Sandy's office and plan the next steps."

An hour later I was parked up in multi storey car park at The Light and popped into the Chinese restaurant on the balcony.

After a good selection of various oriental dishes was polished off I bought a cinema ticket for the multi screen outlet. I viewed the latest Bond epic, which was quite enjoyable, smiling to myself that he always seemed to get the woman in the end. If only...............

Breakfast the next morning was quite an interesting affair. Milo seemed quite subdued as on the previous evening he'd obviously been made aware in more detail of the suffering his poor unfortunate daughter had endured. Elena for her part was a little livelier as if the reunion with her father had restored some normality into her life.

We were all seated in Sandy's office before 9.00 a.m. where he made Milo very welcome. We soon were putting some flesh on the bones of the plan we'd been hatching over the past few days.

Sandy had been busy the previous afternoon while I'd been collecting Milo. Chief Superintendent Rowley had already been transferred out of the way, on secondment to the vice squad based in Brighton, supposedly to add muscle to the local force's efforts. So that was the main potential informer to Michael Grogan out of the way.

Following a three way conference call between Sandy, his brother and a high ranking official from the Home Office, he'd also reached agreement that the assault on The Board Room and the arrest of the Grogan men could be handled by Parker's own team.

When the operation was complete, those arrested would then be handed over to the police for charges and arraignment.

Sandy also had a meeting with one of his men, Duncan Clarke who was given the task of becoming a member of The Board Room.

As Elena, Milo and myself listened to his summary of that meeting, I, for one, could see why he'd been picked for that task.

He was thirty nine years old, had spent twenty years in the army where his speciality was infiltrating enemy lines on reconnaissance missions and he was highly skilled in unarmed combat.

He'd also spent three years on active service in the Balkans conflict and spoke some Croatian and Serbian. He was to start his role immediately and report to Parker by email every morning.

Clarke had been allocated a device for pin-pointing hidden CCTV cameras. He was also to take photos of the interior of the premises on his mobile phone, whenever he could do so without arousing suspicion.

Milo was briefed on the nationalities of the remaining girls and he didn't see any problem getting help from their respective governments in repatriating them. Even those that didn't have their passports when kidnapped, or even those who might have had their passports destroyed by Grogan should have no worries.

Mr Borovic then described to Sandy the sort of contacts he'd built up in the various countries in Eastern Europe. As he'd already told me on the way back from the airport, these included trustworthy government officials and 'untouchables' in various police forces concerned with stamping out the evil trade of trafficking girls for prostitution.

Sandy saw this information as very positive and once our operation had been completed successfully even suggested that there may be an opportunity to establish a long term relationship with Milo's business set up.

When he said this, I stole a glance at Elena, but she spotted me, blushed then turned her head away.

Sandy was going to liaise with the Home Office on the subject of holding in a high security prison, while they were awaiting trial those whom we were to arrest.

He also thought that the freed captives could be secured in our hotel in Roundhay until they could give evidence.

The Home Office felt that evidence by video link would be safer for the girls.

Three more armed men would be added to the security at our hotel to provide us with round the clock protection for our freed hostages.

As the day wore on we put more detail into the planning of the actual assault on the premises. The one thing we couldn't yet determine was the best date on which to carry out the operation. This would depend on the sitreps and intel from Duncan Clarke.

Sandy had tasked him with providing a detailed drawing of the place as soon as possible, to enable us to compare it with Elena's.

He was also to study the staffing arrangements and front door security to see if they'd changed since Elena's escape.

Finally, while posing as a client he was to try and meet as many of the captive girls as possible and provide feedback on them and their current demeanour as well as listening out for any possible mention of Elena and her flight to freedom.

Over the next week, the four of us met in Sandy Parker's operations room for eight or nine hours each day. Sometimes we were joined by Sandy's PA when tasks needed to be allocated and other times by members of his private army when individual briefings were called for.

One of them was given the task of carrying out a full recce of the locality of The Board Room and its surrounding area. It was a prerequisite to be able to get our vehicles into the area without creating suspicion and plan a swift exit once the operation was over.

Duncan Clarke would only draw attention to himself if he started nosing around outside, so the second man would quietly work out the detail for a ground attack in due course.

Our inside man's emails with photo attachments were helpful in building up the detailed planning. The cover he employed was that he'd started a new high powered job in a large plc which had its headquarters on Merseyside.

He was bored with spending nights on his own in a hotel just round the corner from The Board Room. So as not to arouse suspicion, he didn't visit every night, leaving a gap of a couple of days between each visit.

Always this was quite late at night, usually around 22.00 hours; in order that he could leave late and, bit by bit, build up a current picture of the nightly closing procedures in the club. His reports were succinct but meticulous and pretty soon we were reasonably familiar with the layout of the building.

From the initial reports it seemed that there was no change from the security procedures Elena had described to us earlier. That would make our task easier.

We had to get one person in the front door and keep it open to let the rest of team in. Tricky but do-able.

According to Clarke's observations, there were still only two night guards on the premises, one on reception and one in the office. Therefore we could safely assume that Elena had, in Grogan's eyes, been taken out of the picture by the visit of his gunmen to my cottage. Thus he'd probably be expecting to carry on his evil business as before, as if nothing had happened.

The team member tasked with carrying out the exterior recce had also been back to base and given us a full report. This included a detailed street map and photographs of the street where the club was.

He'd been able to secretly take close-up photos of the front of the club by watching the movement of the CCTV camera, then quietly taking his shots when the surveillance camera was looking elsewhere.

A large stone built porch protruded from the front of the building and the entrance doors were built into the centre of this. The porch was around three feet deep which meant that there was a blind spot on either side of the front door where the hit squad could secrete themselves.

Only one of the two solid oak doors seemed to be used, the other remained shut so only one person at a time could go in or out. The streetlights in that area were not brilliant, so concealment was going to be easier for the squad. Their own vision wouldn't be a problem, being kitted out with night vision goggles.

By the middle of the second week of the planning, we were confident we'd covered all bases so Captain Parker set the date for our operation, it was to be the following Monday.

In the week leading up to that, Sandy had all the team in for a full day's briefing. This included Elena and Milo, who were to accompany us on the operation to act as interpreters and liaison with the other girls.

They weren't to be involved with the assault on the premises, but would be brought in to the building once it was secure.

Milo was at first very apprehensive about having his daughter involved in the planned rescue. Elena put up a spirited defence on the basis that she owed it to her friend and the other girls to be there to comfort them and reassure them that they'd be safe from then on. Eventually her father recognised the wisdom of this, but the decision still sat uneasily with him.

By now, I was beginning to feel the adrenalin running through my body, just like when Parker and I were in the Corps going into battle or involved in an undercover operation.

Both of us had some real concerns about how we would be able to arrest Grogan and his main men, assuming they weren't likely to be on the premises when we went in.

So, we had a back up plan if this was needed. We planned to have a reserve team who could hit the home address of Grogan and, armed with a warrant, pick him up then search his house.

Always we had in mind that we had to *BOTH* rescue the girls *AND* secure the imprisonment of the gang, then to capture and put on trial the foreign team behind the human trafficking and drug smuggling.

After each day in the office in Park Square yours truly plus Elena and her father went back to the hotel in Roundhay, and, after an hour's R&R we would dine together.

I was getting to know Milo quite well during our time together. He was a thoughtful man with a quick brain and a real desire to see the break up of the chain that'd been running this prostitution racket for so long.

His own business back in Kotor had been partially set up with Government funding; he also had a second office in Dubrovnik. This had enabled him to quickly gain a solid reputation for helping war victims and refugees.

He had a small staff, which had grown in the last couple of months as the pressure increased on the organisation to provide help tracing persons who had gone missing, especially young women, and, bizarrely, children.

After doing some work on a few files on missing children, it became clear to him that they were being sold into slavery in paedophile rings. What an appalling world we were now living in.

When this terrible truth dawned on Milo he realised that his work would never be done. As soon as his organisation successfully closed one file, another one appeared on his desk. He said to me that his life's work was now clear to him. His qualifications and previous profession as a lawyer gave him the right experience; his exposure to the predicament of many needy people had made this his chosen cause. His daughter's plight, as had been revealed to him since he arrived in England had merely reinforced his determination.

Elena seemed to have changed slightly after her father appeared on the scene. She seemed more relaxed, as if she felt she was back in the bosom of her family again. She and I weren't spending as much time alone together, nevertheless the bond which we were beginning to form before Milo's arrival seemed as strong as ever. She still seemed comfortable in my presence and a couple of times I caught her looking at me, then blushing when I spotted her. On the few occasions when we were alone together we were able to laugh a little and she even joked about her 'assassination' back in the cottage in Cumbria.

"Not many people can have been kidnapped, escaped, murdered then helped put together a hostage rescue, all in fifteen months, can they?" She said playfully one night, as we enjoyed a quiet coffee together in the hotel lounge.

As the weekend approached the team rehearsed their roles again and again, and we asked all the 'what if' questions in order to ensure all angles had been covered.

One of the 'what ifs' we debated at length was the timing of our planned assault.

It was clear that after closing time at The Board Room there'd be very few people there to arrest. However, in any hostage rescue situation, our training in the Royal Marines had shown us that it was essential to minimise any risk to the captives whom we were seeking to liberate.

Thus the potentially low number of men from Grogan's team who were likely to confront us was a considerable bonus in terms of being able to safely extract the girls. We therefore made alternative plans for the arrests of the rest of the gang plus Grogan himself.

Sandy had got all the equipment in place, weapons, vehicles, uniforms, restraints and so on.

We were going to war again, Sandy and I. We were initiating a major hostage rescue situation, not in Kosovo, not in Sierra Leone nor Iraq, but right here in the North of England. The hostage takers were likely to be armed and had already demonstrated a predilection for extreme violence so it would be no picnic for our team. However, we'd be dealing with criminals, not trained soldiers, so we'd be the ones who were holding the whip hand. Roll on Monday.

But before then we'd the weekend to get through. Milo said he would prefer to spend most of Saturday on his own to bring himself up to date with his business activities so would have his head buried in his laptop and mobile phone.

The hotel had internet access so he'd been scanning his emails daily. His colleagues had been keeping him up to speed, and a number of high profile cases needed his urgent attention. He smiled a thank you when I told him that wouldn't be a problem.

I suggested to Elena we have a day out to give her dad some peace and quiet. She jumped at the chance so I examined a road atlas which I'd borrowed from the owner of our hotel. After looking around the various areas of Yorkshire on the pages in front of me, I decided that a ninety minute drive across the A64 would do it.

After breakfast on Saturday, we bade our temporary goodbyes to Milo and set off in the direction of the Leeds ring road and then on to the A64, ninety minutes later we were in the lovely coastal town of Scarborough.

Elena had been quite cheerful on our journey from Leeds and she revelled in the pretty countryside through which we were driving.

The A64 took us through the pretty villages of Stamford Bridge and Malton whose beauty alone made the journey worthwhile. Because it was now the start of the English winter, the road was pretty quiet but I figured in the summer it would be a different kettle of fish.

Doubtless this A-class road, with little or no dual carriageways would be heaving with tourists on their way to the strikingly beautiful Yorkshire coast.

I parked up in The Brunswick Pavilion multi storey car park and we marched off to look for a nice spot for a coffee; we found just the place in one of the hotels on The Crescent overlooking the beautiful South Bay.

We then took a walk past the Town Hall and down on to Foreshore Road towards the fish pier. It was a pleasant late autumn morning, with the weak rays of the sun still creating enough light to bounce off the North Sea and reflect on to the old harbour buildings.

The crisp air soon put some colour in Elena's cheeks and she seemed in a happy state. We walked towards this ancient haven for the fleet of fishing boats, now sadly depleted but still plentiful enough to provide a colourful vista as we approached the quayside.

As we stood in front of the lifeboat station on west pier the sun was shining through the rigging on the trawlers. They were all brightly painted in hues of red and powder blue, peeling in many cases and showing other signs of neglect. Clearly this once busy and profitable fishing port was on its uppers and was just about surviving.

As Elena commented on how beautiful the sunlight was she turned her brightly shining eyes towards me and put her head on my shoulder as we stood there taking in the beauty of the harbour and enjoying the pleasure of each other's company.

I reached over and lifted back into place the strand of her shiny black hair that had strayed into her eyes. As my fingers touched her forehead I felt a tingle down my spine. "Mmm. Take it easy Sawyer." I mused to myself.

"Elena we couldn't visit Scarborough without trying fish and chips, an English gastronomic delight that you haven't yet sampled."

So after exploring the harbour area we sought out a suitable fish restaurant and were soon seated at a square table with excellent views over the harbour.

The table was covered with a plastic table cloth in a blue and white gingham check and had the obligatory vinegar bottle and sauces neatly placed in one corner.

The cheery middle aged waitress soon arrived to take our order.

"Two special haddocks with a pot of tea for two," she repeated in a nicely rounded Yorkshire accent as she wrote our orders down on her pad.

"Do you want your tea now, sir?" I nodded and smiled at this pleasant lady who was a credit to the restaurant.

Ten minutes later we were tucking in to Yorkshire's finest. Lovely crisp batter on the haddock, how it should be, served with freshly fried large chips, none of this micro waved rubbish offered up in the fast food outlets.

Elena cleaned her plate off fully, even devouring the mushy peas which she'd never tried before, along with the generous helping of bread and butter.

As I poured a second cup of tea, lost in thought, the soft Yorkshire tones broke my reverie.

"Can I get you anything else, sir?"

We both looked at her and smiled; I said we were quite full so needed a walk to work off some of the calories. As we were paying the bill, in which I gave her a generous tip, our server suggested a stroll from where we were would take us to Peasholm Park, so that's exactly what we did.

We spent a pleasant and relaxing couple of hours which included a nice walk round the lake in Peasholm. By then it was around 15.30 so I decided we should walk back towards the harbour and catch the sunset.

As we left Peasholm Park I reached for Elena's tiny hand and gave it a gentle squeeze. She didn't resist, just gave me one of her enigmatic smiles, so I held her hand as we walked back to the west pier.

We were just in time to witness the sun slipping low in the sky, past Scarborough's castle on its imposing hill.

As we leaned on the steel railings on the harbour's edge I cupped Elena's chin in my left hand and gently stroked her forehead with my other hand.

She moved her face closer to mine so I gave her a glancing kiss on her forehead, another on the tip of her tiny nose then a short kiss on her parted lips. She put her arms round my neck and kissed me back, looking me straight in the eyes as she did so.

We turned back to the harbour and saw the last vestiges of sunlight as the giant orange ball was swallowed up by the North Sea.

Five minutes later we were walking back to the car park, with Elena's arm through mine and clinging on tightly to me. Neither of us spoke on the way back to the car, enjoying a comfortable silence, happy in each other's company.

Two hours later, back in our hotel in Roundhay we found Milo in the lounge with a pot of coffee in front of him and his laptop closed up but a pile of papers stacked up beside him on the bench seat.

I suggested that he'd perhaps had a busy day. He seemed pleased with what he'd been able to achieve in our absence and was now as up to date with his business as was possible without actually sitting at his own desk.

Later that evening, over dinner, Elena told her father what we'd been doing on the east coast. She enquired if he'd any work to do on Sunday.

When he said he was free I decided I'd take them both to another Yorkshire beauty spot, Fountains Abbey and Studley Royal.

I needed to keep both of them calm, relaxed and with their minds occupied rather than worrying about the operation on Monday.

The following day we drove over to North Yorkshire, via the exquisite spa town of Harrogate and its imposing Georgian terraces and soon were parking the car in the National Trust car park at Fountains Abbey Studley Royal.

We bought a bag of stale bread from the lakeside tearoom and Elena delighted in feeding the plethora of ducks, swans and the occasional goose which noisily came in her direction as soon as they saw her bag of goodies.

There were the usual suspects, mallards with their green shiny heads and beautiful wigeons whose orange red heads were topped by a yellow forehead plus a few tufted ducks whose beady yellow eyes gleamed at the prospect of getting some bread for very little effort. However the 'leaders of the pack' were the mute swans who hissed at any duck which attempted to pick up any bread which the larger bird might have had its eye on.

When the bag was empty I saw that Milo was smiling at his daughter's love of these beautiful creatures. We carried on walking round Studley Lake and on to the impressive Georgian water gardens whose formal geometric design offered us an extraordinary vista.

Then it was on to the huge deer park, where we followed the advice on the notice boards to keep our distance as it was the rutting season and I didn't fancy fighting off a six foot stag with romance on his mind. The deer herd was over five hundred strong and composed of a mixture of magnificent red deer and the smaller species of fallow and sika. It was an impressive sight and the stags were certainly in full voice on that day!! They were busy building up their harems so took little notice of us.

Our final stop was back at the lakeside tearooms for a traditional afternoon tea. Dainty sandwiches and a plentiful choice of tea breads and cakes were deposited on our table along with a pot of tea. We were glad to be back in the warmth, it now being November the air was getting much colder, despite the sun piercing the clouds.

We journeyed back to Leeds, having enjoyed a great day together and I was getting on very well with Milo Borovic, a true and kindly man who'd suffered far too much in his forty odd years on this planet. He was easy to talk to and it was clear that Elena had inherited her strong character and will to survive from both her parents.

Milo talked to me at length about his beloved wife Darinka and told me how he was in the depths of despair when Elena disappeared. The two most important people in his life had been taken from him. He spent weeks looking for Elena and found out that her friend Lucija had been with her when she disappeared.

Both families were unable to find out what had befallen their young daughters: neither the police nor any other agencies were of the slightest help. It seemed that missing person cases were not taken seriously in that part of the world as it happened all too often.

Milo decided that the best way to overcome his grief was to throw himself into his work and broaden out his range of services to help refugees, displaced persons and those with no family to help them. He seemed to have been very successful and his impressive network of high level contacts in both governments and law enforcement agencies was going to be invaluable.

All too soon the day came to an end. After coffee in the lounge Milo bid us goodnight and thanked me for giving him a most enjoyable day.

Elena stayed with me for a while. I asked her if she harboured any concerns about her involvement in our operation. She said all she wanted was the girls to be free and for Grogan and his team to lose their freedom.

She was nervous, but well up for the task ahead. I stroked the right side of her face tenderly and told her she needed to get a good night's sleep ready for a long day ahead. So she smiled and pulled her index finger slowly down my mouth and gave me a dazzling smile then headed off for her room.

CHAPTER 10

D – Day

Monday announced its arrival with a bang, under a dove grey canopy, torrential and relentless rain was driven almost horizontal by high winds. It battered the windows of our hotel like the sound of dry macaroni being dropped on to a marble work surface.

We were scheduled to rendezvous with Captain Parker and the team at 11.00 hours at his operations centre on Thorpe Arch Trading Estate near Wetherby.

This was an ideal location for clandestine ventures. Throughout the Second World War the site had served as an extensive military facility and was, during that time, mainly used as an ammunition store.

As a result, the huge complex had dozens of underground warehouses hidden beneath large semi-circular corrugated structures. Many of these were topped with a deep covering of turf and quite a number of them had a concrete frontage into which were set heavy duty roller shutter doors.

Sandy's site was vast but anonymous and situated towards the back of the development. It was well away from the retail park which was in the centre of the estate.

The building looked neglected and unused, which is exactly how Sandy wanted it, no prying eyes.

Inside however, it was a different story, all meticulous organisation and efficiency. As I drove on to the concrete forecourt, a small door opened next to the roller shutter entrance; two security guards came out and signalled for me to halt.

After checking my ID card plus the ones that Sandy had issued to Milo and Elena they told me to drive through the large warehouse doors and park in the bay on the left.

As I waited for the roller shutters to fully lift, Milo commented the security was very good.

"Wait until you get inside", I chuckled.

As we drove through the entrance he smiled as he saw two more guards wearing body armour and with semi automatic weapons slung around their necks.

The building resembled an aircraft hangar and on the ground floor there was a small fleet of vehicles, including 4-wheel drives, vans and people carriers. Towards the rear was a fully equipped vehicle servicing facility, even a couple of fuel pumps, one for petrol, the other ready to dispense diesel. Once I'd parked the car, the guards showed us to a large goods lift that was also doubling as a passenger elevator.

As I pressed the button the old machinery cranked into life and moved us surprisingly smoothly down to the underground facility. The lift shuddered to a halt, Milo pulled the shutter door open and there was the Boss himself to greet us.

"Good morning all," Sandy said in a cheerful tone, "I trust you had a good weekend and are ready for action?"

Elena looked nervously at her father but they both nodded their assent. He didn't need to ask me for an answer as he knew that I would always display 'The

Commando Spirit', courage, determination, unselfishness and cheerfulness in the face of adversity.

As we followed Sandy we passed large secure storage units where I assumed weapons and ammo were housed. There were also rows of clothing racks on which were hanging hi-visibility jackets, body armour, black uniforms, riot shields, batons, helmets and a selection of footwear.

A number of staff members were milling around, collecting the items required for our hit squad, from a list that Parker's quartermaster had issued. The whole area was continually scanned by numerous CCTV cameras, with alert operators monitoring the screens to which the pictures were being relayed.

We entered the office block and were ushered into a large fully equipped conference room. There were already six men seated in the conference chairs that were set out theatre style. Each chair had a swing out table fitted on to one of its arms, somewhat like those on some airline seats. Sandy showed the three of us to the front row where we picked up a coffee each. There was a clipboard and pen on each of the swing out tables. An LCD projector was at the front, connected to Sandy's laptop.

We were soon into the final briefing session. The Boss put up a large screen on to which the projector displayed the layout of the streets around the target and showed where the vehicles were to park and our exit route.

After a couple of hours of intensive instructions, Sandy called a halt and we all trooped into the fully equipped canteen situated at the end of the office block. There we enjoyed a good solid hot lunch cooked on the premises.

At our table the conversation was kept light and we told Sandy of our weekend activities. Milo and his daughter were somewhat subdued as they weren't used to being involved in military operations but their resolve to participate shone through very clearly, even if tinged with hint of nervousness.

Once the inner man had been sated we were required to report to the Quartermaster for our kit issue. Weapons along with ammunition clips were handed out to those team members who were authorised to carry weapons and their issue meticulously recorded and signed for.

We picked up our black uniforms, body armour and helmets, fitted with full visors. These were to be carried by each individual in the small kitbags we were also given. The kit was only to be put on once we'd arrived at the target location. There was no point in advertising our operation to any onlookers.

In the afternoon session we examined in more detail the layout of the interior of The Board Room. We'd explored any possibility of an escape route our targets might take, so part of the plan was to have an armed man on the back door in case any of the goons tried to flee in that direction. When it came to the detail on the first floor layout, Elena was invited to comment on the facilities. She said to her knowledge, the only rooms on that floor were the bedrooms occupied by the captive girls and one that was used from time to time by Grogan.

The floor above that was a relative unknown to her, except for Grogan's office which was at the top of the stairs. She'd only seen two other doors on that floor so presumably they led into rooms which must have been quite large, as it seemed only three rooms occupied the whole of that level.

The bedrooms weren't locked and they ran along either side of the long corridor that led out from the staircase. We'd determined that the first task after gaining entry was to neutralise the enemy. Only then could we start to liberate the captives, whom we surmised should all be in their bedrooms.

It seemed that if drug smuggling was part of Grogan's operation, then the rooms on the same floor as his office could well hold the clues.

When we'd covered all the angles which we could have anticipated it was the turn of our undercover man, Duncan Clarke to deliver his final briefing to us.

He was to spend the late evening at The Board Room keeping up his guise as a client, as he'd done in recent weeks. He'd ensure he didn't leave until just before closing, so the night guards would see him going out. Then, at the appointed hour, he would regain entry on a suitable pretext and immediately facilitate entry for the hit squad, which would pin down the first guard and move on to neutralise the second one.

We were as ready as it was possible to be therefore the briefings were completed at 18.00 hours. After a final check of our equipment it was time to report to the transport officer and ready ourselves for the short journey westwards across The Pennines.

Captain Parker and myself were in the front 4-wheel drive vehicle, with Elena and Milo. Next in the convoy was a people carrier holding the main hit-squad, a team of six fully focussed men, none of whom you would wish to argue with!!

There was also a further squad of four which was for a separate, but connected operation, and, finally, three ten-seater mini-buses, each with a driver plus one other.

Elena and Milo sat in the rear of Sandy's vehicle, quietly contemplative. She was wearing black slacks and a dark sweater under the warm anorak that we'd bought in Carlisle. For some reason she had her long strapped handbag slung over her arm. I never did understand why you could never separate a woman from her handbag.

As our convoy headed out of Wetherby and on to the A1M South, the rain was easing off and by the time we turned west on to the M62 it stopped completely.

All the vehicles had blacked out windows and were unmarked. As Sandy headed down the motorway it felt like the old days in many respects, him and I in the thick of a dangerous sortie. There was a major difference however with what we were to undertake tonight and our operations in the Corps. Previously we were always on a war footing while tonight was a civilian operation to affect a rescue and break up a major criminal gang. So although we'd be using long established skills, the outcome was going to be somewhat different.

CHAPTER 11

Phases 1 and 2

The tall, thin, middle aged man parked his six months old silver Lexus saloon in his allocated parking space outside the apartment. The car was as much his pride and joy as it was a source of wonderment to some of his colleagues, who questioned how he could afford such a luxury car on his police salary.

After activating the remote central locking, he looked at his watch. Ten minutes to eight in the evening, just the right time for a walk down the Brighton sea front then into one of the eating houses on the promenade.

After a long but boring day in the office reviewing files and filling in forms, he didn't feel up to cooking for himself. In the view of this archetypal misogynist the kitchen was a women's domain, not that of a high ranking police officer.

After ten minutes of brisk walking he passed the burnt out pier and decided to get out of the rain which had started to bear down quite heavily, so he headed for a fish restaurant which was opposite the surviving pier.

He failed to notice the scruffy young hoodie 200 metres behind him who, to the casual observer, was merely wiping his sleeve across his head to take the rain away from his face. In fact he was speaking into a microphone.

"Target still in view, looks like he's going to dodge the rain and go in for something to eat."

"OK, stay with him and confirm destination," came the reply in the man's earpiece.

"Roger that, he's now heading for the fish restaurant opposite the pier. I'll walk past and go in after five minutes, and then we observe radio silence, text messages only."

Sure enough the target went into the fish and chip restaurant and found a table in the far corner and took a seat with his back to the door.

After he'd given his order to the waitress for a haddock special, with mushy peas, brown bread and butter and a pot of tea, he took out his mobile and phoned his wife to update her on his day.

He didn't spend too long on the call as there was little to interest her in his working day. He'd only left his home in Liverpool on the previous evening, but knew while ever he was working down there in Brighton he had to put on a pretence of being the dutiful husband.

His wife had suspected for some time that Chief Superintendent Rowley was far from being a dutiful husband; she knew he was just going through the motions in their sham of a marriage and suspected he was up to no good. Many times she believed she'd caught the scent of another woman when he returned quite late after a day at work.

Mrs Rowley was also at a loss to understand how in the last couple of years he seemed to have considerable amounts of extra cash to play with.

In that time they took more holidays than she'd been used to during their twenty year marriage. He'd also spent a lot of money refurbishing the house, as well as having someone in to remodel her kitchen, also at great expense.

Was this all to keep her quiet, she wondered to herself, as she'd learned to her cost never to question her husband directly.

While Rowley was on the phone, the scruffy hoodie slipped into the restaurant and took a table near the door, having a clear view of the back of Rowley from that vantage point.

He ordered coffee and a chip butty, paying for the bill with his order so he'd be able to make a quick exit when required.

Tucking into his fish and chips, Rowley began to think about why he was here on the south coast. At first, when he was told about his unexpected secondment, he had different ideas to those he now harboured.

He was a vain man, so he'd initially believed that the move was a means of checking him out prior to a possible promotion. However, after the first day in Brighton, he had his doubts, as the tasks in which he was now involved were more routine and certainly not challenging. He was mainly reviewing a number of cold cases in Sussex that the local vice squad hadn't solved. His role was to determine whether he could identify any areas in the original investigation that'd been missed.

On the plus side, the fact that he was reporting directly to the Chief Constable massaged his considerable ego. Little did he know it'd been deliberately set up in this way so as to prevent him trying to corrupt any local officers in Sussex, which he had been doing for many years in his home police force.

His thoughts now came back to this evening, so he finished his second cup of tea and asked for the bill, thinking to himself that in the next week he would seek to clarify the reason behind his transfer.

As the restaurant was fairly quiet, the scruffy hoodie was able to hear his target asking for the bill. He quickly used his mobile to send a coded text, threw his tip on the table and made his exit, handing over the surveillance to one of his colleagues already waiting across the street.

The hoodie walked quickly away as Rowley appeared from the restaurant and turned back towards where his car was parked.

The second surveillance officer followed him at a safe distance and reflected to himself it was clear Rowley had no idea he was being followed, which also suggested he didn't realise why he was here in Brighton.

Directly he was satisfied Rowley was on his way back to the apartment, specially provided for him by the police, the man ducked into an alley so he could ensure his target actually entered his own front door.

Once that was confirmed he turned round and sprinted back to the rendezvous area in the next street and climbed into the back of the unmarked police van where the scruffy hoodie and two other police officers were waiting for him. This was a fully equipped police surveillance van and the radio officer was currently connected to the phone tap on both Rowley's mobile phone and the landline in the apartment.

The team in the van were an elite squad of untouchables, tasked with stamping out corruption in the police force. They reported directly to the Home Office.

They'd listened to the uneventful call that had been made from the mobile to Rowley's wife. But the sound of the ringing out tone of a landline phone now held the attention of the four officers.

"Good evening, The Board Room."

"Can I speak to Michael Grogan, this is Chief Superintendent Rowley?"

The call was immediately put through to Grogan's extension and was, at the same time, being recorded in the police van in Brighton.

"Michael, hello, how are you?"

"Fine John, haven't seen you for a while, what've you been up to?"

"Well I'm on secondment in Brighton at the moment, reviewing cold cases in vice. So, if you need any help while I'm away, you'll need to call my sergeant, Mike Robertson."

"Is he on our side and will that cost me any more or will you cover his wedge out of what I pay you, John?"

The four officers listening to this looked at each other in disbelief, not only were they disgusted at picking up a bent senior officer and at least one other corrupt member of his team, but also they were totally astonished at how openly he and his paymaster discussed matters on an open phone.

Rowley confirmed there would be no further call on Grogan for payment and that Sergeant Robertson was 'already on the payroll'.

"OK, pleased to hear that, I'll call him tonight then, since we plan to move a large coke shipment out at 3.00 in the morning and I don't want any nosey beat copper snooping around."

"Good thinking Michael, anything else you need help with right now?"

"When do you think you'll be back as I've another ten women coming in next week from Sofia for my new operation in Manchester?"

"I don't know, Mike, when do they arrive exactly?"

"Ten days or so, probably next Wednesday night, all being well, my man in Istanbul just got off the phone to me an hour ago. He's already sent the payment to his man in Bulgaria, so I've transferred mine to his Turkish Bank account today."

"OK, Mike, do you want me to provide the usual protection for the Manchester operation?"

"Absolutely, but I want a discount for a second contract."

The two men went on to discuss details of the people smuggling operation and then finished their conversation. Three of the officers got quietly out of the van, leaving the communications officer behind, ready to monitor any further phone traffic. The three got into an unmarked police car parked 100 metres away, with its windows all blacked out. The driver was already gunning the engine as they jumped in.

The scruffy hoodie had taken off his jacket, which had now been left in the van; all of the officers had put on their body armour and riot helmets with visors. The officer sitting in the front passenger seat carried a battering ram. All of them had automatic weapons slung round their necks, they were ready for anything.

The police car roared into life and sped off round the corner, slewing to a halt in front of the ground floor apartment. All four of them leapt out simultaneously and the officer who deployed the battering ram led the way down the short path to the front door.

Two blows with the battering ram, demolished the modern panelled front door and they were inside the building in seconds, the lead man shouting,

"Armed police, stay where you are."

Rowley was sitting in the lounge area when the door fell in. He shot off the sofa in terror when the officers came into the room with their weapons raised.

He still had his jacket on and reached for his inside pocket. Thinking Rowley may be reaching for a gun, the lead special ops officer hit him in a crushing rugby tackle around the waist, knocking the corrupt policeman backwards, causing him to scream at them as his head hit the wooden floor.

"You idiots you're making a big mistake, do you know who I am?"

They didn't wait for a reply but threw him face down, dragged his arms behind his back and hand cuffed him, then threw him back on to the sofa and told him to shut up. The man who had been the scruffy hoodie stood right in front of him and identified himself as a senior officer from Special Operations in the Metropolitan police.

"Yes we know exactly who you are, sir!" He barked into the terrified face of their target.

"Chief Superintendent John Rowley, I am arresting you on suspicion of conspiracy, corruption, perverting the course of justice, and being an accessory to two counts of attempted murder. You do not have to say anything. But it may harm your defence if you do not mention when questioned something which you later rely on in Court. Anything you say may be used in evidence."

Rowley's eyes changed from blazing anger to acute fear and the colour in his face went from angry crimson to natural calico.

With the target secured, if not subdued, the senior officer turned back to his team,

"OK lads, take his mobile phone and his warrant card from him then give him a strip search while I go and talk to our comms man."

The senior officer went back to the surveillance van and gave his instructions to the communications officer and then went back to Rowley's apartment.

Within less than five minutes the hit squad set off with the prisoner in the back of their police car, leaving one officer behind to carry out a thorough search of the premises.

The team were already in possession of enough information to guarantee a conviction, three years copy bank statements showing Rowley had been receiving over £2,500 per month directly into his current account, the most recent credit transfers coming from The Board Room.

His mobile phone records also showed long phone calls to Michael Grogan's house, to Grogan's mobile and to The Board Room.

Furthermore, the day before the two goons had tried to assassinate Elena and me, the police computer log revealed his access code had been used to find my address by searching against my car registration number. Guess that was game set and match.

The communications officer followed his instructions and relayed the information gathered in Rowley's phone conversation with Grogan. He phoned Captain Parker's mobile, but, as Sandy was driving I took the call.

As a result we'd a few adjustments to make to our plan for the evening. We phoned the other vehicles to brief the whole team on the changes.

Many miles away, and about half a mile outside one of the leafy suburbs of Liverpool stood the ill gotten gains of prostitution, drug trafficking and many more serious crimes. This was a three storey, five bedroomed Georgian mansion set back from the road with a very large, and newly built, paved courtyard outside the front door. The house was far too large for one person but Michael Grogan was an exhibitionist and its aura of perceived success served to massage his enormous ego. *'Look at me; I'm another scouser who made good.'*

After taking the call from Rowley, he'd left The Board Room and picked up a girl from one of the massage parlours which he owned in Liverpool, then driven back home.

Whilst The Board Room was for the top end of the market in the evil sex trade, he also catered for the less well off men by running several vice dens in the city.

He told Rowley that he'd planned to go back to The Board Room just before 1.00 a.m. to supervise the drug shipment. But before that he needed to satisfy his sexual appetite. He may have lots of money from his life as a crime lord but he was totally incapable of developing a serious relationship so always had to pay for female company.

He freed himself from the young blonde and rolled over on to his back, reaching for the packet of cigarettes and gold lighter which were nestling on the bedside cabinet.

His guest declined the cigarette he offered her and as she lay beside her boss she looked longingly round the bedroom, wishing she could enjoy this type of luxury more often.

The room was large and the circular water bed was set in the centre of the floor with large mirrors set in the ceiling above it.

There were a couple of large black and white prints of naked women on the walls and an ostentatious full sized alabaster nude statue against the wall that led to the ensuite bathroom.

On the dressing table there were a number of pornographic magazines. No doubts that Michael Grogan had sex on his mind when he was in his bedroom.

As he drew on his cigarette he propped himself up on the pillows and turned to the girl.

"Thanks for that, you can get dressed and go now babe, I've to go back to The Board Room. Help yourself to a shower, there's £200 on the sideboard downstairs, take that and use the phone to get yourself a cab, the taxi firm's number is the second one on the fast dial button."

"Thanks Mr Grogan,"

She eased herself unsteadily from the water bed which rocked as even her slight weight caused the liquid to slosh about in its retention chambers.

She quickly showered then towelled herself dry in front of the full length mirror, admiring her body grudgingly as she did so.

She hated her life and what she was doing, but she'd been abandoned by the man who'd made her pregnant and, with both her parents dead, she'd chosen the world's oldest profession to pay the rent and feed and clothe her daughter, who was just eighteen months old.

Following the death of her parents from substance abuse, she also had to look after her younger sister who was still at school, but who crucially was on hand to supply vital baby sitting duties in the evenings.

She came out of the bathroom just as Grogan was finishing dressing. He was perched on the edge of the bed, pulling on his black moccasin loafers when there was an almighty crash at the front porch and the door crashed open. A shout rang out as four men in full body armour ran into the hallway.

"Armed police, stay where you are."

Grogan froze for a second, then quickly recovered, reached in to the drawer of his bedside cabinet and swiftly snatched out a large automatic hand gun.

He rushed to the top of the stairs, looking down on to the large hallway and came face to face with the first member of Sandy Parker's squad who had his foot on the bottom step. Grogan immediately raised his gun and fired off one shot which hit my colleague in the chest and he fell on his back, motionless.

The other members of the squad had been checking out the downstairs rooms when they heard the shot.

The three of them moved to the foot of the stairwell, two men taking up a position with weapons ready and preparing to go upstairs.

The third man briefly checked his fallen colleague then joined the others. They advanced slowly up the deeply carpeted and broad staircase. It had widely spaced black steel bars on each side forming an impressive open banister with a gold painted hand rail on the top and gold finials positioned every few feet.

As soon as Grogan had fired off his shot he'd moved swiftly back into the bedroom where he found the girl with her back against the far wall, ashen faced and with a fear of the unknown in her eyes.

He immediately grabbed the blonde and pulled her away from the wall then, standing close behind her, he held the terrified girl tightly round the neck with his left arm and with his right hand he roughly thrust the gun against her right temple.

He dragged the poor youngster towards the bedroom door, making sure his body was behind her so she involuntarily became a human shield.

As the two of them appeared at the top of the stairs, Grogan saw the three members of the hit squad advancing slowly upwards towards him, with their weapons raised and the safety catches off.

"Back off or the bitch is history," Grogan screamed in his high pitched, almost girlish voice.

"I'm leaving here, and there's nothing you can do to stop me. Now go very quietly back down the stairs."

As he said this, he flicked his head nervously, causing his pony tail to hit the girl across the side of her face. This startled her and she twisted in his tight grip.

Thinking she was trying to break free, Grogan hit her across her face with the barrel of his gun and tightened his grip round her neck.

This resulted in the girl screaming out in pain and the first man coming up the stairs to shout at him,

"Give it up Grogan, you're outnumbered and don't have a chance of getting past us. There are two more cars full of my colleagues waiting outside."

Grogan didn't answer but started inching slowly forward and pushing the girl in front of him, whilst maintaining the tight grip around her neck.

After what seemed like an eternity, he reached the top step, still holding the gun tightly against her forehead. He advanced slowly, nervously, a step at a time, sweat trickling down his neck, waiting on each stair until the men in black had, in turn, backed down one step.

"You'll never take me, and do you really want her baby and little sister to be left alone in the world?" His voice was more under control now as his mind was working overtime; he quickly examined his limited options.

Did they have reinforcements outside? Probably not, or the shot would have brought others in through the front door. So he figured his human shield would work, but he needed to get them to lower their weapons to reduce the odds against him.

"Lower your guns or I'll shoot her."

"Don't be stupid, Grogan, you can't take all of us out so drop your weapon."

At that point a shot rang out and the girl fell forward on the stairs, her face covered in blood. Grogan fell on top of her with a stream of blood spurting out of his neck.

As the villain's firearm fell through the banister rail, the three members of the hit squad ran up the stairs. The first one pulled Grogan off the girl and the second man lifted her up and gently led her downstairs.

He lifted his visor, and told her she was safe now, whilst also glancing to the area to the right of the stairwell where his fallen colleague had been.

"You OK now Chas?" He shouted.

"Yep, mate, just a bruised chest. Glad my shooting skills are still tops."

His bullet proof jacket had taken Grogan's shot and saved his life, although the impact had caused a temporary loss of consciousness.

When he came round he had sussed the current situation, remained perfectly still and carefully stayed out of Grogan's immediate line of vision. Once again years in our armed forces had provided the courage and the skill he needed.

Once Grogan had moved round the bend in the staircase and was facing the other three squad members, he had his back to the man he thought he'd killed. Chas was able to get his shot off and hit the spot at the back of Grogan's head, right in the middle of his neck.

Grogan was pulled unceremoniously off the stairs and his hands cuffed behind his back. Only once he was secure did they look at his wound. Primary rules of engagement, neutralise the enemy first, and attend to their welfare second. The bullet had passed right through his neck so there were both entry and exit wounds.

He was drifting in and out of consciousness as one of the team ran back into the house with the first aid kit. A gauze pressure pad was applied to the two wounds and a crepe bandage wrapped around his neck.

Chas picked up the house phone and called an ambulance, telling the controller he was part of a special police operations unit and there were to be no calls to the press or any other police unit.

One of his colleagues, Matt, attended to the girl, whom he'd taken into the lounge and set on a sofa. He established her name was Trish, why she was in the house and that she was worried about her daughter and sister.

Matt said he'd get Social Services to go round to the flat and look after Trish's sister and baby daughter while she helped them with their enquiries.

He phoned Captain Parker once Grogan was secured and asked for further instructions and was told that Trish could be a key witness so must be kept away from the local police until it could be established which of them could be trusted.

Grogan came round after about three minutes and was cautioned, having been told he was being arrested on suspicion of human trafficking, wrongful imprisonment, running brothels, murder, attempted murder and corruption, just for starters.

He was searched and his mobile phone removed from his trouser pocket along with a small plastic bag full of white powder, one more offence to go on the charge sheet, smiled Gerry, the third member of the squad.

The ambulance was soon on the scene and the two paramedics gave Grogan a good examination. They cleaned and re-dressed his wounds and put him on a drip before putting him on a stretcher and wheeling him out.

They were given the bare bones of the situation by the squad and were advised that one of Parker's team would accompany them. They gave Chas and Trish treatment and radioed in for a second team to pick both of them up as they thought Trish had a fractured cheek bone and Chas had a cracked rib. Both were made comfortable then they put Grogan in the ambulance, Gerry, his gun still slung around his neck, climbed in with Grogan.

Matt then phoned Parker's mobile to update the commander. I took the call and Matt was instructed to remain in Grogan's house and gather evidence, including recovering any computer he could locate. So far, so good, provided that Grogan survived after his injury, we needed his evidence to track down the Mr Big who appeared to be based in Istanbul.

Parker was pleased with the night's work so far as we carried on down the M62 towards Liverpool. Still dressed in our civvies we pulled in to a motorway services and were soon tucking into burgers and chips. Phase three was not far away now.

CHAPTER 12

Final Assault

After the team had polished off their burgers, chips and coffee, we headed for Liverpool once more.

Elena was becoming a little fidgety now; revisiting the city where she'd suffered so much was clearly causing her some anxiety. Milo kept reassuring her that her input was vital in making certain we quickly got the captive girls to understand we were here to rescue them.

At around 22.30 we pulled into Liverpool city centre and headed straight for an office block which was less than 300 metres from The Board Room.

Sandy's brother, The Chief Constable of a neighbouring police force had organised some meeting rooms there so we could all change into our combat gear and set up our operations room.

Each driver had a swipe card to gain entry to the private underground car park set out of sight beneath the office block.

It was a nondescript nineteen sixties type of building which I understood to be occupied by a couple of Government Departments.

Our small convoy of vehicles parked up towards the rear of the almost empty car park, which was still illuminated. We could see that there were several white vans and a black 4x4 already in situ.

The lift slowly took the team up to the fourth floor and, as we came out on to a wide corridor a uniformed Chief Superintendent warmly greeted Sandy. He introduced himself as Doug Turner and led us towards the operations room.

"Welcome to you all; from the reports we've had so far, the night has been successful up to this point."

Sandy replied with a wry smile, "So I believe, Doug, we've one corrupt senior police officer in custody and one major criminal under arrest, albeit seriously wounded. One of our men at Grogan's house was also able to prove that the bullet proof vests DO work and he got away with damaged ribs. I also understand we've a recording of the chief villain and the main bent policeman that will put them both away for a long time."

Turner was from a select force of police untouchables, answerable to a high command and with no connection to any county police force.

Our assault on The Board Room was to be co-ordinated by him and Sandy Parker. He had brought with him a communications expert, three surveillance officers, a plain clothes sergeant and inspector from his team; they were all fully experienced in dealing with armed suspects and organised crime.

The ops room was already set up for us and from its floor to ceiling windows it had a clear view of the street on which The Board Room was situated.

Three tripods with sets of high powered night vision binoculars were already in place, one of them trained on the entrance to Grogan's centre of so much misery and the other two covered the length of the street.

The whole team were then instructed to put on their combat gear. Elena, as a courtesy, was shown into a separate room to change her clothes, being the only woman present who would be entering The Board Room.

By the time everyone was dressed for action and had made their way to the briefing room, there were two more ladies present.

The first one was a high-ranking officer from Social Services, with special responsibility for refugee welfare. The second lady was from a London based charity which provides housing and other types of vital support to single homeless women and those who'd been trafficked into prostitution.

I noticed at the back of the briefing room, there was a stack of suitcases. Seeing me looking at them, Sandy confirmed that, assuming a successful rescue, we'd be taking all the clothes from the girls' rooms, for their use whilst awaiting repatriation.

The briefing by Parker and Doug Turner lasted forty five minutes as we went over the procedure and again checked everyone understood their role.

Duncan Clarke phoned in to say he'd been at The Board Room until it closed. He'd given a hefty tip to the night man who let him out of the front door. This should ensure the man would remember him when he returned. He confirmed, as far as he could tell, the club procedures at closing time remained the same as Elena had described to us. Sandy instructed him to go back at precisely 01.00 hours in order to kick start our operation.

At 12.40 the team who'd come over to Liverpool with Sandy and myself moved down to the car park along with two of the police officers. We assembled near the entrance leading on to the street where The Board Room was.

The car park lights had been switched off to facilitate concealment. The five members of the initial hit squad were at the front and ready to move into assault mode and take up their positions.

On receiving instructions from Sandy in their earpieces, the first two members of the squad quietly moved into place. They moved in the shadows, keeping tight against the wall of the adjoining buildings like predatory tom cats. Their rubber soled boots allowing them to move swiftly and noiselessly.

The black outfits and masks they wore made them impossible to spot, whilst they themselves could see perfectly well through their night goggles. The two men moved one at a time to the lee of the entrance porch, each waiting until they could see that the CCTV camera was looking the other way before moving forward.

As soon as the first two were in position against the entrance, their two colleagues located themselves in the shadows, 10 metres further back, waiting for their instructions. The projecting porch provided first class cover, while the team waited to make their assault on the door guard.

The fifth member of the armed squad was posted to the back door to prevent that being used as an escape route.

At precisely 01.00 hours Duncan Clarke approached the front door of The Board Room, despite the winter cold, without a coat, as his excuse for returning was that he he'd left his overcoat behind with his wallet in the pocket.

He pressed the buzzer on the intercom by the solid wooden doors and explained why he was there. As soon as the front door was opened he raised his left arm. Sandy barked into the earpieces of the hit squad,

"One and two go, go, go."

The first man pushed past Clarke and kicked the front door inwards, which both trapped the night security man between the door and the inner wall of the entrance and also created sufficient space for the second man to come in.

One of them grabbed the startled guard from behind and put his night stick over the man's windpipe pulling backwards with a hand on each end of the baton. As the guard started choking, the second man quickly taped his mouth and between them they bundled him out into the street.

Duncan held the front door open and the second team from our initial squad ran forward and entered the building. Their two colleagues had released their throat hold on the first door guard and were astride him as they put him face down on the ground. As practiced professionals they quickly pulled the struggling man's hands behind his back and put restraints on his wrists.

The whole exercise was over in less than thirty seconds, carried out with not a word, the only sound being when the door was kicked.

Doug Turner ordered his two police officers forward. The prisoner was dragged to his feet, arrested and read his rights.

Once he was secure in the unmarked police van secreted in our car park the tape was removed from his mouth. He was relieved of his mobile phone and a loaded handgun hidden in a holster under his jacket, a body search also revealed a wicked looking flick-knife.

When the police were happy he was safely secured they set off back to the street, leaving one of the officers behind to guard him.

The four man team were now in the building and started moving up stairs to the office.

The bedrooms where the girls were kept were on the first floor. Grogan's office and some spare rooms were on the next floor.

According to the intelligence gathering we'd secured from Elena they knew the second night security man would be counting the night's takings then putting it away in the safe. Our team members had all memorised the plans of the building and knew exactly where to go.

Their target, therefore, was totally surprised when our lead man kicked open the door to Grogan's office. The guard was a man of about thirty five, heavily built with a broken nose, offset in a face which had weasel like eyes that now were flashing with fire.

Having recovered from his initial shock he leapt to his feet and reached in the top drawer of Grogan's desk for the loaded handgun his boss always kept there.

The first squad member through the door shouted the warning as the night watchman struggled to get the gun from the drawer.

"Armed police, stay where you are."

The night watchman never made it, the butt of a semi automatic weapon hit him hard on the mouth, splattering crimson droplets into the air and causing two of his teeth to fall out on to the desk.

With the team of four now in the room he was soon laying face down, hands behind his back and restraints put on him. So far so good.

Ninety seconds later he too was in the back of the police van, relieved of his weapons and a quantity of cocaine secreted in a small plastic bag, then charged and secured.

As far as the briefing had indicated, there should be only two staff members remaining on the premises after closing. To make sure, Sandy had ordered that, having arrested and secured those two, our team should carry out a full sweep of the building.

First they checked the other two rooms on the second floor, both were locked so they kicked in each of the doors. In these rooms they found neat piles of clear plastic sacks, filled with white powder, which they duly reported back to Sandy. Nice bit of evidence there, as they were clearly not shipping self-raising flour!!

The squad then purposefully moved back downstairs, checking the kitchen, restaurant, casino, lounge, gymnasium, and treatment room and pool area. They went in guns first, barking out 'clear' to their colleagues once they were satisfied that each area was empty.

The lead man then radioed to Sandy that they were ready for the rest of our troop to come in and start to clear the first floor.

Although a fair bit of noise had been made so far in the exercise, we'd discussed this during our briefing meetings, as a potential problem. Elena knew that the girls had been conditioned to stay in their rooms after closing and 'mind their own business', otherwise they were likely to end up with a beating. So it was unlikely they'd dare try and find out what was happening.

In any case it was less than ten minutes into our assault, so the poor girls would still be in the 'what the hell was that?' stage in their minds.

The full complement of Sandy's squad now moved into the reception hall, with me in the second wave then Elena and Milo at the rear.

Sandy moved the two of them into a small room behind the stairs that served both as a cloakroom and also housed the alarm and CCTV equipment. He told them to stay out of sight until it was safe for them to address the girls.

Two squad members went upstairs on Parker's instruction and started knocking on each bedroom door in turn. They knocked hard several times on the door then very loudly issued the command,

142

"Please put on your dressing gown and come downstairs straight away", before moving on to the next room.

Once the guys had covered all the bedrooms they went back downstairs and waited for the girls to appear.

One by one the captives nervously started to come out and make their way down the stairs.

The first girl to come into view was rubbing the sleep out of her eyes and stood uneasily at the head of the stairs. She was a little over five foot in height, pretty, and her floor length dressing gown, an attractive sugared almond colour, provided a nice contrast with her short cropped black hair.

The team leader persuaded her to come down, "Don't worry, you're perfectly safe."

She then slowly and timidly walked down to the reception hall where she was lined up facing back up the stairs.

As each of the involuntary guests of Michael Grogan emerged from her room, she was lined up and waited for her colleagues to come down.

Within around four minutes we had a line of nine girls, then no more activity on the stairs. Sandy looked at me, quizzically.

"Nathan we originally had twelve girls, one known to be missing, one AWOL, should be one more."

"At least, one more, chief, as he may have brought in replacements."

Just as we were about to debate what to do there was a commotion on the stairs.

As we whipped round to face the noise, the team tensed and moved to the foot of the stairs, guns at the ready. Sandy held his hand up and ordered them to stand ready as the cause of the clamour quickly unfolded.

On the second step from the top was a girl with a noose around her neck. The rope extended to about two metres and holding the loose end was an evil looking man.

In his other hand was a hand gun which he was pointing at the terrified girl. He was screaming in Serbian and started waving the gun in our direction.

The girl was very slim and quite tall. Her Eastern European features were attractive and topped with short, dark brown hair, but her face was the colour of frosted steel apart from a poppy coloured weal across her left cheek where she'd obviously had a pistol whipping.

The man was wearing a shiny dark suit, no tie, and sporting dark sunglasses. On the left side of his face from the frame of his shades down to his chin was a wide mulberry coloured scar. So, Scarface was still on the payroll.

The evil looking Serb shrieked again in his native tongue and pulled on the rope, causing the girl to utter a strangulated scream as it tightened around the caramel skin of her graceful neck.

Then it all went deathly quiet, apart from muffled gasps from the girls waiting in line in the foyer. One of then shouted out, "Lucija", then it fell silent again.

In a stand off situation we considered our options and the Serbian was wondering what to do next. I had surmised that Scarface's unfortunate captive was Elena's friend who was with her when they were both abducted from Belgrade Airport.

At that point the eerie silence was rent asunder by a single gunshot, which surprisingly came from behind me.

I whipped my head round and saw Elena standing there with a smoking hand gun in her right hand. I glanced back at the stairs and saw Scarface was holding his groin where his wedding tackle used to be and screaming in agony.

"Wow, what a great shot Elena, he won't be sexually abusing any more ladies. How the hell did you get the gun?" I mused to myself.

The first two members of the hit squad dashed forward. One stood over Scarface with his cocked gun pointing at the Serbian's head and the second dragged his hands behind his back and cuffed him.

They then shook him down for any other weapons, recovering a vicious knife from a belt scabbard behind the man's back.

The third member of the team gently led Lucija down the stairs as Elena rushed forward, and threw her arms round her friend's neck and they sobbed in relief in each other's embrace.

Doug Turner had requested a special ambulance to be on standby outside from 1.10 hours. Its team were now called forward to deal with Scarface.

He was sedated, handcuffs removed, his wound quickly dressed then he was strapped on to a stretcher to which he was then cuffed again. Accompanied by an armed policeman the medics took him off to a private hospital, which was only available to the police, the army and the Home Office, away from the press and other prying eyes.

Sandy had gently taken the gun away from Elena as she and Lucija were in each other's arms. Two members of the original assault force were sent back upstairs to check each room on the first floor. Captain Parker now turned to the astonished girls.

"Ladies, you have nothing to fear, we're with the British Government and Police. You have your friend Elena here to thank for giving us the opportunity to rescue you all. When she escaped she was helped by our colleague Mr Sawyer here, who along with myself served in the Royal Marines and fought against the Serbs in the 1990's.

We've spent the last few weeks putting together our rescue plan and during that time we managed to contact Elena's father Milo Borovic who is here with us to help repatriate you all.

Please be aware that we have also arrested Michael Grogan. We'll pick up the rest of his evil bunch during the course of today, when they turn up for work. So they can't harm you any more.

In a few moments, we'll be joined by two ladies from Social Services and from a Charity who specialise in helping ladies trapped in the UK as sex slaves.

We have suitcases for each of you, so please go and get dressed. Then pack the clothes you were given and any personal belongings you have in your room. We will then take you across to Leeds to a hotel that we control. You will be protected there by our four armed guards.

When the ladies come in for you, please give them your name, the country you are from, what language you speak and tell them the name of your nearest relative and their telephone number.

They will also wish to know if you had your passport with you when you were abducted. The British Government will brief each of your Embassies. We will request they send a government representative in your own country to your home to advise your family you've been rescued and are safe and well. In a couple of days you can phone your relatives to reassure them you are OK.

Michael Grogan and his team are evil and we want them to spend many years in prison. In order to ensure that happens we'll need your evidence. We will, therefore, be taking statements from you in due course and gathering as much information as we can to ensure a safe conviction. Any questions?"

At that point all the girls broke into a round of spontaneous applause and rushed forward to embrace Elena warmly, chattering and shrieking loudly.

Once order had been restored, the search team confirmed that the building was now totally secure.

Sandy then contacted the communication room in our temporary base and requested that the two support ladies be brought forward and that the suitcases be taken in.

I drew Elena away from the excited throng and brought her to the side of the foyer where her father was standing.

"How the hell did you get the gun, Elena?" I enquired with a half smile on my face.

"When you rescued me you threw it on the back seat of their car. I picked it up when you went to fetch your own car. At that point, I didn't know you or whether I could trust you, so I kept it as a safeguard. Once I found out you were a good man I kept it just in case we needed it."

"Good girl" I said, patting her on the shoulder.

Around ninety minutes later, Sandy's squad and the girls were all safely heading back towards the M62, along with the two female support members of the team.

Doug Turner had phoned Superintendent Rowley's bent sergeant, Mike Roberson and, posing as a member of Grogan's team invited him to go to The Board Room to help ensure the drug shipment went smoothly at 3.00 a.m.

He was promptly arrested when he arrived and charged and carted away. Turner then assembled his elite police team, ready to receive the villains who would be turning up to collect the sacks of cocaine stacked up on the rooms on the top floor.

Before we left, Milo and Elena quizzed the girls in their native tongues, to make sure they were all in reasonable health.

The Social Services manager and the lady from the women's charity had completed a brief questionnaire with each of them, to get their basic background details.

Only one of them was married, she had a small child back home in Croatia. The remaining girls were single and had been living with their parents at the time of their abduction.

Whilst pleased with the relative success of the evening, I felt a little frustrated that my own role had been quite passive. I wasn't used to taking a back seat in the middle of an operation.

On our journey back to Leeds, we took two phone calls and were advised that both Grogan and Scarface had been operated on and were stable but still in intensive care.

As expected, at 03.00 hours a team of three from Grogan's drug peddling customer had turned up with a suitcase stuffed with £50 notes money to pay for the large consignment that awaited them upstairs.

They too were picked up and taken to a secure special prison away from contact by the outside world. Their suitcase full of money was kept as evidence.

Turner would now wish to have the men questioned to track down their boss.

Once the gunmetal grey of the winter dawn had spread its pale light over Liverpool, the rest of the staff at The Board Room began to appear.

One by one they were arrested, charged and swiftly taken away. It seemed like our night had proved quite successful. Doubtless Sandy would undertake a full debrief the next morning.

We arrived back at our Leeds hotel at 06.00 hours and once all the girls were safely installed in their rooms, Sandy, Elena and I had a quick coffee in the lounge and wound down a little before Sandy headed off back to his home.

We agreed to reconvene at 11.45 that same morning.

CHAPTER 13

Aftermath

Sandy spent a couple of hours debriefing his team, including Elena, Milo and myself.

He was concerned at the injuries sustained during the operation. Grogan's shooting; the bruised chest of Chas under his bullet-proof vest, Trish's broken cheekbone, Scarface's destroyed gonads and the superficial injuries suffered by Lucija at the hands of Scarface.

By and large, though, he was pleased the injuries on our side were minimal. It seemed we'd been able to rescue all the girls who were still alive, at the time Elena had been a captive, with one of them still being missing, presumed dead. Our major task now was the breaking up of the international operation.

Over the next ten days the hotel bore silent witness to a feverish level of activity. Statements were taken on video, as we knew it wasn't fair or practical to keep all the former captives in the UK until the trials started.

Written statements were also secured and signed off. We wanted to make sure the CPS were able to cover all options when the trial started, so giving them written and video evidence was an insurance policy, in case anything went missing.

The relevant foreign embassies had been given full details of all the girls whom Grogan had kidnapped, with a request to immediately get in touch with their families in the girls' home countries.

Once it was confirmed their families had been contacted, each girl in turn was then allowed to phone her next of kin from the privacy of her own room.

The lady who was with Grogan at the time of his arrest was a cause for concern, so our specialist Social Services lady had arranged for Trish to be taken into their care, along with her younger sister and her baby.

They set her up in a safe house with round the clock protection. She'd given us a full statement regarding Grogan and his activities, after being picked up at his house.

She was able to provide the addresses of another five massage parlours he owned in Liverpool.

In the immediate aftermath of our assault, Doug Turner's untouchables closed each of them down and arrested the staff controlling them.

The girls working in the vice dens gave statements and were released into the care of Social Services to help them sort out their lives, without the need for them to go back to the world's oldest profession.

Over time Grogan and Scarface recovered sufficiently to be taken out of intensive care, but were still kept in separate hospitals in private rooms, under armed guard and still handcuffed to their bed head. There was no chance of our team being caught out by a surprise attempted rescue.

It was reported that Grogan was likely to spend the remainder of his life in a wheelchair.

Scarface would be able to walk in due course but would need a walking stick to support him; his sex life was over.

We were waiting anxiously for them to be well enough for questioning, thus enabling the CPS to put together their full case.

After we'd been back at the hotel for four nights, I asked Sandy if I might slip out for a quiet meal with Elena one night. He concurred and it was arranged for the following night.

I drove out of the electric hotel gates at around 19.30 and headed off into the city centre, still lit up with Christmas lights. As before, we parked in The Light. The owners of that lovely shopping centre had gone to town on their Christmas decorations, with beautiful white tubes hanging from the ceiling; as the lights played on them they sparkled like snow flakes, gently spinning round in the currents from the air conditioning.

After climbing two flights of stairs, we came out into the main concourse and secured a quiet table in the Café Rouge restaurant.

One we'd studied the menus, we tried to relax and talked in general terms during the first course, but when we were both tucking into our rather good main courses I lightly shifted the conversation back to the subject of the rescue operation.

I was concerned how Elena felt about having shot a man. She told me with a grimace that at first she'd been very worried. Then, after sleeping on it, she convinced herself that she did what she thought was appropriate, believing her dear friend Lucija was going to die.

She seemed quite relaxed about the subject, now. I guess the terrible Balkan conflict would've conditioned her up to a point, but, crucially, her protective instinct towards Lucija must have triggered her response with the firearm on the night.

We discussed what the plans were now to ensure long sentences for Grogan and his staff, plus the bent policemen on his payroll who had been protecting his business.

Elena was anxious that the girls who'd been kidnapped with her shouldn't have retribution visited on them. I thought for a while.

"Well, they're very safe where they are right now, Elena. Do you know, whether, like you, they were all kidnapped at random?"

"I can't be sure, but as far as I know, none of them had any knowledge of being followed previously."

"Were any of them offered the chance of coming to the UK with false promises of riches and guaranteed employment?"

"Not as far as I know, Nathan."

"OK, that's good then. If there are any remnants of Grogan's gang around that we've missed, they'll be unlikely to have the girls' home addresses. In any case once they realise that most of the UK team are in custody I don't think retribution will be foremost in their mind.

What they'll be concerned with is self preservation. Their most likely course of action is distancing themselves from Grogan, to avoid bringing suspicion on themselves. So what we must do is quickly close down the overseas operation and prevent them from having the resources in Liverpool or Manchester to start all over again."

"OK, but you should know that although all the girls are delighted to have been rescued, there are one or two of them who want to put all this behind them and go home as soon as possible."

"Right, I'll have a word with Sandy, but they need to understand that we must have all their evidence first. It's also possible that some of them don't have passports.

The ladies from the charity and Social Services, who are helping with the girls' welfare, are working with the embassies to ensure a smooth repatriation and can deliver them safely back to their families.

Until their respective governments are happy with the documentation they'll be going nowhere, but worry not, we're making good progress.

How's your father holding up? He seemed OK whenever I spoke to him and was relatively happy when we engaged in conversation over dinner."

"Well he's fine and obviously delighted to have me back. I think he's looking to return home and put his staff to work and use their collective Government contacts to assist in the repatriation.

He also thinks that his contacts in Interpol will be able to make inroads into the international side of the people smuggling and drugs trade."

"Great we should set up a meeting with Sandy tomorrow, so we can plan how to proceed from now."

Then rather hesitatingly I asked,

"What's your own plan for the future, Elena?"

Her face began to take on the hue of raspberry sorbet.

"Mmm, I may go back home with poppa, depending on what happens here."

"I think Milo and Sandy are talking about a joint endeavour in the future. Your dad's contacts would be of immense help for future operations, just like they're proving to be on this present one.

Some weeks ago, when you and I spoke about what you were looking to do, you suggested the possibility of using your law degree to help displaced people. Have you had any more thoughts about that idea?"

"Well, yes, but the work could be dangerous so I'd need to have someone working with me in case any of the work got physical, or if I had to meet dangerous criminals. My father's firm, he tells me, is full of academics, lawyers and office staff. They don't do armed responses!!"

"OK, maybe you and I could look at that once this mess is all cleared up." We both looked across the table at each other and left our respective thoughts unsaid.

I ordered two coffees to finish off an interesting evening and we spent a few more minutes talking about some of the girls.

Although they did not have much interactive time together at The Board Room, they did manage to get to know each other a little. They'd all been decent law abiding girls before their capture.

They were from varying backgrounds but unfortunately united by the greed of one man and the evil trade which he plied and which had been around on this planet of ours since Adam was a lad.

The night guard checked our IDs and let us in the front door of the hotel. We popped into the lounge to see who was still around.

The room was virtually empty, just the barman still there serving coffee to Milo and Lucija. Sandy had gone home an hour earlier, after an interesting discussion with Milo resulting from a long fax he'd received from Chief Superintendent Doug Turner.

Once they'd arrested all the staff as each of them turned up for work, Turner's men had conducted a thorough search of The Board Room.

The drugs had been impounded as evidence and taken away to a secret warehouse belonging to HMRC, a long way from any possible discovery by the local police.

Doug was still not sure whether there were any more officers locally who were on Grogan's payroll, so the whole of our operation was kept under wraps with no local involvement.

The video tapes which Elena had spotted were also seized with all the incriminating images they contained. The contents of Grogan's desk proved very interesting. A pile of passports were hidden in there, some of them belonging to our girls.

It seemed he thought that his inner sanctum was impregnable; one of his desk drawers contained his black book. The pages were neatly filled in with all his contacts clearly set out, including addresses and phone numbers.

His contact in Istanbul seemed to be one Mehdi Gümüş, a man well known to Interpol and the Turkish police but so far he'd never had his collar felt.

Clearly it would not be long before the demise of Grogan would come to his notice. So Sandy and Doug had decided to start the international operation ASAP.

Milo had agreed to a request from Parker to set his teams back in Kotor and Dubrovnik on the case. He then said that once his usefulness here in Leeds had come to an end, possibly the following week, he planned to go home and take charge of his business again.

As Milo finished telling me this he turned to his daughter,

"So, Elena, presumably you'll want to return with me to Kotor?" That creamy raspberry flush appeared on her cheeks again as she looked first at Lucija, then as she turned to me it started to deepen, so she quickly turned back to her father as she stammered her reply.

"Of course, Poppa, but I may still have things to finish off here."

Lucija stepped in to help cover her friend's confusion.

"Mr Borovic, my parents are coming over next week to collect me, I think Elena wants to wait and see them. Perhaps you could delay your departure until after that."

She glanced at me as she said this and I could see from her eyes that she was being slightly conspiratorial. So that was agreed and we all retired for the evening.

I looked across at Elena before I left the room and gave her an enquiring smile, which she returned before going back to her conversation with Lucija.

"Time to call it a day, Nathan, old son, let's turn in." I muttered.

As I started dropping off to sleep my mind was drifting back to the delectable Miss Borovic, the final image I had, just before falling fast asleep, was of her standing there with a smoking gun in her hand.

Now I knew why she insisted on taking her long handled handbag with her on our journey to carry out the assault on The Board Room.

Much was achieved over the next few weeks. Both Grogan and Scarface were released from hospital into custody and taken to secure units.

All their former captives had returned home to their families in their various countries in the Balkans, amid much rejoicing.

Lucija's parents did come over to collect their daughter, and, after a couple of emotional days with her, they took her back to Croatia to try and rebuild their lives.

Mr and Mrs Babić were hoping it was still possible for Lucija to take up the job that she'd planned to start before she and Elena were taken hostage.

Milo said he would try and help them as he'd done a lot of work for the legal department in Belgrade's town hall. Lucija's parents had a session with me before departing and, quite unnecessarily had felt the need to bring me special gifts from their homeland as a thank you.

Beautifully wrapped in gold foil were two packs of the world renowned Pag Island Cheese and a meticulously crafted model of an Istrian Kažun. These are stone built conical buildings used by land workers as storehouses for their tools and as shelters in inclement weather.

Once Lucija and her parents had departed, Milo made arrangements to take Elena back with him to Montenegro. I took an opportunity, shortly after our night out in Leeds, to walk round the hotel grounds to have a heart to heart discussion with her.

We both realised there was now an understanding between us that was growing daily into something special. However, she'd been through a dreadful ordeal and needed some time to allow the healing process to take its course.

This was best achieved by her being back with her father in her home environment, at least for the time being. So I suggested that when she was feeling better, I would visit her and we could then discuss her future plans.

I drove Milo and Elena to Manchester airport and bade them a sad but fond farewell. The journey across the M62 was a little solemn as both Elena and myself were conscious of the traumas we'd experienced and how that brought us very close together.

When they'd checked in at the airport, Milo said he needed to go and make a phone call to his office so would go and find a quiet corner in the waiting area.

As we watched him walk away, we realised he'd given us the chance to have some private moments on our own. At first there was an awkward silence as we both struggled with our feelings. Elena was the first to speak,

"What now Nathan?"

"Well I need to help Sandy wrap things up in Leeds, after that I must find somewhere to live, and then help him plan the next part of the operation. I also have to keep an eye on you, although that may be difficult as you'll be around 1800 km away."

"You don't need to keep an eye on me, I'll behave myself and count the days for when you come to see me."

"Me too,"

I took her by the hand, stood her up and drew her close to me and gave her a full kiss on the lips. She responded deliciously and moved a strand of her hair out of my eyes.

As we broke free from our embrace we saw Milo walking back towards us with a smile on his face. He gave her the passport he'd remembered to bring with him.

"Well, my lovely daughter, we better go through passport control and to the departure lounge.

Nathan it's impossible for me to say how much I owe you. You have twice risked your life for my daughter and because of you, she's alive and back with her family. Come back and see us soon, please."

At that point he gave me a friendly bear hug and turned on his heels, heading off through to departures. Elena glanced a delicate kiss on my cheek and with a tear rolling down her face, gave me her awkward farewells.

"Nathan, I owe you my life and my freedom. But that has got nothing to do with my feelings for you. Please hurry back to my side." Then she was gone.

On the way home I ran through in my mind the events of those past few weeks.

Chief Superintendent Rowley was brought before a Magistrates Court in Central London. He pleaded not guilty on all charges, so was remanded in custody with the case to be heard by a higher court.

As well as Sergeant Robertson, it turned out that there were two other members of Rowley's vice squad who were on the take. They also were in custody awaiting trial.

Trish, the girl that Grogan had been with at the time of his arrest had been able to put her life back together, with the help of Social Services.

She was now working on weekdays in the café of one of the large department stores in the heart of the city. Her baby was in the care of a nursery during school hours, and the young woman picked her child on her way home from work. Now that Trish was in a better situation, her sister was much happier and performing better at school. Another good result, then.

The Board Room had been totally cleared out and closed up. Assuming that Grogan would be convicted, the building and all his assets would be sold and the money confiscated by the Government.

The same fate befell all his Liverpool brothels. Fortunately, as Grogan kept clear records of all his transactions, Doug Turner's men were able to track down the new place in Manchester that Grogan had discussed on the phone with Rowley. This was also seized and its new line-up of staff was added to the UK prison population.

Using the cigarette butts dropped by our intended assassins at the cottage in Cumbria, two DNA matches were made from Grogan's team at The Board Room.

So unfortunately for them, attempted murder was on their charge sheet now.

I was pleased to find that one of them was the reviled, but now emasculated, Scarface. Wow, what a welcome a eunuch was going to get from his fellow inmates at whichever UK jail was to be his home for the rest of his life.

Doug Turner's team had looked for a link with any unsolved murders of young females in Liverpool. Regrettably a body of a girl aged around twenty two had been found near Albert Dock, her body was covered in bruises and she had a shock of red hair.

They made contact with the family of Mejra in Bosnia and unfortunately the DNA was a perfect match. So murder was now to be on the charge sheet of two of Grogan's men. Turner needed to prove which two.

Now it was time to plan the next period of my life and my long term future.

CHAPTER 14

Turkish Delight

It was now four months since our assault on The Board Room.

I'd managed to find myself an apartment in Leeds on Clarence Dock. A one bedroom property with a luxury bathroom and quality fitted kitchen with breakfast bar, plus a dining room/lounge.

This new development overlooked the River Aire and the Leeds Liverpool Canal, so I'd be able to enjoy great views with my place being situated on the third storey.

The developer had made a brave attempt to create a ready made community with the complex consisting of a number of restaurants, convenience store, hotel, various other shops, coffee outlets and several blocks of smart apartments. A great place for a bachelor pad and it was very handy for the city centre and all that the metropolis offered. Not a bad place for me to settle then, after two decades of travelling the hotspots of the world.

Given the parlous state of the finances in the UK and the number of properties that most developers still had on their books, I was able to secure a large discount, as I was a cash buyer.

I spent a couple of weeks furnishing the place, and then moved the rest of my belongings down from Sandy Parker's cottage in the Lake District.

I decided not to change my car as it was only a few months old. Hopefully the registration number was no longer a threat as Grogan, Superintendent Rowley and their cronies were all behind bars.

So I let Sandy have the pool car back and reverted to my own Seat Ibiza. With the two rear seats folded down there was plenty of space in the back to load it up with my clothes and the few other things that I'd acquired over the years. So the move from Cumbria was achieved in one journey.

The police had finished their forensic work at the cottage, so Parker put it up for sale. I was sad to see the place for the last time but it served its purpose for me and now I must move on.

I gave the place a good clean and tidied up the garden. Sandy had the estate agent's for-sale sign put up at the bottom of the drive, so I left the cottage clean smart and tidy and more than ready for the estate agent to organise accompanied viewings. Almost twenty years in the British armed forces conditioned you to be ready for 'kit inspections!!' Hopefully Sandy would be able to secure a sale before too long.

Before driving back to Yorkshire, I decided to take a last walk to one of the spots where Elena and I had enjoyed a picnic. I returned to the waterside where she'd taken great delight in feeding the noisy ducks and had even persuaded chaffinches to take crumbs from her long, delicate porcelain fingers.

As I sat on the springy, greeny-blue turf beneath the organ pipes of the great towering rocks, I pondered the events of the past few weeks.

This filled me with both melancholy and contentment in equal measure. The longer I sat there with my happy memories, the sadder I became. As I fought with my emotions, I stood up and started to do a forced march back to the cottage, muttering to myself,

"Come on Sawyer, get a grip." I was happy Elena was safe but I really missed being able to see her on a daily basis.

Breathless from my forced march, but with my depressed state long gone, I returned to the cottage and after one last check to ensure that the place was secure I jumped in the car and headed off back to Leeds.

When it came to furnishing my apartment, I was able to get some good prices for quality items, as many retailers were still suffering from the recession, so were happy to 'do a deal'.

The kitchen was fully fitted with a good array of white goods, so I only needed to buy a selection of kitchen utensils and crockery.

I wanted the lounge to be really comfortable so I went to a good shop on Regent Street and picked up a two seater sofa with a matching armchair in leather, a deep buffalo colour that shouldn't show any marks.

That took up a good deal of room in the lounge/diner so I settled for eating at the breakfast bar in the kitchen, and therefore added a couple of bar stools to my purchases. A dark mahogany coffee table, stereo system then a flat screen TV completed the living space.

The bedroom had fitted wardrobes along one wall, so I merely added a bed and a bedside cabinet with a nice table lamp and finally a bedside radio alarm.

The bed was a modern floor level unit with a brown leather frame, complete with a memory foam mattress and pillows.

A few modern art pictures on the walls gave the apartment the final touch and as I looked round I was happy the place was ready for me to settle there, at least for the time being.

As I gradually purchased the various items, I wondered whether Elena would ever grace my new crash pad with her presence. I sincerely hoped so.

The apartment was in an ideal location, a fifteen minutes stroll to the railway station and less than a twenty minutes walk to Sandy's office. There was also a good new riverside walk alongside the water so I'd still be able to do my early morning runs enjoying a pleasant view whilst doing so.

I phoned Elena regularly. I'd left her alone for a week after she returned home. I thought she needed some quality time with her father without having me get in the way. I believed that speaking with me as soon as she had arrived back home would only confuse her.

After that we spoke every three or four days, usually for ten minutes or more. I was trying to take our relationship quite slowly to give her some space. It would have been all too easy for any feelings I had for her to be protective rather than born out of genuine fondness.

For her part, whereas she seemed to have returned my affections, I needed to find out that this was not merely gratitude but something more.

It would have been a travesty if I'd plunged headlong into a romance, only to find out after six months that Elena's feelings were driven by a misplaced sentiment that she was in my debt for rescuing her.

She seemed to have more joy and laughter in her voice than when we'd been brought together in those traumatic circumstances. Hopefully that meant she was beginning to put her ordeal behind her.

She had one bit of good news to tell me once she'd been back home for three weeks. Her father used his influence in Belgrade to secure agreement that Lucija's original appointment in the city legal department still stood. After a month's R&R Elena's friend felt able to take up her post and started her new career over a year late.

Milo and his team had been working hard with Interpol to establish what they knew about 'Mr Big' in Istanbul, whom we now believed to be known as Mehdi Gümüş.

His Turkish operation seemed to be quite extensive and he certainly lived a millionaire lifestyle, with luxury homes in both Istanbul and Northern Cyprus and several Mercedes saloons.

He was known to be involved with people smuggling, drug dealing and prostitution, and was suspected of being behind several gangland murders.

The Turkish Police had never been successful in arresting him; this was almost certainly due in no small way to his army of bodyguards and the bribes that he quickly handed out, when the heat was on. I thought to myself that if the whole of Interpol hadn't been able to bring him to justice, then we were going to have a tough job.

This was where the plan I'd put to Sandy could now be put into action. The discussions started in his office the day after Elena and Milo had returned home.

Sandy and I read through the Interpol files on Gümüş. They were extensive and unbelievably comprehensive, but they'd clearly not led to a satisfactory conclusion.

"Why, then, Sandy has there been no arrest, and no prosecution?" I asked, once we'd finished reading the catalogue of heinous crimes that were linked with this man and his bunch of ruffians.

"Pockets have been lined, families have been threatened, indeed some have been viciously attacked and forced into silence. The man's very powerful and ruthless and will stop at nothing to protect his interests, Nathan. I think we need to take a different tack if we're to bring him and his empire down."

"Over the last few days while taking in the data that's in these files I've been thinking long and hard about how we can best approach this. I believe I may have a suitable line of attack to put to you.

Now that Grogan's operation no longer exists, one of the Turk's main sources of overseas revenue and profit has gone, so he's probably not best pleased.

The files we've read from Interpol don't indicate that Gümüş had any other customers in the UK. Therefore, when we closed down Grogan's operation, it must have hit him hard. My suggestion is we set up a phantom UK operation to look like it's going to replace the one Grogan operated.

We make it look as authentic as possible, with a few carefully scripted press releases that speak of rumours of a new operation to fill the vacuum left by Grogan's demise.

We could then make sure Gümüş heard about the new operation and saw it as a possible new outlet. You know the sort of thing?"

"Mmm, we could do an exposé on the drug trafficking and the people smuggling, without naming Grogan or any of his team as their trials are imminent. We wouldn't wish to prejudice any court proceedings.

We could then indicate in the articles it's rumoured the next big area for drugs and sex slaves is West Yorkshire with Leeds the possible option."

"That's the sort of thing, boss. The press stuff also needs to be fed to Turkey to get Gümüş on the hook.

Then, my plan would be to contact him, posing as the head of a new Leeds operation and ask if I could go and see him, to discuss a possible business relationship.

I'd clearly need a different name and passport, as he may just have heard the name *Nathan Sawyer*; in any event, I'm supposed to be dead!!

Once I'd set up a meeting I could be wired and try and persuade him to supply me with drugs and girls. We'd set up the sting jointly with Interpol.

Once sufficient evidence had been gathered in any of the meetings, the cavalry comes in and makes the arrest. Simple enough in my view. Risky, of course, but simple."

"It's not as easy as that, but at least it's a starting point. The man is dangerous and a known killer and never goes out without at least two bodyguards. From the reports we've just read, he carries a gun, so do his minders."

"I know, but that's just detail. It can't be any more dangerous than the ops you and I did in Bosnia in 1995 with the Rapid Reaction Force. Let's put something together, we need to take this bastard out of circulation."

As I gazed steadily at my former commander I could see a twinkle in his eye, so I knew then I was on the right track.

He wanted to bring down this evil operation just as much as I did and sending me in under cover was an ideal solution from many aspects. I knew so much about Grogan's operation I could certainly pass myself off as a man planning a similar set up.

We agreed that this embryonic plan could be worked up into a viable tactical proposal.

During the next week, Sandy met with Doug Turner and with senior officials from the Home Office and the Foreign Office.

At first, the Foreign Office guy was reluctant for us to get involved as the criminal we were targeting was a foreign national, over whom we'd no jurisdiction.

The man from the Home Office, though, was a different kettle of fish, quite aggressive and very keen to help. The

Home Office was putting in a very significant effort to try and stem the ever burgeoning trade in drugs and the escalating flow of captive sex slaves from Eastern Europe.

Both of these criminal activities were causing considerable police work plus additional efforts from Social Services and the NHS and thus were putting a huge strain on the budgets of several UK government departments.

Once Justin Forester, the Foreign Office official, had listened to the arguments from his Home Office Colleague, he relaxed quite considerably and provided some good input to the meetings.

By the time we reconvened, the guys from Interpol reported that Gümüş had now gone over to Northern Cyprus. By the looks of his luggage, he was planning quite a long stay in his villa outside Girne (Kyrenia); the house was in an expensive coastal development at Ozanköy.

This news brought a smile to the face of Justin, who revealed that less than twelve months ago he'd completed a three year assignment as a military attaché to the British High Commission in Nicosia, with special responsibility for Northern Cyprus.

The fact that the Turkish Republic of Northern Cyprus isn't recognised as an independent country means that there are no embassies or consulates north of the Green Line, the heavily guarded border which separates the north from the south of this beautiful island. He therefore was based in the only capital in the world that's divided.

From his base in South Nicosia he worked extensively in Northern Cyprus and the information he'd gathered whilst performing his tour of duty was going to be invaluable to me. We therefore agreed to meet at his office the next day where Justin would fully brief me on what background he felt I'd need on my trip, as I was no longer going to Istanbul, as we'd originally planned, but to a sunny island in the eastern Mediterranean.

After a second group meeting had taken place and the framework of our plans was beginning to take shape, our high level team requested the allocation of a senior team from Interpol to the project. The various members of our party then convened together in one of the Government's offices on Whitehall. Sandy and I both attended to put the final touches to the agreed framework.

Once we'd done that, the finer details would be left to Sandy and Doug Turner, plus Interpol, with input from myself. I had a considerable amount of additional information after my long and very worthwhile meeting with Justin Forester. He also arranged to have a new passport couriered to me, and for this exercise I'd be known as *Max Kelman*. That would take some getting used to!!

To establish my cover, the Home Office PR department started sending releases out to the press. A dummy company was set up as a front for the operation with an address that was controlled by the Home Office.

We secured a number of commercial estate agents' brochures for suitable properties that might pass as potential outlets if we'd actually been going ahead with the set up.

I'd take them with me to show to Mehdi Gümüş, to give him the impression that my intentions were credible and large enough to be of interest to him.

We had letterheads and business cards printed showing my pseudonym and a spare phone line in Sandy's office was dedicated to that company with the name of the phantom business being Executive Entertainment.

The theme of the press articles was the Government's concern at the increase in organised crime, especially drugs and prostitution. There was mention of an increase in these activities in Leeds, the third largest city in the UK.

The series of articles appeared over five consecutive nights in one of the quality nationals and the press releases were also sent to the major nationals in the Balkans and Turkey. Hopefully the seeds were sown and would make my initial contact with Gümüş a little easier and my undercover role seem completely authentic.

We decided to advise Milo of our planned operation, both as a courtesy and to see if he could bring anything else to the party through his own contacts.

I told Elena, in what turned out to be an extremely difficult telephone call, what our plans were. She took this quite badly and expressed her concern for my safety in a tearful exchange of views.

I talked to her about the benefits of trying to ensure no other young ladies had to go through what she'd experienced. Whilst she recognised the sentiment of this, she was clearly worried about what could happen.

It pained me to bring her grief whilst I was so far away, but I believed that being honest would maintain the trust between us we'd developed since we first met on that fateful October night.

We completed our planning and the travel arrangements were organised for me.

On a Wednesday in late spring I boarded the 09.45 scheduled flight from Leeds Bradford Airport to Larnaca in Southern Cyprus.

After a good, quite long, flight, during which I tried unsuccessfully to have a nap, we touched down on time at 16.30 hours local time.

After a relatively swift transit through passport control I collected my baggage and went through customs. I looked out for my name on a placard.

It took a while to find it, mainly as I was looking for 'Nathan Sawyer' instead of my temporary moniker 'Max Kelman.' Once I'd clocked a foreign office type holding up my new name I was soon shaking hands with him.

Less than five minutes later we were sitting in a green Land Rover, sporting CD plates. I'd been collected by a pleasant and cheerful youngish man, probably no more than twenty eight, who introduced himself as Howard Rhodes a military attaché from the High Commission. He was to drive me over the border, take me to my hotel in Kyrenia and act as my liaison during my engagement.

My host was dressed in smart casual clothes. He had a pleasant demeanour and a slight West Country burr in his voice. We soon established his home town was Cleeve, near Bristol Airport just a few miles from where I was brought up. We, therefore, had an immediate rapport, especially as he was interested in rugby union.

Rhodes had been thoroughly briefed about my assignment and was in touch with the Interpol team, who were already on the island but wouldn't be looking to meet me for a week.

They were a team of four and wanted to check out whether Gümüş had a daily routine, where he went, what he did and whom he usually had with him. Once they were satisfied they would then meet me, away from the public eye, and we could work out our plan to bring about the arrest.

Howard gave me a mobile phone and charger which he said was the only one I should use whilst on the island. It was scrambled and totally secure with a variety of fast dial numbers programmed on to its simcard, carefully chosen by the High Commission to cover most eventualities. Finally there was a red panic button which would bring in the cavalry if needed.

I asked him about arms as I was concerned that Gümüş and his men were known to be carrying when they were out and about. My assignment had been organised as a UK Government operation and, as such, I was on secondment to MI6. Thus, I'd be supplied with a weapon.

It had been agreed with Sandy, as the operational commander, that a password would be issued, to be known only by myself, Howard's staff and the Interpol team.

Thus if anyone should contact me, their first ID check would be to use the codeword 'Bluebird.' If one party uttered this then the correct response was 'Campbell.' If at any time this was found to be compromised, Howard would change it.

We speedily went through the border crossing and I was furnished with my Visa, officially stamped and as official as it was going to get.

A little over an hour after we'd left Larnaca Airport we pulled up in front of my hotel. It was around a mile outside the coastal town of Kyrenia, a small but vibrant port due north of Lefkosa (Nicosia).

Howard dropped me off, at which point a uniformed hotel employee appeared from nowhere to take my case and carry-on bag into the building that was to be my home for at least the next two weeks.

I bade a temporary farewell to Howard who said he would be back at 10.00 hours the next day.

I was to spend a few days familiarising myself with the island and acting as a tourist to establish my cover. My liaison officer had arranged for a pool car to be delivered to my hotel the next morning. Until then my time was my own. As he took his leave of me, Howard gave me a black leather briefcase and asked that I familiarise myself with the contents straight away.

The tall, smiling male receptionist came out from behind his desk and shook my hand warmly,

"Welcome Mr Kelman, if you could fill in the registration form and let me have your passport, my colleague will show you up to your room. As we aren't too busy at the moment, I've upgraded you to a superior room."

Whilst filling in the simple form, I remembered to use my new name and the address that the Home Office told me to use. It was one of their safe houses in Leeds and any attempted contact that may be made there by our target wouldn't present a problem.

The receptionist advised me of the restaurant opening hours and told me my passport would be available to collect the next day. My passport looked genuine with a number of visa stamps in it and the deep red covers had been distressed to make it look a few years old.

I went in my room and a few minutes later was sitting out on my balcony, sipping a coffee I'd made from the hospitality tray.

After a while, I set my cup down and collected Howard's brief case which I'd left on the bed. I took it on to the balcony and snapped open the two brass locks.

I checked the security code on the locks. They were both set at 000, so I pressed the internal lever and set them to my own code.

What was in the case was interesting, and immediately added to the already high esteem in which I held Howard. There was a detailed map of Northern Cyprus, with all the Turkish military bases hand marked on for me, town maps of Kyrenia, Nicosia and Famagústa plus a Turkish phrase book and a tourist guide for Cyprus. In a separate compartment in the bottom were a bug detector and a Beretta 92FS handgun, complete with a lightweight holster and three magazines, each packed with fifteen rounds.

I picked up the bug detector and switched it on, giving the room a full sweep, the furniture, lamps, telephone and bathroom fittings.

After covering all possibilities, the machine gave a satisfying short bleep and came up with a green light, so all appeared to be clear with no extraneous listening devices in place.

The note from Howard that was attached to the machine suggested that I make this part of my daily routine. A suggestion I was happy to follow, now that I was a spook, albeit in a temporary capacity.

I unpacked my case and hung my clothes up, then decided to do a bit of exploring in this little piece of Turkey. I was also quite hungry by this time so set my sights on a cup of Turkish coffee, after which I would look for a half decent restaurant.

CHAPTER 15

Playing the tourist

I took a quick look around the hotel before going for a walk into Kyrenia which took me about twenty minutes. I went past a casino, a military archives establishment, the town's ambulance station and a handful of shops and houses.

As I reached the town centre I stopped by the town hall to photograph the large statue of resplendent white doves in front of the building.

Turning round to my right I politely declined the offer of a taxi from the multitude of drivers standing by their cars on the rank in front of the bus station. By now I was slipping nicely into my role as a tourist.

I walked down a narrow one way street, lined with shops on either side, a large number of them mobile phone shops; this 600 metre parade led me down to the old harbour, which turned out to be a veritable delight.

I stopped at the first café on the side of the harbour and ordered a coffee. As I sipped the dark hot nectar (at last, proper coffee) I took in the amazing view and started to get my bearings, using the tourist map Howard had given me. It was important to quickly familiarise myself with the layout of the town.

From my table I was facing the castle so the inner harbour was on my left. As well as a number of imposing modern yachts, there were some magnificent old schooners which I looked forward to viewing more closely in due course.

To my left, the harbour wall had a wide walkway of about 400 metres in length which led out to a small lighthouse.

This was clearly a promenading area for the locals, as many Turkish Cypriots, young and old were walking arm in arm, or standing smoking on the harbour's edge, many were sitting on the benches that were placed at strategic intervals, engaging their companions in animated discussions.

Further round to the right of the café I could see a selection of restaurants, many of which had outside tables alongside the edge of the extensive marina.

As dusk was beginning to fall, the castle was now floodlit. The other arm of the harbour wall passed under the castle walls so I took off in that direction after paying for my coffee.

This area was going to offer plenty to explore over the next few days. On the face of it, though, it presented little opportunity for clandestine meetings. However, my target was known to spend a lot of time in Kyrenia so I needed to familiarise myself with the layout of the town centre and its various main areas, including this interesting harbour district.

After nonchalantly strolling around, taking a number of photos, I started looking around for a restaurant, having to fight off the men who were stationed outside each establishment and who vociferously entreated me come inside,

"For the best table, at the best price and the best food in Cyprus!!"

I smiled at each of them and courteously declined, with a promise to come back another day. Eventually, I settled on a smart but quiet place, specialising in fresh fish, by the name of Trypiti Restaurant.

I took my time over the meal to enable me to look at the people who were promenading past.

As well as those who were clearly locals, there were many who stood out as Brits, mostly aged sixty plus.

In addition, there were small numbers of quite smartly dressed individuals, younger lean looking men, mostly in pairs, who were clearly from elsewhere and had a swagger in their gait. With their tanned skin and aquiline nose they would either be Italian or possibly Spanish, more likely the former.

I took my receipt and walked back along the promenade taking a slightly different route back, up some steps, passing a large luxurious looking casino.

Outside were a few taxis looking for trade and a small number of thirty something men in shiny suits and dark glasses, milling around. They seemed to be vetting anyone who wanted to go into the place.

They were well muscled, scowling and had pale skin with high cheekbones. It seemed to me like the Russian Mafia was already well represented in this area.

Needing to keep an eye on that situation, I looked in their direction and tried a smile which was returned with an even deeper scowl.

As I walked past I looked back, I could see that the one with his back to me had a bulge at waist level so, presumably was packing a handgun.

I also saw another guy looking in my direction. He was dressed in the relatively poor garb of the local working class, had black hair and moustache. When I looked back at him he quickly looked away and moved off up a street on the left.

I eventually came back to the town hall, retracing my steps towards the hotel. As I came past the forecourt of the ambulance station I heard footsteps about a hundred metres behind me.

I stopped and turned round, there was no-one there, as far as I could see. As soon as I carried on, the footsteps started again so I walked as far as the lay-by in front of the military archive and secreted myself behind a large tree.

The street lights were pretty poor so my stalker wouldn't be able to see that I'd stopped, as my rubber soled shoes were making no sound.

I waited until he'd just walked past the tree then grabbed him round the neck from behind, forcing his head backwards and causing him to struggle for breath.

"OK, who the hell are you and why are you following me?"

I relaxed my grip, slightly, to give him chance to reply. I was only slightly surprised to hear him say in a croaky voice,

"Bluebird."

To which I answered.

"Campbell" as I let him go with my apology "Sorry mate but I didn't expect a tail so early in my operation."

"OK Mr Kelman, I'm Hakan Çöteli, I'm a Turkish Police liaison officer working with your High Commission. I've been asked to keep a discreet eye on you if you travel on foot in Kyrenia.

I won't be able to follow you in a vehicle; that would be too obvious to the target, but if you can let me know each time you go into town on foot, I'll be there.

I'm armed and I know who the target is and will also be liaising with the Interpol team, so between us we should have a successful operation.

I better go now as I can't afford to be seen with you. My name is in your mobile phone, you can call me any time. Also the red panic button goes straight through to me."

"Great Hakan, many thanks. We'll find somewhere to meet up that's safe over the next few days. Have a good trip home; I should be OK getting back to the hotel now, hope I didn't hurt you too much." He smiled and was gone in an instant.

I quickly walked away so as not to compromise my minder and within another ten minutes was back at my hotel, thankful the High Commission was looking after my interests. Back in my room I did another sweep for bugs, again it proved negative so picked up the mobile that Howard had given me and called Sandy to give him a full report of the day's activities.

I then went onto the balcony with a coffee and admired the swimming pool, with its underwater lighting. After a few minutes, feeling relaxed, but tired after a long day, I went back into the bedroom, five minutes later I was in bed, fast asleep.

My bedside alarm went off at 06.30. I donned my tracksuit and went down through reception to a running track opposite the hotel.

After a few stretching exercises on the side of the football pitch, I set off round the track. After completing eight laps in a time that pleased me I called it a day and headed off back to my room.

As I walked back I switched on my mobile, by the time I had gone up to the third floor landing, my phone beeped with a message alert. I opened the message as I was going through my door,

"Phone me ASAP, Sandy."

I did so after getting showered and dressed. In a startling but interesting conversation, Interpol had reported to Sandy the wife and two young children of our target, Mehdi Gümüş had been kidnapped from their home in Istanbul and then his house had been blown up.

No ransom demand had been made but the police picked up a related call to his mobile. They also had phone taps on the phones at both his residences. Sandy read out the transcript of the call to me. He said the caller was obviously Russian as he started off the conversation to Gümüş in his native language before reverting to heavily accented English.

"Good evening Mr Gümüş. We understand you've been taking away our trade in the UK running your so called business from your rat's nest in Istanbul. Our colleagues in Moscow say that must stop. Here are your instructions. Stay where you are in Cyprus, do **not** go back to Turkey and close down your operation there immediately."

Gümüş's reply was swift and to the point.

"Fuck off you Russian pig; you're all talk, what's the matter can't stand the competition?"

"You may wish to think about it Mr Gümüş, we've destroyed your house in Turkey and your wife and children are now our guests. You may wish to speak to your beloved wife right now."

Our target's wife and her husband exchanged some brief words, sufficient for Gümüş to know that any threats were genuine. Once the Russian was back on the phone he laid down his demands to Gümüş.

These were described to me fully by Sandy:-

The drug and people smuggling operations in Turkey were to be shut down immediately

Gümüş must provide evidence to the Russians he'd done that

He must hand over his supplier and customer contacts to the Russians

He mustn't go back to Turkey but should now arrange to live in Northern Cyprus permanently

If he did not do all of this within fourteen days, his wife and children would be killed

Once he'd complied with all their demands, his family would be free to join him in Cyprus.

Gümüş was given no chance to reply for as soon as the last demand was read out, the Russian terminated the phone call.

Sandy asked me to think over how our plans might now have to be changed and asked me to call him back later in the day.

"Great start to my mission!" I mused as I went down to breakfast.

Sitting out in the early morning sunshine on the terrace in front of the restaurant, I helped myself to the tasty buffet, cereals followed by cold meat and cheese and a pot of ground coffee.

I was just finishing off my coffee when my mobile rang, it was Howard. He asked me to meet him at the new harbour in half an hour.

There was a café next to the ferry terminal. A ten minute walk from the hotel took me past the magnificent and huge monument on the roundabout. After going down a dusty dual carriageway I went through a modest housing estate, a large military establishment on the left, then through the gates of the docks.

I found the simple café to the right of the ferry terminal and got myself a table on the outside terrace where a number of dock workers were having their breakfast.

I'd just ordered myself a coffee and phoned to advise Hakan Çöteli, my minder, where I was when Howard Rhodes joined me.

I asked the waiter for a second coffee then looked around at the rest of the tables to see if there were any interested parties. Apparently not, so I thanked Howard for the briefcase and its contents then told him of my meeting with Hakan Çöteli the previous evening.

Rhodes was surprised I'd sussed my minder, so I just smiled to myself and made no comment. I'd felt I may be under threat last night so had taken appropriate action, I think Hakan realised that.

It was then I surprised him even more with my updating him on our Turkish target, and what had happened with his call from the Russian Mafia.

"So Max, clearly our original plan is now somewhat compromised."

"I figured over breakfast that I should let the guys from Interpol continue their surveillance of Gümüş and they should carefully monitor his phone calls.

His movements should also be carefully monitored now. Once we have a clearer picture of what he's planning then we can establish how to proceed.

In the meantime I'll keep my head down whilst actually looking for suitable quiet places for you and I to meet the Interpol team."

My pool car was waiting for me in the hotel car park on my return. It had local number plates; it was, therefore, not allowed over the Green Line.

I debated the possibilities with Howard. My initial thoughts were that the Russians may well be doing our job for us. But then I thought, the problem hadn't gone away, it would merely be a changed nationality. Same problem, different language.

Howard would get his staff to produce a dossier on any Russians who were on Cyprus at the moment and who may be known to them.

I told him I'd ensure I was armed each time I was out from now on. We might get caught in the middle of a gang war if we were not careful, so the feedback from our surveillance over the next few days would be crucial.

I thanked Howard for his input and he left me after we had a further ten minutes debate on the situation.

I walked back to the hotel and picked my car keys up from the reception, where my passport was also returned to me.

I reached the car park and found my car, a red Ford Fiesta, against the whitewashed wall.

A first parade maintenance check revealed that all appeared to be in order, apart from the petrol tank was almost on empty. I'd spotted there was a filling station on the main road, quite near the hotel, so would use that on my way out.

I ran up to my room which had already been serviced by the maid. I did another bug sweep; again negative.

Strapping my gun holster around my waist with the holster in the small of my back, I then put the first ammo clip in the gun, put a second clip in my jacket pocket and secreted the weapon in the small of my back.

Slipping on my light weight shower-proof jacket which concealed the gun, I went down to the car after looking at the map to decide where I was going.

I'd checked the guide book over breakfast and made a list of places to go where I might find suitably quiet meeting places. Before driving off I phoned Hakan to stand him down as I wouldn't be around Kyrenia for the rest of the day.

After filling up with petrol, I turned right, following the sign for Bellapais Monastery. In a few minutes I reached the outskirts of this pretty and ancient village, parked up in the small car park, paying the attendant as I left. After a couple of minutes' brisk walk I reached the tiny square in the village centre.

After buying my entry ticket I toured round the Abbey and figured there were a number of spots where quiet conversations were possible, if required. The only problem was the holiday season was starting to gain momentum so doubtless tourist coaches would soon be filling the place.

Once I'd exited the Abbey grounds I retraced my route to the main road near the hotel and turned left and after a couple of miles I was heading out of Kyrenia on the coast road towards Güzelyurt.

My journey took me past a number of modern monuments to the conflicts in the fifties and the seventies that engulfed this magical island. The countryside was also awash with military establishments all of which had numerous armed soldiers standing guard on their gates, preventing access and stopping any attempt to take photographs.

Way out in the countryside, I found a tiny café right alongside the beach. It was quite anonymous and had seen better days. It had a sort of thatched roof that was gradually being blown away by the strongish wind coming in hard off the Mediterranean Sea.

I pulled on to the large unevenly surfaced car park and took a table next to the beach. I paused to admire the wonderful breakers which the wind was bringing crashing down rather angrily with a resounding boom on to the tawny coloured sand.

I ordered a Turkish coffee and cheese and ham sandwich from the middle aged man who clearly owned the place.

This would be a good place for meetings. It was off the main road and not very smart so wasn't likely to attract our target or his bodyguards as casual visitors.

I took a second coffee before setting off towards Güzelyurt, after checking I wasn't being followed.

Once I'd arrived in this busy town I found there was a magnificent mosque in the centre. I parked in a side street near this photogenic place of worship. Just across from the mosque stood the famous and beautiful Icon Museum, residing in the Agio Mamas Church. In the grounds of the museum, there were a number of quiet benches, nestling among the trees and statues along with antique relics.

I marvelled at the scented air as I walked around. It was heavy with perfume from the exotic blossoms that were now in full bloom on the low shrubs bordering the gravel paths.

"Why is it always the places of beauty that attract conflict and violent acts?" I thought, as I sat there drinking in the clean and beautifully perfumed air, but still frantically trying to think through our next steps.

I kept coming back to square one; we really needed to know what action the Turks and Russians were going to take, as that would dictate our best route to a successful conclusion to the mission.

In retrospect, then, I was happy that so far I'd found two places for quiet meetings, time to go back to the hotel and have another conversation with Sandy. Hopefully, the surveillance team would've come up with something we could use.

As I was motoring back, I was enjoying the fact that in Cyprus, like at home, driving was on the left, so I could allow a part of my brain to continue to think, whilst still concentrating on the road.

I parked up and took the stairs two at a time up to the third floor. I passed a couple of stocky guys coming down the stairs, wearing thick dark glasses. White Europeans, by the looks of them, they hardly glanced at me as they dashed past. "Hmm, they're certainly not tourists and where have they been?"

I entered my room with caution, nothing appeared to have been disturbed and the bug sweep also seemed OK.

I had a long phone conversation with Sandy, most of which centred on the report he'd received from the guys at Interpol.

They'd determined from listening in to the traffic on both the house and mobile phones belonging to Gümüş that he was gathering his cohorts around him in Cyprus and had set up his team in Istanbul to try and find out where the Russians were who'd abducted his family.

They also discovered that he held a meeting each morning in Kyrenia. He went to the same hotel at 11.00 hours and usually had animated discussions with about half a dozen of his group.

The hotel was alongside the promenade, right in the centre of Kyrenia. It had an outside area with tables along its frontage that provided great views of old Kyrenia Town centre. Attentive but unobtrusive waiters were on hand to bring coffee, tea and snacks as required.

On the right of the hotel, a short way from Kordonboyu Caddesi was a taxi rank and beyond that a small square with the obligatory statue of Atatürk, one of which seemed to occupy every village square or town plaza.

I suggested to Sandy that I should spend some time on the next day observing our targets from a distance. He agreed, but also emphasized that Gümüş seemed to be getting his army together and was maybe about to try and fight fire with fire. What he didn't want was for me, or any other members of our team, to be caught inadvertently in a cross fire. I was therefore instructed merely to observe to start with, without being seen.

"Also Sandy I believe a couple of Russians are in my hotel, possibly staying here, in the same block as myself. I'll ask my minder Hakan to try and find out who they were; as a member of the local police force, he would be able to ask a hotel about its foreign guest check-ins."

I finished my call and phoned Elena to see how she was getting on. She was well and clearly delighted that 'Mr Big' was now beginning to feel the heat.

I asked her to enquire if her father would be able to find anything out about the whereabouts of the wife and children of Gümüş in Istanbul through his contacts. I figured if we had a chance of finding that out we may be able to use the information to get to the man himself.

As far as you can have a relationship on the phone, I was starting to recognise the tenor of Elena's voice and each time we spoke, we were drawn inexorably closer together. This time not forced together by circumstances but keeping in touch through choice.

Her voice was soft and delicate, like a little china bell and I just loved the sound of her girlish laughter, wishing that she was by my side in person rather than just a voice on my mobile.

I then phoned Hakan and asked him if he could find out anything about the two guys I'd seen in the hotel.

"OK, Max, I'll make enquiries and call you back."

He was somewhat concerned when I told him about the recent problems that had befallen Gümüş. He said with sadness in his voice that the last thing Cyprus needed was gang warfare on the streets.

"I'll be around tomorrow from 11.00 as your back-up when you're observing the target in Kyrenia."

Hakan phoned me back within an hour. Two Russians had checked into my hotel and were in two rooms in the same block but on the floor below and round the corner from me. My room and balcony couldn't be seen from where they were.

What was of real interest is they travelled from Istanbul, but their home addresses were in Moscow and Interpol had issued a blue notice in respect of both of them to all its member law enforcement authorities.

There are seven types of notice that can be issued from Interpol's headquarters in Lyon, France. A 'Blue Notice' is in respect of 'Individuals of interest in relation to a crime.' So these guys would, likely as not, be part of the crew that were looking to take over the Turkish operation.

I certainly needed to be even more careful now and had to blend in even more. If either side in the internecine warfare crossed paths with me it was imperative I should pass their scrutiny, no matter how casual.

"Hakan, I'll eat at the hotel tonight so you can enjoy the night off. That'll also enable me to see if the Russians are around."

"OK, Max see you tomorrow."

I went down to the restaurant at 20.00 hours, it wasn't quite warm enough to eat outside as a sharp wind had got up, so I asked for a table at the far end of the restaurant where I could see who came in.

I was shown to a spot next to the large picture window that overlooked the pool and given a menu from which I was to choose my starter. The waiter advised me that I would then select the main course from the extensive hot and cold buffet laid out in the centre of the vast dining room.

After I'd asked for a soup to start with, I furtively looked around the room to see who was in. No-one that I should concern myself with, I thought, there were just around twenty or so middle aged and elderly couples, busily getting as much as they could from the 'all you can eat' buffet.

I was just about to get up and have a look at the choices for my main course when the two Russians walked in, still wearing their sunglasses and looking like extras in a gangster movie.

They quickly glanced around the room then walked straight back out again. A couple of minutes later I heard a powerful motorbike start up in the car park to the rear of the restaurant.

"Were they out hunting or was this eatery just not lively enough for them?" I mused. No matter, I would keep my head down and continue to play the single thirty-something visitor.

My meal was pleasant and uneventful and the service attentive without being obsequious. I finished off with a coffee in the bar, idly watching the two TV screens that were on in there. Nothing of interest so I went back to my room and flicked through the thirty or so channels until I found The BBC news channel which enabled me to catch up with world events.

I rose at 06.00 before the alarm had gone off and, after my run and shower; I strapped on my weapon, sent a text to Hakan then set off in the car towards St Hilarion Castle and to carry out a quick recce of the location.

After a steep climb up the mountain which involved frequent gear changes in my tiny car, I drove past an army base with a huge bronze statue of a soldier at the front gate. I then wound my way round a number of hair raising bends to the tiny parking area located under the shadow of the imposing castle.

I walked a few yards into the small open air café which had about ten tables. After ordering a simple breakfast and coffee at the kiosk, I took my seat at a table on the side away from the car park.

I was able to look down towards the road which looked like a piece of grey ribbon unravelling in a green baize cloth a few hundred metres below me.

I had a perfect vantage point to see any individual or any vehicle approaching. It was obvious why the location was chosen for building a castle over 1500 years ago.

Perching on the edge of a high cliff, St Hilarion and its sheer cliffs must have provided superb protection against potential invaders.

I figured it would be a first class meeting place for my first conference with the team from Interpol.

I took a number of photos looking up towards the castle, making sure the guy in the café saw me. I paid for my breakfast noting that mine was still the only vehicle in the small parking area and then headed off back to the hotel.

So, although the castle was open from 9.00 hours, no visitors had appeared up till 09.45, so that might be a good time of day for me to arrange a quiet confab.

I parked up at the hotel forty minutes later and set off on foot towards Kyrenia town centre, advising Hakan by text that I was on my way to the area where our target's favourite hotel was located.

I kept checking behind me and was happy to see that I wasn't being followed. Just before 10.50, I arrived at the square where the statue of Atatürk dominated the open space.

I walked slowly along the promenade to the boundary of the hotel. No sign of any Russians at the moment so I carried on until I was level with the hotel's outside dining area and crossed the road without looking in the direction of the café.

Once I was on the other side of the road I again pointed my camera towards the statue then panned around to the waves beating in from the Mediterranean Sea and took a couple more shots.

There were a few young men casting fishing lines off the beach. Out in the open sea a large oil tanker hugged the horizon.

I was casually scrutinising the knots of people in the immediate vicinity to see if anyone else was people watching. I couldn't find any so I looked hard at the tables in front of the hotel.

I had a photo of Gümüş on the mobile which I now looked at and then I glanced towards the few people seated at the tables. Sure enough there he was, in the right hand corner with four of his henchmen who were watching, grim faced, while he waved his arms about as he engaged them in animated discussions.

I continued watching for ten minutes then decided to walk past the front of the hotel for a closer look. There was nothing worth noting there and certainly wasn't any point in listening to their conversation as they would be speaking Turkish, a language of which my knowledge was zilch. What I was able to determine was that the five of them were quite paunchy and hardly looked like they could handle any hand to hand combat. None of the party of five paid any attention to me, they were too engrossed in what their lord and master was postulating.

From my discreet glances, I could see there was a hint of a bulge under the jackets of the ones who were facing me, so they were obviously expecting trouble. I wondered how experienced they were at small arms fire.

I walked along the promenade for a few minutes, idly appearing to take photographs, then crossed the road again and walked back towards the target.

Just as I was within 30 metres of the place, I saw a powerful motorbike parked on the same side of the road as me. It was facing away from me, but I stopped dead when I saw that the two sitting on it were the Russians who were staying at my hotel. The engine was still running and both of them seemed to be looking in the direction of the hotel's outside tables.

I decided there was no point in risking their seeing me so I turned round and quietly walked out of their sight. Once I couldn't be seen from the hotel or the bike, I phoned Hakan and asked him to keep an eye on the Russians and phone me back once they'd left.

I'd spotted him in the taxi rank sitting on a concrete bollard, blending in beautifully, exhibiting the appearance and languid demeanour of the ordinary local that he actually was.

He called me back in less than ten minutes to report that after five minutes of observing Gümüş and his team, and without being spotted, he'd watched the Russians leave. I told Hakan I was now walking back to the hotel and wouldn't require him during the rest of the day.

As I made my way back I had a message alert on my mobile to phone Sandy when I was free. I managed to make the return journey to my hotel in fifteen minutes and took the lift up to my room, not wishing to pass Gümüs's adversaries on the stairs just now.

My room was its usual immaculate self, thanks to the efficiency of housekeeping at the hotel. The usual sweep for bugs again proved negative, so I took a soft drink from the mini-bar and phoned Sandy.

He was in a meeting, so his PA said she would have him call me back as soon as he was able.

I moved out on to the balcony with my orange juice. Just as I sat down I heard the roar of the motor bike as it came to a halt in the hotel's car park. I wondered where our friends from Moscow had been on the way back from watching our target, as they should have been back before me.

I stayed out there for another thirty minutes and then went back through the French windows into my room when Parker called me back.

I updated the boss on the events at my end.

"Sandy I now have a few potential meeting places where I could hook up with the guys from Interpol. What do you have for me?"

He had been in a meeting with Doug Turner when I originally phoned him.

What he told me made my blood run cold and his revelations made it crystal clear to me that we should now proceed with even more caution from this moment.

I also concluded that the heat would now be on and there would be no holding back by the two sides.

CHAPTER 16

This is War

I'd seen innumerable horrors in Sarajevo and Africa with the Royal Marines and although I wasn't inured to the suffering that humans could inflict on each other I wasn't easily shocked.

So, when Sandy reported that a Russian national had been found hanging by his ankles from a railway bridge in Istanbul, my throat went dry and I felt cold.

His throat had been cut and he'd been left hanging there and allowed to bleed to death. A wooden placard had been nailed to his chest; a long nail driven through his flesh in each corner, doubtless causing excruciating pain and suffering.

On the placard was a message, written in Turkish reading 'This is War.'

Once the Turkish Police had identified him, they were able to determine he too was the subject of an Interpol blue notice in connection with the importing and sale of narcotics and human trafficking.

Sandy went on to tell me that, rather strangely, the traffic from both the home and mobile phones of Gümüş was very innocuous, just routine stuff. It was almost as if he'd suddenly realised that he was being watched.

"Maybe, boss, it was more likely he felt the Russians were going to be listening in to discover his response to the kidnapping of his family."

"Good point Nathan, you're probably right."

We went back to the subject of the dead Russian. Sandy asked how I felt this might impact on our operation.

"In my view the placard is 100% accurate. This will now be open gang warfare, with many tit-for-tat killings. What we don't want is for us to be caught in the middle of that whilst just trying to arrest one man – especially as we're in a foreign country." I paused for a moment to gather my thoughts before carrying on.

"I think Howard Rhodes should set up a meeting for me with the Interpol team ASAP. They'll have been observing the guys from Istanbul as well and may well have more Intel than I've been able to gather so far. I think we should meet at St Hilarion Castle this afternoon, to pool our knowledge and plan the next steps."

"OK, Nathan, I'll set it up, but this will turn ugly very quickly, so you need to have your wits about you. I don't want any casualties on our side this time."

"Don't worry about me boss, you trained me well, remember?"

We spoke for a couple of minutes more, then he was gone.

In order to avoid bumping into the two Russians who were staying at my hotel I decided to stay in my room for the moment.

So, on to room service to order a salad for lunch, along with some fruit and a pot of Turkish coffee, which, when it arrived was strong and sweet, as it should be.

After I polished off my meal, I lay on my bed and had managed half an hour's shuteye when the shrill ring tone of the company mobile broke my reverie.

Sandy confirmed the meeting with the Interpol team in one hour's time at St Hilarion Castle.

I had a quick wash, strapped on my weapon, popped on my jacket then quietly opened my door, looking in both directions, there was no-one around so I padded towards the lift.

When I reached the ground floor it was quiet so I turned left and walked through reception and out of the front door. I turned left and after 200 metres took the first left and then down the street to the hotel car park.

It was a bit of a circuitous route but avoided going past the restaurant and pool. I didn't want to bump into the Russian heavies any more than I needed to.

As I pulled out of the car park I could see that their motorbike was parked up at the opposite end of the car park to where I'd left my car.

Fifty minutes later after an uneventful journey, and having made sure that I wasn't being followed, I parked at the St Hilarion Castle café.

There was just a mini-bus there with the name of a tour operator painted on its side; it was in the process of disgorging around ten middle aged tourists, chattering excitedly in English. The tour guide took them up the gravel path to the ticket office to gain entry to this beautiful monument. I walked over to the kiosk where I was pleased to see a woman was now serving; I had a niggling concern in my mind that the man that had been there to serve me breakfast earlier would think it strange if I made two visits in the same day.

Just as I sat down with my coffee, a black four wheel drive Mercedes started wending its way up the S bends below me.

The driver eventually parked behind the kiosk and three men got out. They looked like hippies, with long hair, scruffy jeans and were carrying small backpacks.

Two of them walked over to look at the castle from the path that led up to the ticket office. The third one walked casually over in my direction, totally ignored me and came to rest ten feet past my table.

He leaned on the wall and looked over the edge in the direction of the road on which they had just driven. After a few minutes he moved to my side looked me straight in the eye and smiled,

"Bluebird,"

So I was pleased to respond with "Campbell."

As he sat down, his two colleagues joined him and we exchanged introductions. One of them went off to get some coffees.

They were German nationals, an inspector, a sergeant and a constable and by the looks of their appearance were well used to working under cover.

Their fourth team member was following Gümüs as our quarry was on the move in his car. The inspector, Jan Heinemann, briefed me on their backgrounds, he ran a squad of around ten who were tasked with bringing to justice the people behind the people trafficking that was growing like a terminal cancer on the continent of Europe.

In the various intelligence reports they'd received, the top dog was described as being Russian whilst Gümüs had been viewed as a relatively small time drug dealer.

Over the past few years his ambitions had grown, he started with a chain of brothels in Istanbul and Ankara. He'd then become increasingly aware of the UK sex industry.

He discovered that, in London, a number of Eastern Europeans and Russians were working as prostitutes but under duress, not through choice.

Thus his interest in providing sex slaves became a passion and caused him, over time, to take business away from Moscow. This caused a long burning fuse to be lit, as the Russians didn't like people treading on their turf.

Jan and his team had some difficulty in pinning anything on Gümüs as he was both good at covering his tracks and at dishing out bribes to ensure that certain law enforcement officers looked the other way.

They'd issued Interpol blue notices on Gümüs and several members of his squad, but getting concrete proof was proving difficult.

My inside knowledge and the evidence collected from The Board Room and Grogan's team was going to prove invaluable to them. Now, though, the potential for increased hostilities had changed and the apparent start of a gang war was putting a totally different perspective on the situation.

There was a second team within Jan's squad and this group was tasked with carrying out surveillance on the upper echelon of the Russian heavy mob.

They reported that instructions had been issued to liquidate the hostages they were holding and send Gümüs his family back in body bags.

Apparently the guy who met such an obscene execution in Istanbul was the son of the Russian number two. Thus their patience had run out and the Turk had a price on his head, his family were surely doomed to suffer a terrible fate.

The Russians in Northern Cyprus believed Gümüs felt he was safe on the island and was unaware he was being watched.

Jan and his team felt powerless in the broader scheme. They'd been unable to motivate the local police in Istanbul to put more than a token number of men on the search for the wife and two children being held hostage.

The Germans were unsure whether that was because the Turkish Police were less interested in helping out a dangerous criminal or whether, like Michael Grogan, the Turk had key police officers in his pocket.

The immediate concern expressed by the Germans was ascertaining what additional instructions had been issued to those Russians who were known to be in Cyprus.

On the assumption the order had been given for the three members of Gümüs' family to be liquidated, it was not unreasonable to suppose they would move against the man himself very quickly.

As we were all here on the island and unable to easily influence events that may take place in Istanbul, we decided that we should continue to try and achieve what our original objective was – the arrest and arraignment of the man running large quantities of highly expensive lethal drugs into the UK and organising human trafficking on a large scale.

It would seem that our target was still happy to have a visible presence in Cyprus, almost as if he thought he was indestructible, or that his entourage would be able protect him should any member of the opposition raise their head above the parapet.

He continued to hold his 11.00 meetings with his team in the highly public centre of Kyrenia. His phone traffic had still not revealed anything new, so continued observation was suggested for the next forty eight hours.

The original plan which I'd put to Sandy of me posing as a potential new customer for Gümüs was clearly not appropriate now, so we agreed to dispense with that strategy.

I hadn't been used to watching and waiting too often in my military career. We were usually straight in and out, objective achieved.

I debated with Jan and his men whether we should take a different tack and make a direct approach to Gümüs and warn him of the threatened attack.

Just as I suggested that, Jan's mobile rang. He took the call and listened to the caller with a grim expression across his youngish face. He finished the call and turned towards me.

"That was the fourth member of my team. He's parked just around the corner from Gümüs's villa at Ozanköy with a clear view of the house.

A van has just pulled up outside the villa. The men on board opened the back door and dumped three body bags on the road. One of the bags was adult sized; the other two were much smaller.

They immediately drove off after dropping their cargo. They were wearing black overalls and ski masks. I guess now it really will be open warfare."

"OK, Jan, what if we arrested our target plus his men and kept them in protective custody? Maybe we could cut a deal with him, a reduced sentence for providing us with the evidence against the Russians?"

"We could do Max, but does Gümüs really know enough about his enemies to provide the information we need to take action against them?

His gang and the Russians have never traded with each other, as far as we know. So Gümüs wouldn't have the intimate knowledge of their empire that we could use in any court case.

As far as we know, both sides work in isolation, even though they are operating in the same market. I just feel that there may be a sudden eruption of bloodshed on this beautiful island which would be a great shame after it's been partially successful in putting its own violent past behind it. We must work hard to prevent that, whilst still not losing sight of our original objectives."

The sergeant, Jurgen, interjected with his thoughts.

"Why don't we phone Gümüs and suggest we have some business for him. We could tell him we tried the Russians but their price for a drug shipment to the UK was too high. We might offer a down payment of cash to gain his interest.

I know the original plan was for Max to do this and carry a wire, but we should be trying to flush out Gümüs and getting him to talk about his own business. If we're skilled enough, and given his hatred of the Russians, we could set up a honey trap."

"But what happens in the next few hours is going to be crucial. Surely once he knows about the body bags he'll be looking to retaliate. I can't believe he won't want to meet violence with more of the same. I'm certain that having his family wiped out will have him seething with rage."

Jan had made his decision.

"OK, here's what we'll do. Round the clock surveillance on the villa at Ozanköy. Whenever our target leaves his house we'll follow him, but we'll leave one man behind.

The first time Gümüs leaves, our man will enter the villa and plant listening devices. The taps on his phone calls are not telling us a great deal, but maybe, in the relative comfort of his house, his dialogue will be more revealing.

As far as we know he lives alone and we've discovered his minders stay somewhere else but, as well as the daily meeting in Kyrenia, we know that at least some of the team visit him at his villa.

There's no sign of any guard dog or intruder alarm so it should be easy enough to plant a few bugs. We have three vehicles between us so we can change them around to avoid suspicion. One of them is a panel van with our radio comms in it. The bugs can be listened to up to 5 kilometres away. We'll keep recordings of anything we hear."

"There are four of you, plus me, but in case you don't know, the High Commission has given me a minder, a Turkish Cypriot police inspector, Hakan Çöteli. He looks like a local, which is what he is so he blends in nicely.

He's armed and is used to working under cover plus he has the intimate knowledge of the whole island. We could include him in our team. That would give us a team of six, one of whom has Turkish as his native language, which could be very useful, especially once you've planted the bugs."

"Sounds good, Max; will you contact him and set that up? Do you have a secure phone?"

"Yes, provided by my liaison officer."

We put my temporary number into all the mobiles of the Interpol team and I took their numbers and did the same. I also gave them Hakan's number and then phoned him and asked him to meet me at Bellapais Abbey in forty five minutes.

I took my leave of my German colleagues, who before leaving, also confirmed they were armed and they checked I was also.

I suggested we might need bullet proof vests at some point. They didn't have any with them, so I agreed to ask Howard to supply a set of six.

I pulled in to the village car park at Bellapais, no attendant this time so I walked quickly up to the café by the entrance to The Abbey and took a seat at the rear of the place, away from the street.

I had only just sat down when Hakan appeared, so I ordered two Turkish coffees and then briefed my minder on the current situation. A worried expression came over his face as I was giving him all the bad news.

He paused for a moment and then responded, in a quiet voice as a few of the other tables were now occupied.

"I agree with your thoughts, there could be a gunfight on our streets within a couple of days.

I've been able to hear snatches of conversation when Gümüs and his team meet. He's very angry, as you would expect, but it appears he wanted to wait for a few days before doing anything.

Now that his family have been killed he may think differently and wish to take immediate action. So I'll wait for a call from Jan, then meet his Interpol team and get myself set up in the van to listen for any news.

If it would help, I also have two more colleagues in the national police force who are used to working under cover and could help us with surveillance, being local, they would be inconspicuous, and, of course, they speak Turkish so could position themselves near enough to hear what Gümüs is saying."

"That could be useful Hakan, presumably they're totally trustworthy and, most importantly they are skilled in the use of firearms and not frightened to use them."

My minder smiled and patted me on the arm in a touching and friendly gesture.

"They'll shoot to kill if ordered and both of them have been wounded in service by drug dealers so have a vested interest in bringing this gang to justice."

"OK, my friend, give Jan this information when he phones you and I'm sure he'll respond positively. I'm going to try and get us some bullet proof vests from The Embassy, unless you can provide any, Hakan."

He replied he could get brand new ones from his stores, British made and lightweight. We shook hands and went our separate ways.

When I got back to the car I phoned Sandy and gave him an update. Fortunately he agreed with the amended plan, which we'd need to keep revising as the facts unfolded.

At the moment we had to gather information to try and keep one step ahead. I drove back towards Kyrenia and parked my car in the hotel car park.

Having bought a sandwich and some fruit at a nearby green grocer, I went up to my room unobserved, apart from one of the hotel staff who greeted me with a warm smile.

I wolfed down the sandwich, a banana and apple, whilst stripping my weapon down and giving it a thorough clean and check. Old habits die hard.

I then changed into clothing more suitable for potential combat. A few minutes later Jan Heinemann phoned me to say that Gümüs had taken his car out, so one of our team had picked his lock and let himself in and had been able to plant bugs in four different locations.

Then Jan and the rest of the surveillance team had followed the Turk to The Peanuts Restaurant that was on the opposite side of the double U shaped bay, just round the promontory from Kyrenia Harbour, near the modern outdoor amphitheatre.

As our target was on his own they waited for a few minutes in the van, which they'd parked in the street outside the restaurant.

They turned the vehicle round on arrival so it was pointing in the right direction if they needed a quick getaway, as the street formed a cul-de-sac. One lesson you always are taught in the forces, so presumably in the police as well, is to leave your vehicle ready for immediate access, and a quick getaway, if necessary. There are no brownie points for wasting time turning the vehicle around, or finding you're blocked in while the enemy escapes.

Jan picked up Hakan on his way to the villa, so my minder was still with them. After a few minutes Gümüs was joined at the restaurant by two men, they appeared to be looking through the menu so they clearly planned to spend some time together.

Jan had taken some digital photos of the two new arrivals using his telephoto lens and said he would send them to my mobile to see if I knew them, so he hung up.

I couldn't believe my eyes when I saw the photos and called Jan back immediately.

"Jan, what's going on? Those two guys are the Russians staying at my hotel. You've issued a Blue Notice on them. Do any of your team speak Russian?"

"Yes, I do. OK I'll go and take a table along with Hakan, so we can listen in two languages." With that he was gone.

I'd seen the sign for the restaurant a few hundred metres from my hotel so I went down to the car and shot off down there.

Parking in front of the amphitheatre, I walked down towards the Interpol van and quietly tapped on the window. As it was dark, I used the password and was let in on the blind side from the restaurant. We had to play a waiting game, whilst keeping a close eye on the restaurant through the night vision glasses we both had. There was nothing we could do until we were able to hear the conversation between what we'd originally thought were warring factions.

After an hour the two Russians finished off their meal, stood up and shook Gümüs warmly by the hand and walked off down the street behind our van. The Turk paid the bill then walked in the opposite direction and headed to his car with an ambling gait.

His large Mercedes was parked near my Fiesta in the car park area in front of the amphitheatre. Shortly after Gümüs left, Jan and Hakan paid for their meal and got back into the van.

They looked puzzled and it soon became apparent why. They'd been sitting near enough to be able to hear most of the conversation between the three villains. Fortunately, the Russians and Gümüs were not able to converse a great deal with each other in their respective languages, so during most of the meal they were speaking English.

Jan spoke first. "It appears that there's a split in the Russian organisation and these two are part of a team that want to set up an alliance, a sort of joint venture, with Gümüs. They aren't the ones who killed his family and they want to start working with the Turk, with a view to establishing a satellite organisation here in Northern Cyprus.

They have sufficient information on the guys who carried out the killing to enable our man to seek revenge against them."

Hakan added, "In return for that information and providing Gümüs with some fire power, they want half of his business and access to his supply chain for narcotics, plus they'll provide him with an endless supply of Eastern European girls to be used as sex slaves."

I didn't like, nor did I believe, what I was hearing. After my experiences of the last few months, I knew that it would be highly unlikely that the Turk would want to share his ill-gotten gains with anyone, especially a former competitor. Something was not quite right; I had a hunch that we were being misled into backing a horse that would never run.

While Jan and Hakan were relating what they'd been able to hear from the Russians and Gümüs, the sergeant, Jurgen, had been keeping his binoculars focussed on our target's car.

He remarked that Gümüs was speaking animatedly on his mobile. Just as he finished speaking, there was a throaty rumbling noise a couple of hundred metres behind us, which I instantly recognised from the hotel. I needed instant action around me so I shouted a warning as the rumbling grew louder.

"Quick everybody get down, out of sight."

Just as we all crouched down in our seats, the Russians' motorbike went slowly past us and then stopped 200 metres away from where my car was parked and opposite where Gümüs was now sitting. Again I shouted, this time more urgently.

"OK guys, looks like they're going to kill him, weapons out go, go, go."

I was first out with my gun in my hand running towards the bike, I instinctively took off the safety and sprinted towards the motor bike.

I'd covered the first 50 metres when one of the Russians put out his right arm and pointed towards Gümüs's car.

I shouted a warning but within a split second the sky was lit up with a bright orange flash and a deafening explosion assaulted my eardrums, so my words were lost in the ether. The pillion rider had been pointing his remote detonator at the bomb they'd planted under Gümüs's car. The vehicle was lifted about a metre off the ground and shattered into a thousand pieces. A plume of orange flames shot about 20 metres in the air and there was a second explosion as the petrol tank went up.

The mistake the Russians made was staying where they were to admire their handiwork, which gave me sufficient time to cover another 50 metres and be within shooting range. I aimed my weapon and fired off three shots in quick succession.

The first bullet hit the man on the pillion who had detonated the bomb and he fell off the bike. The second hit the petrol tank and the bike went up in flames, the force of the explosion throwing the driver off the vehicle and into the road. The third shot must have failed to hit a target.

Within a couple more seconds I was alongside them both and the Interpol guys were just 10 metres behind me. I pointed my weapon at the rider, who was shocked but not badly injured, motioning for him to kneel down. He did so and by this time Jan was upon him and cuffed his hands behind his back. The passenger lay motionless in the gutter. Hakan felt his pulse and shook his head.

"I'm afraid he's dead, Max."

Jurgen ran over to where the fire was burning brightly and sending out two huge columns of thick, choking black smoke as all the plastic components on board started to burn. Gümüs's lifeless body was laying face down a few feet behind the vehicle. His limbs were splayed out at grotesque angles such was the force of the explosion. It seemed that the war was over just as soon as it had begun.

Jan pulled the surviving Russian to his feet and read him his rights in English. Hakan was busy on his mobile, calling up the emergency services and the police.

People had started to come out of the nearby apartment blocks and we badly needed to keep them away from the crime scene. Hakan stationed himself at the top of the road to meet the ambulance and fire crews and direct the police when they arrived.

As the fire and ambulance station was less than a mile away, the emergency services were on the scene almost immediately. A pair of fire engines was the first to arrive, their siren piercing the warmish night spring air.

Hakan showed them his police ID card and advised them briefly what had happened. The first one stopped some way away from the blazing car and its crew unrolled their hose and started the onboard pump, aiming a powerful water jet at the conflagration.

The second engine attended the blazing motorbike and soon had the flames doused leaving just steam and thick acrid black smoke as the tyres were still burning quite fiercely.

An ambulance was next to turn up and Hakan directed the driver to where the surviving Russian was being held. Two paramedics jumped out and went over to Jan who showed them his Interpol badge told them what had happened. They gave the man a quick check over then asked for his cuffs to be removed, so he could be put on a stretcher. Jan unlocked the restraints while Jurgen held the prisoner's arms, put him on the stretcher and cuffed him to the aluminium struts on either side.

The paramedics protested in Turkish at this but Jan merely pointed to the burning car then back to the Russian and mouthed 'BOOM' very loudly, spreading his hands theatrically in a circle as he did so. The ambulance men understood his mime and soon changed their tune as they smiled grimly.

As the stretcher was being loaded, three police cars arrived and screeched to a halt disgorging ten uniformed officers and one plain clothes guy who was an inspector.

He waved Hakan to come down and join him and instructed his men to control the large crowd that had now gathered.

Hakan shook his colleague's hand warmly, then introduced him to Jan, Jurgen and then to me. We briefed him on the events, some of which he knew as he was aware of the operation we'd been conducting and had been ready, with his men, to provide backup to Hakan and the rest of us if we needed it.

The area was taped off and searchlights put up to illuminate the crime scene. The officers were all armed and looked like they would use their weapons if the need arose. They first of all made sure that no members of the public got anywhere near the action. The first ambulance started its siren again then went off with the Russian who had been driving the motorbike. He was accompanied by Jurgen to ensure he made no attempt to escape.

A second stretcher was brought out, along with a black zip-up body bag. Pretty soon the body of the second Russian was secured and taken away to the morgue in the second ambulance.

The fire brigade now had the fire from the car under control and their second appliance had almost succeeded in putting out the blazing motor bike, which was just smouldering now.

Once the fire was safely doused the police officers were given clearance by the Chief Fire Officer that the immediate area was safe so they started combing the ground around the remains of the bike. They were tasked with finding the remote detonator for the bomb which would be game set and match in terms of securing a conviction.

I'd seen the pillion man stretching out his arm, the driver had placed the bike in position, and as soon as the passenger's arm was stretched out the bomb went off. So the detonator would be the defining evidence in the subsequent court case when all the facts had been gathered.

After less than ten minutes of scouring every inch of the ground within 5 metres of the spot where the bike had parked, the hand-held electronic detonator was found. It was collected carefully by the senior officer, who was wearing latex gloves, and the remote device was then bagged and labelled.

That was a good result for us as the Russians hadn't been wearing gloves so there should be a good set of prints on the detonator, maybe two sets.

A large police people-carrier had been called up along with an army truck. The officers in the police vehicle were to stay overnight protecting the crime scene and keeping away the curious members of the public, who were growing in number by the minute.

The army truck brought a contingent from the bomb squad, all fully kitted out in their protective suits. They were to segregate the bomb components from the remaining debris to be used as evidence and make sure there were no additional devices that had failed to explode.

Jan and Hakan now wanted me to go with the police inspector and themselves to the police station and file our reports and make statements.

My car had been damaged by the car bomb which killed Gümüs so I gave my keys to one of the police officers who would arrange for it to be picked up. I accompanied Jan and Hakan in the German's van. Before we set off, we had the bomb squad check out the vehicle, just in case. They found nothing.

Jan's mobile rang shortly after we drove away, so he stopped for a moment, checked out the caller and gave the phone to Hakan. Great news! The telephone tap on Gümüs's mobile had picked up his phone call while he was sitting in his car just before the bomb went off.

The conversations were in Turkish and after listening to the recordings Hakan was able to tell us that the phone call was to three of his colleagues here in Cyprus, asking them to take down a shipment of cocaine to a warehouse situated on the road to Bellapais at midnight that very night.

The plan was for the Russians to come to collect that consignment the next morning and pay for it in hard cash.

Once he'd shared that information with us Hakan excitedly called his fellow inspector and arranged for an armed plain clothes squad to go to the warehouse and pick up the remnants of Gümüs's team.

They were successful in doing this and caught the three Turks with about $100,000 worth of Bolivian marching powder in their three vehicles.

So, now we had a dead Mr Big, his three henchmen in custody, facing long jail sentences plus his enemies were either dead or under arrest.

Not exactly what we had envisaged in our original plan, but a good result nonetheless and there were no casualties on our side, which was a considerable bonus.

We all gave our statements and I had to hand in my gun as evidence. Doubtless a post mortem on the man I'd shot would discover the bullet from my gun. Perhaps a second bullet had been lodged somewhere in the twisted metal that was all that was left of the bike. That was a job for forensics.

I was then allowed to leave and given a lift back to my hotel in a police car. I stopped off at the bar for a quick and welcome cool soft drink and figured it was too late to phone Elena but I'd been instructed to call Sandy at any time if there were any important developments.

So I went back to my room after paying for the drink and made the call. He was delighted with the news and asked me to brief Howard first thing in the morning, and then have him arrange to fly me out of Cyprus.

I was to make sure there were no loose ends to tie up with Interpol and the local police before agreeing a departure date with Rhodes. He finished the call and told me to call him again in the morning.

I'd been used to killing people in battle and when fighting in wars, usually it was kill or be killed or take out an enemy position to enable the squad to move forward. Now, though, I was a civilian, and it felt different and thinking about tonight's killing kept me awake for a while.

I ran over in my mind the events of the evening, first asking myself whether I had followed the correct procedure. Eventually I concluded that I'd acted properly.

I had shouted a warning and prevented the enemy detonating a second device. With this clarity of purpose in my mind I was happy that I wouldn't have done anything different and eventually I drifted off to sleep.

CHAPTER 17

Finishing the jigsaw

Thumping my alarm into instant submission, as its shrill beep rent asunder the early morning half light, I jumped out of bed at what was the usual time, heaved on my track suit and threw myself into my early morning run with a fair degree of vigour.

I felt the need to work off a lot of anger so I pounded round the track faster than normal and did a few more circuits than was my usual practice.

Looking back on last night's episode I was infuriated by the thought that all of us had been taken in, being led to believe the Russians and Turks wanted to work together. The reality was Gümüs was to be summarily executed by the very men whom he believed were about to go into partnership with him.

It was clear that dealing with the criminal fraternity required many different skills and these were significantly more complicated than I realised.

On the sixth lap round the track I consoled myself with the thought that brains far more experienced than mine in catching criminals had also got it wrong. Jan and his team, plus Hakan and his colleagues all believed the Russians were apparently offering the Turk a joint venture.

I felt a little better as my limbs started to feel the effort of having run over 2000 metres, so called it a day and went back into the hotel to shower and have breakfast.

Going through the hotel lobby I saw a uniformed policeman speaking with the receptionist. I wondered if he'd be going up to the bedrooms in which the two Russians had been staying.

I decided to have a reasonably large breakfast so started off with a large bowl of cereals then picked up a number of different cheeses and various local cold meats. I finished off with several slices of plain bread and filled a bowl with some strawberry jam, which according to the sign alongside its serving dish, was home made. It turned out to be delicious.

I finished my mini-feast with a couple of cups of black coffee. Now I felt able to take on whatever was thrown at me today. Hopefully it'd be less traumatic than yesterday.

After I'd eaten my fill I sat at my table for a few minutes, contemplating how we would put the last few pieces in to the jigsaw. I then went back to my bedroom and phoned Elena.

I was delighted to hear the joy in her voice when she realised it was me. She immediately asked for an update on my activities.

Elena gasped when I told her about the bomb. Although I underlined that Gümüs was the man who'd organised her kidnapping along with all the other girls, she had some difficulty in understanding that he could be liquidated so easily by his enemies.

On the basis of being completely honest with her I described my own involvement in the incident with the Russians. She was shocked and the line fell silent for a while until I heard her sobbing at the other end.

I endeavoured to deliver some soothing words that I hoped would spur her into a better understanding of where we were up to in this terrible affair.

"Listen Elena, the man who had you kidnapped is now dead, three of his men are in custody, two men are dead from the team who planned to take over his empire and a third is in custody.

In addition to that, all of the people in Liverpool who held you prisoner for over a year are now in prison, awaiting trial. Most important of all, you are now safe and have me to look after you for as long as you wish me to. So, I think all things considered we've done pretty well."

"Nathan all of that's true, I've just not been used to violence in recent years. The war with the Serbians cast a shadow over my childhood and cost me my mother's life. I suppose I'll get used to it over time and, hopefully there will be no more conflict that involves me, however remote it might be.

I guess if you still want to look after me, then my healing process will be on track. You do still want to look after me, don't you, Nathan? Please tell me you do."

"Of course I do, now more than ever, and I can't wait to see you again when we've drawn a line under all of this activity.

I hope you and Milo are now making some progress in his business so we can put some effort into that when I get back to reality after being in a war zone again for some time."

By changing tack in bringing up the subject of her father's business, I appeared to have calmed her a little as she was speaking almost normally now and the excited tone was back in her voice.

We continued our conversation for a further fifteen minutes then I had a quick word with Elena's father. I asked him how he thought his daughter was shaping up now that she was back in her homeland.

Milo said he felt she made little steps each day and he was pleased she continued to make progress and was gradually inching her way back to being her normal self.

I briefly related to Milo the events of the previous evening. He said he had mixed feelings, some relief that two evil empires seemed to have been hit quite hard in the last few days but mixed with some degree of sadness that I'd personally liquidated one of the Russians.

I found this somewhat surprising, given what his daughter had gone through and his own experiences in the Balkans conflict in the nineties.

Next stop was a call to the High Commission and a discussion with Howard Rhodes to fully update him on how our evening had panned out and how we should close down the Cyprus end of the exercise.

Howard drove over and met me in the lobby bar but it was busy with tourists so we went into the upstairs bar above the restaurant where we could enjoy more privacy.

A middle aged English couple were sitting at the far end of the huge bar area watching an English Premier League match on the giant TV screen, the rest of the place was empty. As the commentary on the TV was quite loud we were quite happy sitting at the other end of the room, safe in the knowledge we couldn't be overheard.

As we drank our coffees, I gave Howard a full run down on recent events. He took a deep draught of coffee and paused, thinking hard before he made comment.

"I think you should stay here for another three to four days, Max. We'll have lots of bureaucracy to deal with as we've had one murder and one killing and have made a number of arrests here on the island. In addition there have been several murders in Istanbul, all of them linked and involving the same two criminal gangs.

As well as the form filling, statements and so on, we need to make sure there will be no more killings. My other concern is your identity.

Although it was dark when you saw the bomb go off, we need to check whether there are any other people from either gang on the island, just in case they recognised you and might be looking for retribution.

I think perhaps we should base you at in our offices for the rest of your stay. It's secure there, nobody would know you in Nicosia and we can easily set up meetings with the Interpol team and the local police.

If you were to continue to stay here in Kyrenia it's like living in a goldfish bowl. The locals know when a stranger is around and soon find out what he's up to. I phoned Sandy Parker before I left this morning and he's in agreement with my proposal."

"Sounds a sensible idea Howard, I guess I could be a target if I stay here, if Sandy is OK about it, then so am I. I should check out of here, then. Where would I stay when I move?"

"Yes, we'll settle the bill here then I'll drive you to Nicosia and check you into one of our regular hotels. It's nice and central, still in the Turkish part and not too far from Alexander Pallis Caddesi where the High Commission is."

At that we went up to my room so I could pack my case, ready to check out. I suggested we sweep the room for bugs one last time. This time the machine gave off a loud beeping and the red light came on, so clearly I was now under surveillance from someone.

We therefore maintained silence until we left the bedroom and after checking out walked on to the front street and turned left to the car park. There was no sense in walking through the hotel and past the swimming pool as we didn't know who was watching me.

As we drove towards the capital, I reminded Rhodes I was no longer armed since Hakan and his team had taken my handgun as evidence. He smiled and told me that an armed bodyguard from his staff would be allocated to me and then he used his hands free mobile to arrange for the man to be waiting at the hotel.

Once we'd negotiated our way through the traffic in Kyrenia, the journey to Nicosia was relatively easy. We were soon passing through Girne (Kyrenia) Gate and joined the queue of traffic which was inching slowly down Girne Caddesi and in due course we arrived at my new temporary home.

We stood at the reception desk of The Saray Hotel for a moment or two while the guy on duty carried on with what he was doing, so Howard shoved his ID under the receptionist's nose. His peremptory attitude immediately melted away once he saw whom he was dealing with.

Howard asked for a room for me for three nights with an option to extend if necessary. As I was filling in my registration form, a tall, well muscled and lightly tanned man with short cropped black hair approached Howard and they shook hands. He sported a dark drooping moustache that gave him a Turkish appearance. I noticed the bulge in the small of his back at waist level, so he was carrying a weapon and I guessed this was my bodyguard.

Sure enough that is exactly who he was and he shook me warmly by the hand and introduced himself as Chris Palmer, ex Special Forces. Although he was English, his Mediterranean appearance meant he could blend in nicely as a local, which could be useful for undercover work.

I took my things up to my room and then quickly went back down to the lobby, the three of us immediately setting off for the High Commission.

We soon got to work when we were seated around Howard's meeting table. We went through the Intel reports, firstly concentrating on the new arrivals in the last forty eight hours.

There were a large number of foreign visitors on the manifests and very many entry points, Ercan airport providing direct flights via Turkey; Larnaca in the Greek part of Cyprus disgorged many more, with easy overland transfers to Northern Cyprus. In addition ferries regularly came in from Taşucu to Kyrenia and from Mersin to Famagusta.

So we had many large passenger schedules to go through, looking for travellers originating from Russia. As far as the Turks were concerned the names of the gang controlled by Gümüs were being flagged up by the immigration authorities. None of them showed up in the last two days and no Russian nationals appeared to have landed in the same period. So who'd been bugging my room?

We then checked with the Turkish Cypriot Police. They had remanded the Russian motorbike rider in custody, charged him with murder and had decided he would stand trial in Cyprus.

They felt that if there was a request for the trial to be moved to Russia then perhaps justice wouldn't be served. The Turks from Gümüs's team had been caught red handed with the large consignment of cocaine so a trial date was set for them; in the meantime they were remanded in custody. They were certain to receive a long sentence. In fact life sentences if the vicious murder of the son of the Moscow gang leader in Istanbul could be pinned on them as well as the charges for drug dealing.

We turned our attention to the whole episode at The Peanuts Restaurant. Could Jan, Hakan and myself have done anything differently? How did the Russians manage to plant the bomb without being seen? Why were we all taken in by the apparent setting up of a joint venture between Turks and Russians? Did I take the correct action in jumping out gun blazing? Could we have prevented the violence?

After a great deal of debate, it was agreed that given the circumstances we got it as near right as we could have done.

Howard had kept in close contact with Sandy Parker who was still in command of the whole project and we had to be sure he felt the job was well and truly done before drawing a line under the whole Cypriot operation.

Sandy had suggested that we wait a couple more days to see if any more members of either of the two bunches of criminals arrived in Cyprus. As well as potential new arrivals there was also the problem that someone wanted to listen to my conversations by bugging my room. That had happened after the bombing so there must still have been some villains on Cyprus who were alive and not in custody.

We decided Hakan should investigate who'd bugged my room. The hotel had CCTV cameras, so it shouldn't be too difficult to see who else had been in my room apart from the housekeeping staff. A phone call to him brought the swift response that I would have expected; he said he'd go directly to the hotel and requisition the video tapes.

The following day Hakan came to Nicosia to report on his findings. Howard set up a video player in a conference room and we watched what Hakan had found. The normal mid morning traffic of the chambermaids was innocuous enough, but in mid afternoon the previous day two burly white Europeans in shiny suits went into the room I'd occupied. They were wearing cheap black sunglasses and

I could see they were two of the men I had clocked outside the large casino just off the sea front at Kyrenia.

Our surprise was mixed with some incredulity. How had they established that yours truly was somebody other than an unaccompanied tourist? How did they know where I was staying? What was their relationship with the dead Russian and the one in custody?

We decided to try and find out the answers as the last thing we wanted was any more killings. So Hakan arranged for a small detachment of his undercover colleagues to join him to track down the guys and find out what they were up to.

Kyrenia was a small town and strangers stood out easily so finding the two men proved to be not too difficult. They were staying at the hotel where Gümüs held his daily coffee meetings. We decided we should pay them a visit so arranged to go there the next day.

Hakan, Howard, me and one of Hakan's team went down there in the early morning as the Turkish Cypriot police had reported from their observations that the two had breakfast at 08.30 hours every day.

We took three tables in different parts of the restaurant to enable us to converge on our targets as soon as they appeared.

At exactly 8.30 hours the two men took their table. Once they were seated we converged on them and we each pulled a chair from adjoining tables.

Hakan pulled his police badge and asked them to put their hands on the table and keep perfectly still. The younger of the two men smiled and said in English with only a hint of an accent,

"OK, it's very public here let's go out on to the rear terrace where we can speak in private."

Hakan held one arm of the young man and his colleague took the other man and they were led outside.

The two local police officers frisked the men and relieved them of their side arms. We all sat down and Hakan asked them why they were on Cyprus.

Both of them laughed loudly and looked at each other then slowly opened their jackets. The Cypriots quickly cocked their weapons and stood up, in the ready pose.

Both prisoners slowly drew identical shiny black leather folders from their inner pocket and laid them on the table. I picked them both up and flipped them open, then I, too, started laughing.

"They're Russian police officers and by the looks of it part of some special operations team."

At that point everyone relaxed and the weapons were restored to their owners. We all introduced ourselves to the two men.

Within a few minutes a waiter approached us on the terrace so we ordered breakfast then set about listening to the story that the Russian policemen had to tell us. The older of the two men introduced himself and his colleague.

"I'm inspector Sergei Yaravoya and my young colleague is sergeant Alexander Krylov. We're members of a special unit that's tasked with stamping out people trafficking between Russia and other European countries.

For two years we've been following one of the largest gangs and building evidence against them. Then we found Gümüs was building a large empire from Istanbul and was providing sex slaves to the UK market. Because of his success he was treading on the toes of the Russians, so we've had him under observation as well for the past six months.

We'd hoped we might be able to bring down two separate operations. Then we found Gümüs was really beginning to feel the heat from the boys from Moscow, so was planning to move his operation here to Northern Cyprus. We followed him to the island and kept a tight watch on him and his minders.

We've recruited several locals to help us with the surveillance and were advised by one of them that Gümüs was in a meeting at a restaurant with the two Russians.

We drove down from our hotel, had just parked the car and were only a couple of hundred metres away from the place when the bomb went off and then we heard the three shots.

We watched the scenario unfold and weren't sure who the men were in the van and were concerned about who the guy was who'd fired the gun. We traced him back to his hotel and bugged his room."

"Yes, I found that just before I checked out." I said with a grin.

I explained the bare bones of our mission and a little of the history of the UK operation that Grogan was running and how Gümüs had been supplying him with drugs and girls.

They were pleased at the number of arrests that'd been made in England which meant that, at least for the time being, there was no ongoing outlet for either the Turks or the Russians in The UK.

Howard expressed surprise that Sergei didn't know of the Interpol presence on Cyprus, as part of our team. Usually the High Commission would know if friendly foreign law enforcement teams were around, especially if a UK team was also in the middle of an assignment.

Sergei explained that because much of the police force back in Russia was corrupt they had a small team of untouchables who reported to the highest authority and whose movements and operations were totally covert. The only way they could be successful, especially if the Mafia was their target was to go totally underground and advise no-one what they were involved in.

"We haven't seen any Russians and no known accomplices of Gümüs on any passenger list in the past forty eight hours."

He surprised us with his reply. "They're already here. The original team was four men. You've killed one, and have a second man in custody; the other two Mafiosos are still here.

They'll want to take over what Gümüs was planning to set up on Cyprus. I think we should pool our evidence then we'll have enough to arrest them. I also think we should meet your Interpol team."

He then turned to me and asked with an expression that was half smile and half frown, "Where the hell did you learn to shoot like that?"

"Almost twenty years in the Royal Marines with active service in Kosovo, Iraq, Afghanistan and the trouble spots in Africa. My ex Commanding Officer, now retired, is running this operation and we're here as a joint UK Secret Service and Interpol team.

So far we've done pretty well in getting most of the top dogs off the street or into the morgue. We too have our fair share of police corruption, Sergei.

One of the reasons that Michael Grogan was able to run his evil empire in Liverpool is because he had police protection. Those policemen are now in custody and their trial is imminent.

We have the statements and video evidence of all the girls, we have recordings of incriminating phone calls and we have Grogan's records of his dealings with Gümüs. I think between the people round this table and the guys from Interpol we can really close down the two operations permanently."

"Good, Max, I'm pleased you're on our side and I'm sorry we thought you might be part of the opposition – but you found the bug in your room anyway. Is that why you moved out?"

"Sure. We couldn't afford any more bloodshed so were planning to wrap the whole thing up, using the High Commission as our base. It seemed from the appearance of the bug that my presence had been compromised so we decided to pull me out of there."

"OK guys, I think Russian police expenses can just about manage to pay for these breakfasts. Here's my card with my mobile number.

If you can set up a meeting with the Interpol team we can plan how to finish off this assignment then we can all go home. We know our two targets are staying in a rented house near Güzelyurt so we could meet on the way there and discuss how to proceed."

"I've sussed out a café that would be an ideal meeting place and is just a short distance away from Güzelyurt."

We agreed for the meeting to take place the next day at 10.00 a.m. Sergei said he would have his men track the movements of the two Russians, who were probably going to be hanging around their house and keeping out of sight for a while to distance themselves from the two men on the motorbike.

I left with Howard and Hakan and Hakan's fellow officer and we decided to walk for a while and discuss the events of the morning. We went along the promenade past the statue of Atatürk and were soon on the side of the old harbour under the walls of Kyrenia Castle.

We stopped alongside two magnificent old wooden schooners that were moored alongside the harbour wall. They were both two-masters, the first a black and white beauty called Neptün and the second was a real peach with its prow proudly displaying Forsa as its name.

Her timbers were in prime condition, even though the craft was probably close to a hundred years old. The hull and masts were a crisp marine blue whilst the superstructure was unpainted, a matt varnish protecting the dark wood planking. I mused that a trip on one of those old ladies would be quite an experience.

Hakan brought me back to earth. "I think tomorrow we should be planning to arrest the two remaining Russians, but even though there are many of us, I don't think they'll surrender without a fight, do you?"

"No, I don't Hakan; so I guess we could do with the body armour you were going to get for us."

He confirmed he'd bring the vests in the morning and then we broke up and Howard and I headed towards his 4x4 and back to Nicosia. I phoned Sandy as we travelled back to the capital. He was happy with the next steps and found some amusement in the fact that I'd been bugged by the good guys!!

When we arrived back at the High Commission we joined up with the officer who'd been checking on incoming Russian passengers or Turks who were on our identify and report lists.

He reported that a known Russian was due to come in direct to Ercan Airport from Istanbul, having travelled the first leg from Odesa in The Ukraine.

He was on an Interpol blue report and a known Godfather in The Russian Mafia. The man, known as Ivan 'Big Bear' Romanov had two other Russians travelling with him, also the subject of Interpol blue reports. Looked like **THE** Mr Big was on the way to see what the Turks were doing to his mob.

Howard decided we should find out where they'd be staying and also work with Sergei on the surveillance of the house where his two gang members were holed up.

While Howard phoned Sergei to give him the news, I contacted Sandy and apprised him of developments. He said we should set up a honey trap for Romanov once we found out where he was on Cyprus. If possible we should bug the house his colleagues were occupying.

I rang off quickly while Howard was still on the phone to Sergei and suggested that we could follow up Sandy's request. He smiled and gave me a thumbs up sign. A couple of minutes later Howard ended the call and turned to me with a grin.

"The Russian police are ahead of us. The two living in the house took their car out and Sergei's team were able to gain access while the place was empty and plant a number of listening devices. After what I'd told him, he figured that they may be on their way to collect their boss and two others from Ercan Airport."

I suggested there was nothing we could do until we knew for sure where the Godfather was ensconced and whether we'd learned anything useful from the bugs in the house at Güzelyurt.

He agreed and suggested we write up our reports since we needed to be absolutely sure that the evidence to the courts was properly presented and documented fully.

After a long afternoon in front of the computer screen, thumping the keyboard, I was satisfied I'd covered all the events, and in the right chronology.

Then we received the important phone call. Romanov and his two minders had indeed been collected at the airport, and had stopped off to check in at The Denizkizi Royal a four star hotel west of Kyrenia and a short drive from where the rest of his mob were in the Güzelyurt area.

The car was then driven back to the house, without Romanov or his minders. Half an hour later the three of them were seen to take a large saloon from the hotel car park and drive into Kyrenia and on to the site of the bombing. They stayed for a few moments then went back to their hotel and didn't leave again that night.

Howard joined me for dinner that evening. The hotel restaurant was on the top floor and had a wrap around outside terrace with panoramic views over the City of Nicosia from three of its sides.

The dinner was of the highest quality, with service to match. We both enjoyed generous helpings of various types of meze to start, then for our main course, bursa, which consists of kebabs in rich spicy tomato sauce.

My companion was an amiable guy and we mostly kept our discussion away from the reason I was on this beautiful island.

He was single and had served a three year commission in the Royal Green Jackets, with active service in Iraq before being seconded to the Foreign Office. His service finished just before the regiment was amalgamated with several light infantry regiments and then became known as The Rifles. The RGJs have been awarded more Victoria Crosses than any other unit, fifty six in total.

Cyprus was his second assignment; his first two years on secondment had been in the High Commission in Colombia where he had advised the local military in their never ending struggle against the drug barons and the FARC, the local guerrillas who spent their lives kidnapping and imprisoning senior politicians.

He also set up some training for their weapon handling, using the skills he learned in his regiment. The Green Jackets were typically used as shock troops and marksmen, with their motto *Celer et Audax*, Swift and Bold.

Twice he'd been wounded and had been decorated for rescuing two of his squad in Iraq while under heavy fire from local militia. Like me, he had no family and no wife and was reasonably happy with his lot, though not sure where his next role would take him.

After some decent Turkish coffee we called it a night and went our separate ways, Howard back to his home, me down to my room, ready for an early morning meeting on the way to Güzelyurt with the rest of the team. Before leaving, Howard gave me a briefcase, equipped with another weapon and three magazines full of ammo.

Our drive was uneventful and we found Hakan and his sergeant there already. Within a few moments the squad from Interpol arrived with the Russian police being the last to join us.

We pushed two tables together at the far end of the café overlooking the beach but far enough away from the kitchen and serving area to give us privacy.

The only other customers at this time were a couple of young white Europeans, the girl gazing wistfully out to sea while her male companion was messing about with his mobile phone.

The Interpol team said they believed that there were no remaining members of Gümüs's gang on the island.

The Russian police reported that their surveillance and listening in had indicated that whilst Romanov and his two bodyguards were sleeping at their hotel, they would be spending daylight hours at the house occupied by their two colleagues.

They seemed to have three items on their agenda:-

Find out who shot and killed their bike pillion rider and 'take care of him'

See if they could bribe their way into where the surviving bike rider was held and get him released

See if there were any more Turks left from Gümüs's gang who could be 'persuaded' to give the Russians sufficient information about the operation he had on Cyprus and whether the Istanbul operation could be breached

In the last call from Romanov's mobile to the house, he said he was getting his man in Odesa to transport ten more unfortunate girls to a rendezvous point in Sofia, Bulgaria, this very afternoon as he had a new client for them in the UK. He instructed his man to accompany the truck to ensure safe delivery of the cargo. Sergei had deputed a squad of his select team of untouchables to lie in wait for the truck. Hopefully they would not only secure the arrest of the right hand man of their quarry, but also save a bunch of young girls from suffering what Elena had endured under Michael Grogan's tyranny.

They'd also been able to establish that Romanov was planning to travel to the house at 13.00 hours that afternoon with his minders. So we could, given a following wind and a fair bit of luck, clean up completely in one day.

It was clear that we would have enough evidence if the arrests were made in Bulgaria. The taped phone calls and conversations in the house also made reference to the bombing and the fact that the Russian had ordered it. With our pooled resources and the exchanges of evidence, we now had a massive case against Romanov and his team.

The plan was to hit the Russians' rented house at the same time as Sergei's colleagues were to ambush his men in Bulgaria. We were all tooled up and ready here in the café, Sergei took a call which confirmed his informers had seen Romanov plus two men leave their hotel.

The Cypriot's colleague who was watching the house reported that the Russians had arrived and had entered the house.

It was time to split. We went our separate ways so as not to draw attention to ourselves.

Howard and I went back towards Kyrenia and stopped off at a magnificent and fairly new war memorial. It was guarded by three immaculately turned out Turkish Cypriot soldiers.

There was a condolence book that we looked at with a degree of personal sadness as we both knew what it was like to lose comrades in arms.

Only Turks were allowed to write in the book so we wandered to the front of the obelisk which overlooked the beach.

As we turned back to look at the lovely plaza that had been built as homage to the fallen, Howard pointed out there was a small exhibition of military vehicles and armaments used in the 1974 conflict. We had a quick look round that then set off back towards the target site.

We turned right out of the monument and set off for what would hopefully be the last piece of this complicated jigsaw.

The satellite navigation took us to the target in half an hour and we parked in a side street directly opposite the Russians' rented house.

Hakan and his sergeant had pulled up at the street on the other side.

Jan then arrived and drove past our position and parked up.

Sergei was the last to arrive and pulled up right in front of the house, blocking the exit.

We had agreed that Sergei would be the 'platoon commander' for the exercise, so we waited for his signal. When he gave that, we all jumped out with weapons ready and Sergei's colleague Alexander hit the front door with his battering ram and shouted out his warning in Russian.

"Armed police stay where you are."

The response was a screamed oath and a burst of automatic gunfire. Alexander stood back from the door, as he did so, one man came out of the front door firing a handgun at random, not knowing where his target was; Jan took him out with two shots.

Two more men came out with automatic weapons and sprayed the front street, failing to hit any human target, but peppering a couple of our vehicles with bullets.

They stopped for a moment on the large paved area in front of the villa.

That was enough for Sergei to try getting a shot off from his position crouched behind his vehicle.

He picked off the one on the left with two shots to his upper body and the man went down in a seemingly lifeless heap.

In a nanosecond I covered the few metres that separated me from the third Russian.

I was on his blind side as he glanced towards his fallen comrade so I hit him just below his waist with a full blown rugby tackle.

He fell backwards on to the block paving and the force of my weight caused his arms to stretch out above his head and send his gun flying, it landed a few feet from his right hand.

As he tried to struggle under my body I head butted him and brought my forearm down hard across his throat.

A couple of seconds later Hakan and his colleague forcibly turned the man over so he was face down and cuffed his hands behind his back.

One of them kept his pistol rammed against the nape of their captive's neck. The guy Sergei had shot hadn't moved but was still alive, so he was also cuffed and laid face down, hands secured behind his back.

As I stood up Sergei waved for the rest of the squad to go inside the building as Romanov was still there along with one of his men.

We all had our weapons at the ready and as we went through the front door we could see that the corridor led straight through to the lounge.

One of the squad kicked open the lounge door and we all burst in with Howard Rhodes bringing up the rear. As we entered the room we stopped dead at the scene that confronted us.

Romanov and his henchman were standing in front of the sofa with their weapons in their hands.

Between them, ashen faced and trembling, was a young Turkish Cypriot woman. Her hands were tied in front of her and the two Russians had their pistols held tightly against the temple of their terrified prisoner.

Romanov shouted out in surprisingly good, but very heavily accented, English.

"Put your guns down and move to one side, we're coming out. We'll shoot her if you try to stop us."

We all glanced at each other and shrugged helplessly then realised we had no choice, so we complied with his request, slowly putting our weapons on the floor in front of us.

At that point, the girl screamed as Romanov's minder pushed his gun harder against her head. His immediate response was to lift the gun back and strike her across the left cheek with it, drawing blood from her pallid skin. As he did so, I detected a movement some feet behind me. Glancing over my shoulder I saw that Howard Rhodes had taken off back to his 4x4.

The girl stopped screaming and glanced down anxiously at the blood that had trickled down on to her cerise coloured top.

We spread out in a line in front of Romanov. The lounge was large so we were around 10 metres from our quarry.

The Russian indicated that we should move aside and open a gap in the middle of our line so they could come out.

As we complied and parted our group in the centre, the two men each grabbed the girl with their free hand and took a step forward, roughly pushing their human shield forward a couple of steps as they also moved tentatively towards us.

At that point two reports from a high velocity rifle rang out with no perceptible time lag between them. The first one split Romanov's head in two, the second one smashed the right shoulder of his fellow thug.

I spun round in astonishment to see a grim faced Howard Rhodes walking down the corridor with his rifle held across his chest.

Hakan rushed forward to help his female compatriot and put a comforting arm round her, whilst showing her his Turkish police badge.

He untied the lady and sat her down gently in an armchair, which he turned round so she wasn't facing the carnage.

We all stooped down and instinctively picked up our weapons.

Jan took the safety off his gun and stood guard over the remaining Russian, who was screaming with pain and in no state to argue, his shoulder blade being completely shattered.

Hakan's colleague took out his mobile and called in both the ambulance service and extra police to secure the premises.

The young lady turned out to be an employee of the owner of the house, which was usually rented out to holiday makers. Her routine was to go in twice a week to clean the property.

At least she was not badly injured, but nonetheless, as a precaution, she was taken away in an ambulance. Her husband had been called to accompany her.

They were escorted by an armed Turkish Cypriot police officer for their protection. Hakan took her contact details to secure a statement in due course.

Alexander read their rights to the man I'd tackled and the two wounded Mafiosos, the one outside, still being unconscious until the Russian policeman with a surprising degree of callousness threw a bucket of water over him to bring him round.

Although the man was badly wounded he was dragged to his feet and made to stand up while being cautioned. Sergei caught the look of surprise on my face and murmured by way of explanation.

"These bastards kidnapped his eighteen year old sister near Odesa and trafficked her to Holland where she killed herself to escape a life of enforced prostitution."

After the paramedics had done their best to make them comfortable and ease their pain, the ambulances took away the wounded prisoners, cuffed to their stretchers and accompanied by armed police escorts.

As the last member of Romanov's gang was put into the ambulance, Sergei took a call on his mobile.

His squad that had been dispatched to Sofia confirmed they had been successful in stopping the truck belonging to Romanov at the border between Romania and Bulgaria, well before they reached their intended destination of Sofia.

They arrested Romanov's number two, plus the driver and an armed guard. In the back of the truck they found a large quantity of cocaine and ten bewildered and frightened girls.

So between the activities here in Cyprus and Romania, Romanov's vile empire was destroyed and a group of young ladies had been saved from going through a living hell.

While all this was going on, I took Howard into the kitchen and put my arm round him. He wasn't sure whether his actions were justified so was a little upset, to say the least.

"Listen, Howard, we were almost on a war footing, these guys clearly proved to be unpredictable and had demonstrated their willingness to use their weapons indiscriminately, even against unarmed women.

We were up against it and couldn't afford to take the chance that the Russians might shoot the girl; you did what I would have done. I'm only glad you are ex-Green Jackets and your shooting skills are still there, bloody amazing shooting, mate."

He relaxed a little and suggested we re-join the rest of the team and await our orders.

CHAPTER 18

Back to Reality

The police photographer did his job at the house very professionally and thoroughly; covering every room, all the outside areas, and taking close up photos of the bullet holes in our vehicles.

The forensic team gave the place a thorough going over, gathering plenty of evidence including a large stash of cocaine, other drugs and several more firearms, with a large number of boxes of ammunition and a substantial quantity of bomb making equipment. Looked like this gang meant business.

The SOCOs took away a desk top PC and several laptops; there was plenty of incriminating stuff and a whole load of contacts stored on their hard drive, phone numbers, addresses and email addresses of all of Romanov's business contacts. Sergei and Jan were going to be busy picking up all these crooks and sending them down for a long time.

What I found astonishing was how the Russian felt he was untouchable; he made no attempt to hide what he was doing or cover his tracks. His arrogance was nothing short of breathtaking.

Didn't do him any good though, with his brains now being scraped up off the living room floor.

The whole of our team then went back to police HQ to prepare our statements and file our reports.

The original plan hadn't been to perform as a hit squad but circumstances dictated we met force with force or be taken out ourselves, possibly along with innocent civilians.

The man Jan shot died on the way to hospital. The man who was in the house with Romanov had an emergency operation to amputate his arm. The surgeon ascertained it was so badly damaged from the bullet from Howard's rifle it couldn't be saved.The Russian that I'd disabled was not badly injured, just a bloody nose and a bruise at the back of his head where he'd hit the floor.

He was taken to an emergency court hearing after being charged with attempted murder. He was remanded in custody for a trial that would doubtless ensure he stayed on Cyprus for a long time, but not in the accommodation he would have originally chosen. Another good result for our operation seemed to be on the cards.

Following an x-ray it was found that the cleaning lady held captive by Romanov had only suffered bruising to her face, caused by the blow from his minder's handgun.

After treatment and an interview with a trauma counsellor a police car was assigned to take her and her young husband back to their home.

She seemed worried her employer would hold her responsible for the mess in the rental home. Her fear eased when the police assured her the authorities would arrange for the property to be cleaned and have the bloodstained carpets replaced.

Thank goodness she wasn't badly hurt and mercifully was the only local injured during our operation. The way the Russians came running out of the rented house spraying shots from their automatic weapons, there could've been a bloodbath.

Given all the gunfire at the property, together with the bomb blast and associated shootings, the local press were getting almost hysterical and jamming the police switchboards.

Local residents were becoming increasingly alarmed and ugly rumours were already circulating that another Greco/Turkish conflict had sprung up on Cyprus. Given that there'd been peace, even though it was fragile, for many years, it was felt necessary to make the truth public. Inspector Hakan Çöteli, therefore, called a press conference.

He gave this statement before submitting to a barrage of questions from the local and international TV, radio and print media. He introduced himself to the gathered press then carefully read his prepared statement.

"Ladies and gentlemen you will know about a bomb being detonated earlier this week near one of our famous restaurants, immediately followed by gunfire and a second explosion. Then today a gunfight near Güzelyurt may well have been brought to your attention.

I wish to reassure you that this isn't armed conflict carried out by fanatics or insurgents who wish to destroy the peace on our beautiful island.

All these events were associated with the planned break up of two very large, dangerous and evil criminal gangs in Istanbul and Moscow.

The operation was set up and run by the British Secret Service jointly with Interpol and our local police major crime squad, of which I'm commander.

The British team has already closed down a major vice empire in the UK and has arrested over twenty people in the north of England who were involved in drug smuggling, people trafficking, murder and prostitution.

They were working alongside Interpol, our local police here in Cyprus, the Russian Secret Police and with members of the UK High Commission.

Unfortunately there have been fatalities amongst the crooks and a number of members of the two gangs have also been wounded but the only local civilian casualty suffered a facial bruising and is otherwise fine.

The two foreign factions had started a gang war in Turkey. It spread to Cyprus where the criminals on each side were planning to set up a base to run their evil trade, in Asia and in Eastern Europe.

Because the team I worked with were operating under cover, it isn't possible for their identities to be revealed.

I can assure you that here, in the UK and near the border between Bulgaria and Romania we've rescued almost thirty female hostages and closed down substantial Russian, English and Turkish criminal outfits.

There's now no chance of organised crime being brought here and we've saved many young ladies from a life as a sex slave.

The innocent girls, from good backgrounds in the Balkans, who were liberated in England, had been forced into prostitution for over a year.

Our team freed them and all the persons who held them captive are now in prison themselves.

We've also confiscated several very large consignments of cocaine and other drugs so have stopped that getting on to the streets and causing all the misery drugs bring.

I regret we weren't able to give you any information earlier but it was essential to the success of our operation that our undercover team weren't compromised.

I can't yet give you the names of the criminals that we have arrested nor those who've been killed until the court papers are complete."

Hakan finished his statement to a round of applause, as the press were clearly pleased with the outcome of our operation.

He then invited questions which he allowed to go on for another ten minutes before closing the press conference.

After a couple of days of statement writing, form filling and fulfilling other legal requirements I figured that my duties in Northern Cyprus were complete.

I'd kept Sandy fully in the picture from the moment I left the house at Güzelyurt and also had long and, at times, quite difficult telephone conversations with Elena.

Sandy half expected that there would be bloodshed, given the reputation and volatility of the two gangs and was pleased that we'd wrapped it all up with no casualties on our side.

His final comment was "Just another day at the office then, Nathan, eh?"

Cheeky bastard.

He was able to tell me Chief Superintendent Rowley's trial had taken place and although he'd pleaded not guilty on all counts, the evidence against him was watertight and completely irrefutable.

The jury took less than two hours to find him guilty on all counts and he received a fourteen year jail sentence and lost all his police pension rights as well as his job.

Two weeks into Rowley's sentence in one of the UK's highest security jails, two supposed armed robbers he'd banged up for long sentences for crimes they hadn't committed were both surprised and delighted to renew their acquaintance with their nemesis.

After their collective evening meal the two prisoners crept up behind the corrupt ex policeman, having decided to see if he could fly when they threw him from their fourth floor prison balcony. He couldn't.

When I first contacted Elena with a brief summary of all the news, she broke down in tears and spent quite a few moments sobbing into the phone.

I dearly wished I could've been there to comfort her, so I tried manfully to do my best down the phone line. She expressed her regrets at the deaths that the operation had caused but was obviously pleased the two obnoxious gangs had effectively been shut down.

There was clear delight when I told her another truckload of girls had been rescued on the Romania/Bulgaria border from a future life as sex slaves. During our conversations, she also kept asking me two questions I couldn't answer but which kept haunting me.

"Nathan, how long will Michael Grogan and his gang have to spend in prison? And when can you and I see each other again?"

The answer to the first one came at the end of the week. After a two week trial, Grogan, still confined to a wheel chair, was found guilty on all counts and received a life sentence, with minimum tariff of twenty five years.

Scarface was also convicted and got a twenty year sentence with an order from the judge that he be deported back to Serbia at the end of the term.

The rest of Grogan's team were found guilty and each received long prison terms.

The Government having seized all of Grogan's assets, duly disposed of them, so his ill-gotten gains were no more.

Social Services managed to arrange for all the English girls from Grogan's various brothels and massage parlours in north west England to be put on a special programme to help them get their lives back in order.

The intention was that the girls wouldn't find the need to go back to the evil trade that they'd been forced into by the scouse pimp.

Back in Cyprus, Sergei and his team, Jan and his squad plus Howard and me all worked hard putting together the evidence to guarantee convictions and long sentences for the men who'd been arrested in Istanbul, Romania and Cyprus. We checked and re-checked all our facts and after four days felt that the files we'd prepared were perfect and would achieve their objectives.

We decided we should wrap up the exercise and return to our respective bases, but first we should go out for a farewell dinner.

It was a good night, with a selection of meze, kebabs and great Turkish coffee to finish off with. To add some further spice to our evening, there was also a selection of local entertainment including a Turkish Cypriot girl singer with a good voice and a young and highly attractive belly dancer, who for some strange reason reminded me of Miss Borovic. Must be the long black hair and great body, I mused.

The location, next to The Bellapais Abbey was pretty spectacular and as I looked round the rest of the tables from our place on a raised dais by the large picture windows, I felt a sense of history.

Since the fifties this was a village that had seen much pain and witnessed many groups huddling together with coffees in hand to discuss the problems that the Greeks and Turks were creating for each other in the 1950's.

Despite the grim end to our assignment, and the eclectic mix of Germans, Russians, Turkish Cypriots and Brits we had an enjoyable farewell gathering, helped by copious amount of local wine, and we agreed to keep in touch in the future.

After the restaurant's taxis dropped us back in the centre of Kyrenia, Jan and his men picked up a second cab to carry them on to their hotel, Sergei's team walked to theirs which left Hakan and his men, Howard and me.

I bade a fond farewell to my minder and his colleagues at which point our driver arrived, as requested by Howard, and took him and yours truly back to Nicosia.

I spent a further day in the capital as the scheduled flight to Leeds/Bradford was only on Wednesdays. We were at the end of an exercise that'd been successful but for which the outcome was totally different to how we'd planned it to end. I'd known there would be danger when I set out on the exercise but as it turned out, two episodes of bloodletting and violence had come as a big surprise.

When Howard Rhodes was driving me to the airport in Southern Cyprus he asked how I thought the assignment had gone.

"It's difficult to say as this is my first op in Civvy Street. Obviously, as you know from experience, the rules are different to when you engage the enemy as a member of the armed services.

As a civilian, things aren't the same, of course, but as we were working with police forces from three countries, being directed by a man working with the UK Home Office and the UK Foreign Office, I guess we did what was absolutely necessary under the circumstances.

We were never intended to be a hit squad but things moved so fast and we had lives to protect so meeting fire with fire was our only option. I genuinely think we did the best we could since we were under fire and had come pretty close to being wiped out by the bomb blast. "

"I guess so, and given the violence that each of the warring factions has meted out to the other in recent weeks, this was bound to escalate and probably would have resulted in innocuous local Cypriots getting caught up in the violence.

So, job done and two supply lines for drugs closed down. In addition, between what you did in the UK and what has been achieved here we've made a big advance in reducing people trafficking."

We were more or less in agreement, then, and changed the subject to more normal matters. Howard believed that, as he'd been in his present post for a while, his next career move would come along pretty soon. He was immensely satisfied he'd helped prevent Cyprus being used as a staging post for organised crime barons.

"I hope my involvement in the exercise would be seen as a positive by my lords and masters, Max."

After I checked in my bags we went and had a last coffee together. I'd handed back my High Commission briefcase and weapon in Nicosia and now just needed to use my passport for the last time as Max Kelman before returning to some sort of normal life as Nathan Sawyer, whatever that meant!!

Howard and I shook hands warmly then embraced as comrades in arms. I left him with a mixture of warmth and sadness then went through passport control and into the departure lounge, eschewing the chance to waste time and lots of money in the overpriced shops.

Unlike on the outward journey, this time I was able to get some sleep, just managing to keep awake long enough for a coffee and some snacks when the flight attendants came round and with their trolley.

Pretty soon I'd be back to doing my own cooking so I figured I'd better make good use of the in-flight service. While munching away on the snack I took my mind back to my time on Cyprus and concentrated my thoughts on what I'd been able to see of this beautiful island when I'd been on my own and not dodging bombs and bullets.

My flight to Leeds left punctually and touched down on time at 20.35. Passport control was pretty swift and then I'd a short wait at the luggage gondola.

After catching the mini-bus to the off-airport parking, I picked up my car and made the thirty minute journey to Clarence Dock. I'd been instructed by Sandy to wind down my operation in Cyprus and he'd arranged for the High Commission to get me on the Leeds/Bradford flight.

His office had a spare key to my apartment and was aware of my flight details consequently I asked the boss if some provisions could be brought in to my apartment to await my return.

I wasn't too surprised, then, as I put the key in the lock, to see that there was a light shining under my front door. As I opened the door a delicious smell of freshly cooked food hit my nostrils. Which was a nice surprise but nothing compared to the sight that greeted me.

Standing at my cooker with long black hair tumbling over her slim shoulders, which moved in rhythm as she stirred the casserole, was a young lady whose shape and form I instantly recognised. I dropped my case and bag and moved towards her as she turned round and smiled in that enigmatic and unnerving way that I'd come to love.

"Welcome home, Nathan, or should it be Max?"

I threw my arms round Elena's neck as tears poured down both our cheeks. I kissed her gently on the forehead then tapped my finger on the end of her nose.

"What a great surprise, what are you doing here?"

She broke free from my embrace and turned back to the cooker to switch off the casserole. Then she threw her arms round my neck and kissed me hard and long on my compliant mouth.

As I looked into her eyes there was a sparkle there, a joy, that previously I'd only ever seen occasionally but never shining with such intensity.

"Does that answer your question?" She said, giggling like a schoolgirl.

"I can't think of a better answer, but how the hell did you get here?"

"I was called as a witness for the prosecution in Michael Grogan's court case and also for the final day in the case against Scarface, which was yesterday.

Sandy arranged for me to stay at the hotel in Roundhay and to be brought in to the court with two of his men, fully armed, as bodyguards for the two days.

He also told me you'd be coming home on Wednesday so I asked if I could be here to give you a proper home coming. Sandy just smiled and gave me the key and his driver brought me here."

"Well, I couldn't have asked for a more pleasant surprise and homecoming, so come over here Miss Borovic and I'll show you how much I've missed you."

I kissed her long and hard on her full, sweet tasting lips then held her at arms length and kissed her again.

Eventually she came up for air and stroked my hair and ran a caring finger over the wound on my forehead where I'd head butted the Russian gangster.

"Looks like you've been in the wars again; you'd better tell me all about it over dinner."

Having now found out why Elena's mobile had gone straight to voice mail when I phoned her earlier in the day, I quickly put my bags in the bedroom then checked over my mail as Elena busied herself serving dinner.

The post revealed very little that was new, bank statements, CV acknowledgements from various executive recruiters, a poll tax demand from Leeds City Council and an interesting letter from Justin Forrester of The Foreign Office. He invited me to phone him on my return as he'd a project he thought might interest me.

The first course was soon served up on the breakfast bar, so I perched on one of my new stools, and looked down at my dish which contained a mouth watering spicy black bean and lentil soup.

My unexpected and clearly accomplished hostess served it with some fine seeded bread rolls and a delicious bottle of wine that she proudly told me she had brought with her from Croatia so we could celebrate my return. She then pressed me to tell her the full story of my time in Northern Cyprus.

I did so, sparing her no detail, which induced her to gasp in surprise and with a look of horror at several points. Although she'd known some of the facts from our phone calls, I was now giving her the fully story with all the gory details.

As we were enjoying her delicious offering of beef stroganoff with Basmati rice, she stopped eating for a moment and turned her head towards me. The colour had ebbed away from her classical features somewhat, as she realised how near I'd been to the explosion from the bomb the two Russians had placed under Mehdi Gümüş's car.

"Nathan, we knew this operation may be dangerous but I didn't know that it'd have so many ways in which you could've been killed."

"I'd realised the sound of the motorbike meant that the two Mafiosos were going to take Gümüş out. That's why I got out of the van with my weapon ready to fire if necessary and shouted for the others to do the same.

At the instant the bomb went off I'd shot the first Russian and disabled the second one, so we weren't really in any danger, Elena."

She looked at me intently and gave me a grim smile of acceptance of the situation. We spent the next half an hour going over my time on assignment with her interrupting me on a regular basis to clarify various points.

I finished the update by telling her that Chief Superintendent Rowley had been killed and that gradually all the people who'd caused her nightmare were now dead or in custody. Again she gave me a grim smile and nodded her head a few times.

"OK, that's enough about the war we've been waging, let's sit in the lounge and relax."

We refilled our glasses with the last of the Dingač wine and sat on my brand new leather sofa, carefully placing the glasses on the coasters on the coffee table.

She took great delight in telling me the wine came from a vineyard which was on the Peljesac peninsula right alongside the spot on the coast where Dubrovnik nestled and where her father had one of his offices.

Milo had a close friend who was a top wine merchant so was able to pick out a couple of good bottles, from a fine vintage, for Elena. I murmured in thanks that I hoped to be able to explore Croatia in the near future, so she smiled and relaxed a little as we stopped talking crime and punishment.

Sitting alongside Elena, I glanced round my apartment and liked what I saw. Before I set off for Cyprus I'd thought to myself I was getting it sorted out with furniture and fittings but wondered how long it would be before Elena saw it.

Now she was here I was anxious to know if she also shared my passion for my crash pad. She told me she'd been dropped off there by Sandy's driver that morning and had spent a little while looking round the area and agreed I'd made a good choice.

"As well as the location I love the apartment, it's ideal for one person, although it would be a bit of a crush for two." I looked at her as she said that but couldn't read anything in her eyes so just let it go for the moment.

"Well, I don't know how long you plan to stay in Leeds, Elena, but we could manage for a few days, if you wanted to keep me company."

"OK, I'd like that and I've an open airline ticket to return home so don't have to worry about that."

"That's settled then, let's wash the dishes then have some coffee.

I'd like to go to Liverpool in the next few days to see the hotel owners who were tortured by Michael Grogan's men. I feel I owe them that. Would you be up to coming with me?"

She paused for a while before nodding her assent so I gave her a quick kiss on the forehead then made my way to the kitchen.

After we washed the pots, Elena went to make some coffee while I unpacked my cases. Once I'd done that I went back in the lounge with some spare sheets, a pillow and duvet and put them on the armchair.

"You can sleep in the bedroom Elena, I'll take the couch." She looked at me quite embarrassed and the raspberry blush appeared back on her cheeks, just like the one I'd seen as she was leaving to go to home.

"No, this is your place, you take the bed."

I stood my ground and insisted she was the guest so should take the bed, and I'd spent many nights in far less comfortable situations. She again smiled and eventually conceded.

We retired for the night and I settled myself on the sofa, a very happy man. Within minutes I was asleep and had a dream free sleep until the smell of strong coffee wafted in the direction of my nostrils eight hours later.

I sat up with a start to see Elena standing over me with a cup in her hand, and a delicious smile on her face. She leaned over and kissed me.

"Morning Nathan, how's the sofa?"

"Fine, I slept well and happy, well because I was dog tired, happy because you're here."

After showering and getting dressed I joined my delightful houseguest for the breakfast she'd prepared. Bacon, eggs, sausage and even black pudding, she'd remembered everything, what a star!!"I could get to like this", I thought to myself.

Elena must have been up quite early as she was already showered and dressed when she'd brought my coffee, bed made, breakfast started, what an organised young lady.

We decided I should arrange to see Sandy that afternoon. I phoned him and fixed up to go to his Park Square offices at 15.30 hours.

I had Miss Borovic to myself for six hours, life couldn't be better.

Elena was dressed for walking, I thought, and that's just what we did. We put on our anoraks, set off along the banks of the River Aire and the Leeds Liverpool canal, and walked arm in arm or holding hands for a good couple of hours.

Elena was fascinated by the locks on the canal so I explained to her how they allowed the narrow boats to climb hills. Not only was I enjoying her company again, but took great pleasure on being able to show her things that were new to her and had not been part of her experiences in Montenegro and Croatia.

As we stood in front of the lock gates on the canal just behind the Novotel, Elena took my hand and brought it up to her lips and kissed my fingers soothingly. I took both her hands in mine and brought them up to my mouth and brushed them tenderly with my own lips. I then put my left arm round her waist and pulled her head on to my shoulder.

We sat down on the parapet wall next to the winding handle for the lock paddles. We stayed like that for a few seconds, with a comfortable silence between us. I then pulled her gently round so that we were face to face.

"It's now over six months since your little altercation in Liverpool. In that time, I've thought about you almost every minute. We've been apart for several weeks, since you went back to Dubrovnik with Milo. I've missed you terribly and you can't begin to imagine how delighted and surprised I was to find you at my apartment last night.

When I'd free time in Cyprus and when I was planning this apartment I kept asking myself, what's Elena doing, what will Elena think of this, will Elena like the colour?"

"Strange, Nathan, I've been thinking the same. Wondering what you were doing, whether you were safe. At first I was struggling with my emotions, was I drawn to you because you saved my life? Were my feelings enhanced because you arranged the rescue of all the girls? Had I grown fond of you out of a feeling of gratitude?

Then I started thinking differently, the time we spent in your cottage was special, I'd been through hell for over fifteen months. You treated me with respect, you were kind to me, and you made sure I recovered from my beating. You made me laugh again; you showed me how to enjoy the natural world, birds and beautiful countryside.

I enjoyed your company from the first time we met and each time we spoke on the phone I was wishing I could see you in person, Nathan.

When I found out that you were coming home and I was going to be in England for the trial, I just knew I had to see you."

I looked at her long and hard, kissed her firmly on those soft yielding lips then gently pulled her up and we walked off, hand in hand. We walked for quite a few minutes in soft silence, each with their own thoughts. I broke the stillness first.

"Elena, what's your work situation at the moment, are you committed to working for your Dad, or do you still want to establish your own legal practice?"

"My father doesn't want me to work in his business. He's enough staff but would be happy to give me some work to help his firm out.

I want to become involved in legal matters and especially in helping people who've been kidnapped and people who've been displaced through civil war or are refugees for other reasons.

Daddy's determined that I should make my own life and not worry about him. He's so happy I'm safe and he's told me I must do what's right for me.

I was wondering to myself while you were away, what your plans were and if you've chosen your future career path yet. Are you still going to work with Sandy, or was the assignment just because you got involved by accident?"

"I certainly had no plans to join Sandy's private army, I've been involved in conflict all my working life and was happy to come out of the Royal Marines with my head held high, having done a good job, and having avoided getting killed for almost twenty years.

I was pleased to carry out this last op, as in a perverse sort of way I started it myself by rescuing you. We've achieved a great deal, all of the people involved in your kidnap and many more are now either dead or serving long jail terms.

Those we arrested in Cyprus are likely to spend many years in jail. But I don't see myself doing that kind of stuff full time. Where do you see yourself setting up your legal practice?"

"Where to do that is something I haven't been able to sort out in my own mind. I was hoping if you'd decided what you want to do, then it would help me to make my own decision."

I paused to collect my thoughts as my heart was pounding. What did Elena want me to say? Was she looking for me to be in her life or was she just looking for advice?

"When I got back last night, there was a letter from Justin Forrester at the Foreign Office, suggesting he had something that might interest me.

While you were getting ready this morning I phoned him. His department is looking to bolster their team in Eastern Europe by appointing someone with military training to act as a liaison with the European Commission on matters relating to asylum seekers and refugees. They're flexible about where the person is located."

"So if you and I found that we're still looking to spend our lives together, and you accepted the offer, you could possibly move to be near me, even to Kotor or Dubrovnik?"

"Of course I would be delighted if our lives could continue to be closer together but I've the small problem of having bought my apartment, here in Leeds. We need to think long and hard about how we want to go forward from here, don't we? Let's go and see Sandy this afternoon, then we can have a long talk when we return.

I also want to plan our visit to Liverpool to pay my respects to the couple who own the hotel where I stayed."

CHAPTER 19

End Game

The meeting with Sandy went well and he was happy with the debriefing. There was some detailed discussion over the amount of bloodshed in Cyprus but given how unpredictable the two rival factions had proved to be, he accepted casualties were inevitable.

However, he clearly needed to justify to the Foreign Office the killings that had taken place during the operation. Fortunately there were no serious injuries amongst our law enforcement team.

One UK arrest that was added to the list was the person who shopped me in Liverpool when I set fire to the BMW that'd been used to hunt down Elena.

It turned out from the evidence against the bent police officers the person who gave my car registration number to Michael Grogan was an illegal immigrant.

He was employed in one of Grogan's brothels as a doorman so he got a prison sentence for conspiracy and was to be deported once his sentence had been served.

Another satisfactory result and it seemed that we were gradually removing all the villains from the street. I just hoped that they wouldn't be immediately replaced by another bunch.

I managed to discuss the opportunity that'd been offered to me by Justin Forrester. What Justin told me on the phone was, in fact a cover as he couldn't discuss the role on an open phone.

If I took on the opportunity I would become a Spook and be involved in investigation, surveillance and bringing to justice people smugglers and also be involved in tracking down criminals who ran child paedophile rings.

There would be occasional elements of danger but not with the intensity I'd experienced in Northern Cyprus. Captain Parker thought I should take it and felt I'd have little difficulty in renting out my Leeds apartment for a decent monthly amount on a shorthold tenancy basis.

So, I'd a lot to think about. Maybe yomping outside was beginning to take a turn for the better.

Elena and I returned to Clarence Dock as dusk was creeping in. The late spring sun was dancing off the water, creating a magical sprinkling of light and shade as we walked across the car park to my place.

I held Elena's hand tightly as we looked at the light refracting seductively on the dark waters.

We went inside and sat down heavily on the sofa in unison, causing the leather cushions to groan in protest. I put my arm round Elena's shoulder and pulled her pretty head on to my shoulder.

"Sandy's given me more details of the role that the Foreign Office wants me to take."

"Nathan, I'm not sure that I could face the fact you might be facing danger every day. But if you really want to take on this role it would be a huge opportunity for us to make a difference to the lives of many people. Once you had the facts to hand, I could come in with the legal support."

"I was lucky last week to come away relatively unscathed and in a way, you were lucky that someone was around in Liverpool when you were getting your beating.

If we can prevent that happening to any more girls, then the question of me experiencing the odd bit of danger will make it all worthwhile. Also the thought of kids being abducted to order by paedophile rings across Europe churns my stomach.

I'd like to go down to London and explore my options with Justin in more detail. You could come with me and I could show you our fine and exciting capital city.

I don't think it'd be a good idea for you and I to set up a business together. I'd have no problem with us coming together on projects but I think to work too closely would harm our relationship, which in my view is coming along quite nicely."

"OK, Nathan, let's do that. We have two parallel lines of decision making to follow. First the question of a career for both of us and then how we can proceed on a personal level. When we were effectively living together in the cottage in the Lake District we got to know each other quite well, even though we were brought together by accident after you walked into a difficult situation.

We're from diverse cultures and entirely different backgrounds but, despite this we seem to have got on with each other very well in my view.

As we spent more time together, shopping, cooking, walking in the mountains or sitting by a stream in Cumbria I thought to myself 'I like this guy'.

Then when you kissed me in Scarborough I felt a tingle running down my back.

When I got on the plane with my dad to return home, I'd to fight hard to hold back my tears.

Daddy spoke to me at length when we arrived back.

He told me that he wouldn't stand in my way in whatever career I chose or whom I chose to be the man in my life.

He did say if I thought you were the man for me I should make sure the feelings I had for you weren't out of some misplaced gratitude.

When you went to Cyprus, I was worried. I genuinely was scared that you might get hurt, or even worse as I'd seen for myself what these evil men could do to anyone who got in the way of their profits.

I was so happy when you told me it was all over and you were safe and coming home. When I was called to court as a witness, I asked Sandy if it'd be alright for me to be here to catch you unawares."

I kissed her lightly on the cheek then tapped my finger affectionately on the end of her nose.

"It was a lovely surprise when I returned home and found you here. Since we first met in Liverpool, you've been in my thoughts every day. Even when I was buying the furniture and stuff for this place I kept asking myself, 'I wonder if Elena would have chosen that or would Elena like this?'

When I was away I was trying to keep in touch with you whilst at the same time giving you some space to get your thoughts straight without me getting in the way.

If you did harbour any feelings for me, I also wanted to be sure they weren't false. I think we're both now beginning to see we really do mean something to each other."

After I'd said that, I pulled her head towards me and gave her a long hard kiss. As I did so her lips parted and she searched my mouth with her tongue and slid her body on top of mine. We locked in a passionate embrace for what seemed like an eternity. I stroked her silky black hair and broke away, not wanting gratuitous sex to get in the way of establishing a relationship.

"Elena, let's take this nice and slowly, and make sure we both know what we want and we don't allow our physical attraction to each other to cloud our judgement.

Why don't you stay here with me for a few more days, and then go home and a few weeks after that we could take a couple of week's holiday.

That would give us a taste of being with each other all day every day in a home environment, then the holiday would allow us to enjoy some free time and see if we enjoy the same things."

"That works for me, Nathan; I could stay here for another week or so, if that's OK. We can go to Liverpool and see the couple from your hotel then take the train to London to see Justin."

We made the arrangements to go to Liverpool the following day, travelling by train direct from Leeds to Lime Street, then a taxi to the hotel.

I rang the door bell and it was quickly answered. Despite their ordeal the young couple were genuinely pleased to see me and to meet Elena.

They showed us in to the comfortable and immaculate lounge where coffee was served along with some delicious home made shortbread biscuits.

I gave them a full run down on what happened in October and since then.

They weren't called as witnesses in the trials, as they were still recovering from their injuries but their written evidence had formed an important part of the prosecution's case against Grogan and his gang.

They became quite upset as the story unfolded, especially when they heard Elena's story and the attempt on our lives in the Lake District.

Whilst shocked at the events in which I was involved in Northern Cyprus, the couple were pleased that the whole operation had been instrumental in cleaning up the city of Liverpool and also smashing two people smuggling rings.

Their injuries were now healed and having heard that justice, in some cases summary justice, had been done, their minds were now beginning to mend.

They'd received a payment from the criminal compensation funds which helped a little and were now planning to sell the hotel and move from the area.

I apologised several times for the problems I'd caused but they wouldn't hear of it. The couple, Nick and Maria were resilient and happy that, despite their terrible ordeal, all the villains were now off the street, as far as we knew.

We stayed for about an hour then took a taxi back to Lime Street. I'd asked Elena whether, now that she was safe, she wanted to have a quick tour of the city where she had been held captive for so long.

She agreed to this so we started off by going to the Beatles Story on Albert Dock, and then had lunch in the bistro at the Tate Liverpool.

We walked round to the front of the Liver Building where she'd been beaten by the two Serbian thugs. Walking freely in that area seemed to lift a cloud from Elena's mind and she smiled at me, whilst holding my arm tightly.

We finished off with a visit to both the Anglican Cathedral and Paddy's wigwam, as the Catholic version was known by the locals, then a quick look at the Cavern and the statue of John Lennon.

Elena marvelled at the wonderful old architecture where she'd spent so long without being able to see any of it. She also saw the huge amount of building work taking place as part of the regeneration work resulting from Liverpool recently being European City of Culture.

Just as we settled in our seats on the return train journey my mobile rang. It was Justin Forrester; we arranged to meet on Tuesday at 10.30 at his office. I asked him if he could book me a couple of rooms in a suitable hotel for three nights, so I could show Elena some of the tourist spots of the capital.

As we went through the barriers at Leeds station we decided to walk back to the apartment. I walked wherever possible, using wheels as a last resort, old habits die hard, keep fit, keep alive was my motto.

We turned right out of the station concourse and made our way down Neville Street past the Hilton Hotel. As we reached the bridge, we dropped down the steps to follow the towpath alongside the Leeds and Liverpool Canal.

We'd walked a couple of hundred metres in the pastel shaded evening light, enjoying each other's company by the water and the tranquillity of dusk.

It was then that the man approached us; he was sitting on one of the benches strategically placed in this nicely refurbished area.

"Excuse me guv, can you spare some change for a coffee?"

His manner wasn't threatening and he was reasonably well dressed and clean, not your typical beggar. I'd noticed that he had a slight limp as he got up and approached us. I answered him calmly and clearly, holding on tightly to Elena.

"Maybe, but why are you here, mate, don't you have any money, what's the story?"

"Sorry to bother you, sir but I'm skint. I was invalided out of the army, the Royal Engineers, after picking up a bad leg wound in Afghanistan, did twelve years but my compo hasn't been approved yet and they haven't sorted out my pension. The landlord kicked me out of my little flat today when I got behind with the rent."

"Where are you planning to sleep tonight?"

"I've got a place in a Salvation Army hostel about a mile from here, sir."

"Stop calling me sir, what rank were you; don't you have any family?"

"I was a corporal and I'm a single man with no family still living. I had a brother but he was killed defusing a bomb in Iraq six months ago. My dad served over twenty years as a sapper, both he and my mother died from lung cancer in their late forties, which is why I don't smoke or drink."

"OK, I was a stripey in the Royal Marines and I've just come out after eighteen years. I'm Nathan Sawyer and this is my girlfriend Elena Borovic. What's your name?"

Elena looked at me and smiled rather coyly when she heard the girlfriend bit.

"Royal Marines, eh, good job I didn't try to mug you sarge," he said with a grin,

"I'm Steve Cooper."

"OK, Steve, have you got your clothes and things at the sally army?"

"Yep, that's all I have as the flat was furnished."

"Right this is what we'll do, here's twenty quid. Get yourself something to eat and a coffee, no booze, mind, do you understand?"

He nodded as he answered, "As I said, I don't drink sarge, never have done."

"Right, when I came out of the Corps I took on a short term assignment for my ex Captain, Sandy Parker which I've just finished.

His operation's based in Leeds and he runs a private army, working with the police and the Home Office as well as helping with quite a lot of clandestine military stuff overseas. He only employs ex military who have come out with a good record and only personnel who are clean, no drugs, no excessive alcohol.

Many of them continue in active service with him, but if you're injured he also has many other roles that you might be able to fill.

I'll take you to see him on Monday morning if you want, let's see if he can find a position for you in his operation. We can also speak with SSAFA and ask them to put you in touch with one of their case workers to help you with some permanent accommodation.

Knowing Sandy, he'll also get your landlord blacklisted by the City Council and have his business closed down for throwing out a wounded soldier."

"Wow that would be great, many thanks, sarge; Captain Parker must be a very powerful man."

"He certainly is, but you can judge for yourself on Monday.

I'll pick you up at 10.30, go and get yourself a bite to eat and make sure you're booted and suited when I collect you. Don't let me down. Here, write the address of where you are," I said, handing him a pen and paper.

"Thanks again sarge, you can count on me." He wrote the address down then shook me warmly by the hand and kept hold of my hand as a tear started to appear in his eye.

Elena leaned forward and patted him on the arm and said,

"Enjoy your evening meal; I'm sure things will work out for you."

Steve eventually let go of my hand and his emotion prevented him getting any more words out so he limped off and lifted his arm high above his head in a farewell gesture without looking back.

Elena put her arm through mine and held me tight as we continued our walk home.

"That was rather kind of you, Nathan. You seem to make a habit out of helping people."

"When you're in the armed forces, you learn to depend on each other and look after your mates. He's clearly a good sort who'd been let down by the system and a crooked landlord. Let's hope Sandy can do something to help the guy."

Elena nuzzled her fragrant head into the crook of my neck and held me even tighter. Less than ten minutes later we were back at my apartment.

We cooked a simple meal, macaroni cheese, and while we were eating spent some time planning.Elena would stay another ten days before returning home. We decided to take a two week holiday in about six weeks, by which time we'd hopefully have worked out our career options.

I continued playing the respectful host and slept on the sofa, which wasn't ideal but not too uncomfortable. Elena and I found that living together didn't present any problems. We'd done so for a few days in Cumbria but the circumstances there were much different.

During that time we weren't as close as we'd become since she'd been with me in Leeds, both in the hotel and in my apartment.

Having spent most of my adult life with almost entirely male company, it was taking some adjustment, having a lady in my life. As I'd never had a serious relationship I told myself I must take it a little slowly as I not only didn't want to make a mistake but equally didn't wish to hurt Elena.

So far, so good, though, we seemed to be making good progress and were living as man and wife, after a fashion, but without sex getting in the way to confuse our thinking.

At the start of the weekend we spent an hour on the internet booking our holiday. We decided to go to the Portuguese island of Madeira so booked our flights and our hotel independently, rather than through a tour operator.

First we booked Elena's flight from Dubrovnik to the UK, then our flights to Funchal. We elected to stay at a hotel on the coast, west of the island's capital and only half an hour's drive from the airport.

We debated what accommodation we should go for and eventually decide on a double room with a sea view.

With that done we decided to explore Leeds, something we hadn't had the time to do when we'd been staying at the hotel in Roundhay Park.

We started off with a little retail therapy, buying some clothes for the holiday followed by a trip to the supermarket for more food supplies leaving the purchases in the car while we continued to take in the delights of the city centre.

We then went to a museum and art gallery, next to the town hall as I thought we needed to delve into each other's interests as part of our getting to know each other.

We'd discussed culture to some extent when we were in Cumbria and both enjoyed visual arts so wanted to explore this and maybe at some point enjoy performing arts as well.

Next to the art gallery is the Henry Moore Institute where we also spent some time before going back into the art gallery for a snack lunch in the beautiful and aptly named 'Tiled Café'.

By the end of Saturday we realised our interests were seemingly parallel and made for an enjoyable and relaxing day.

We decided to spend the evening chez nous and watch TV which was an education to Elena. Although we had ninety six channels there seemed to be nothing to watch of any substance, so we settled for a film in the end.

Sunday I woke quite early so prepared a cooked breakfast while Elena was showering. I shouted that her meal was ready and a couple of minutes later she came out of the bathroom with a towel round her head and wearing her towelling dressing gown. Her soft skin was glowing pink from the shower and she was looking radiant. We ate our breakfast with relish and discussed what to do for the rest of the day.

Whilst clearing the dishes away the towel fell away from Elena's head and as she bent down to pick it up, the top of her dressing gown parted to reveal a very appealing cleavage.

She caught my eye as she picked up the towel and blushed then went back towards the bedroom, stammering that she needed to dry her hair.

I went up tight behind her and put my arms round her waist and kissed her lightly in the nape of her neck then slowly moved my hands up to where her breasts were proudly nestling behind their towelling covering. I cupped one of them in each hand and kissed her hard on the neck and whispered,

"Don't worry; I can wait until we get to Madeira, but only just!!"

An hour later we set off to Ilkley where we went for a long walk on the famous moor. In the early summer sunshine it was just like a scene from a travel brochure.

The rain of the past few days had freshened the grass which was soft and springy under foot and displayed a thousand shades of green. The various rock formations were covered in bright green moss and lichen and the small trees had their full growth of leaves proudly displayed.

We spotted a couple of brown hares running across a grassy mound beneath the Cow and Calf rocks. As we took the footpath through the wooded area we startled a roe deer which stopped its grazing, looked at us then leaped over the dry stone wall and was gone in an instant.

The walk was hard going with plenty of steep ascents and descents through small ravines and gulleys. Elena laughed out loud as I tripped over a tree root and almost fell flat on my face. As I recovered my composure, she took a step backwards and fell on her butt. Divine retribution I call that.

Feeling the benefit of our long and fairly strenuous walk in the clear fresh air on the moor we set off on our drive back to Clarence Dock.

Once we were there, I phoned Sandy to let him know about Steve Cooper and our visit the next day. Elena also phoned her father to update him on her situation.

Monday morning came and Elena said she would stay in and clean the apartment while I collected Steve and made the journey to Park Square.

When I turned up at the Salvation Army hostel at 10.25 the man was standing outside waiting for me, smartly dressed in immaculately pressed grey flannels, regimental blazer and tie and a crisp white shirt. He was carrying a folder in which he told me were his discharge papers, a reference from his CO and his citations, plus details of his tenancy and his landlord's name and address.

We were shown into the meeting room by Sandy Parker's secretary and she suggested we help ourselves to coffee.

Out of politeness, I proposed that we should wait for our host. He appeared a couple of minutes later, at which point Cooper shot out of his chair and stood ramrod straight to attention. Sandy smiled and spoke softly,

"Thank you Steve, we're all in Civvy street now, so please make yourself comfortable and have a coffee then tell me about yourself.

Hi Nathan did you enjoy your surprise on Wednesday?"

He smiled then listened while Steve started to describe his history. After a few minutes Sandy stopped him and asked him for the details of his flat and his landlord.

"Do you know where he's from Steve?"

"He told me he's an Iraqi, sir."

Sandy asked his secretary to pop in. He gave her the landlord's details and asked her to get the 'persona non grata' wheels in motion immediately. A team of armed police picked the man up within an hour of Sandy's instructions and a search team went through his house with a fine tooth comb.

Once they found his passport and checked him out it turned out the man was an illegal immigrant and had been one of Saddam Hussain's key torturers who'd fled Iraq when the tyrant was toppled.

His house contained a number of illegally held weapons, a quantity of drugs and several books and videos on bomb making. He apparently had been in the UK for over three years, but no-one knew he was here, not even the tax and VAT authorities.

Seven days after kicking Steve Cooper out of his apartment, the manacled Iraqi was taken on a military aircraft back to his home country where he was put on trial for treason, a capital offence.

He was banned from ever re-entering Britain and there was a total UK-wide news blackout to prevent the do-gooders and the human rights activists sticking their noses in.

The man had never worried about other people's human rights, including thousands of innocent Iraqi civilians, women and children and an honourable but impoverished British soldier by the name of Steve Cooper. So the Iraqi's so-called human rights were not an issue.

His UK assets were taken over by the local authority which set about refurbishment and then putting them into their housing stock.

Once the first property was completed it was furnished and Steve Cooper installed as a Leeds City Council tenant, the first two months rent free whilst his army pension was sorted out.

The guard who escorted the Iraqi landlord on the British military plane had been given an envelope by Sandy Parker, which was to be handed to his prisoner at the moment he was entrusted to the Iraqi police.

The British Army sergeant followed his orders and the prisoner opened the envelope, read the card inside then threw it at the sergeant who smiled when he picked up the card and read it. It had Captain Parker's name printed across the top and the following message hand written across the middle:-

"That will teach you to fuck with a brave British soldier."

Back in the present, Sandy gave Steve a full and searching interview, focussing especially on his role in the Royal Engineers.

It turned out he was an armoured engineer, operating and maintaining Trojan and Titan vehicles.

Steve proudly spoke of his active service time and gave many examples of having got broken and damaged equipment up and running again and back on to the front line.

After an hour Sandy stood up.

"OK Steve, you start Monday and spend a month understudying my head of engineering who retires in five weeks. Then you'll take over from him.

You'll be based at our operations centre in Wetherby, I'll have a contract drawn up for you to sign on Monday, here's a compliments slip with the address for you to report to at 08.00 hours.

In the meantime, my secretary will give you an advance on your salary for you to live on until pay day. You can pay it back over three months.

I'll ask a SSAFA caseworker to call on you at the sally army to get the details they'll need to chase up your compensation and your army pension. Clear?"

Cooper again shot out of his chair as he stood ramrod straight.

"Sir! Thank you sir."

"My pleasure son, you've earned the right for some luck to come into your life. Nathan will fill you in on what we do on the way home, see you Monday."

With that he was gone. Doubtless he wanted to move along the repatriation of Cooper's landlord.

I gave him the full run down on Sandy's business as we drove back to the hostel and also some of the detail from Elena's story and my time in Cyprus.

When we pulled up in front of the hostel, I walked round to the passenger side and shook Steve by the hand. He reached into his pocket and took out the money that Sandy had given him and peeled off a £20 note.

"Sarge, I can't thank you enough, here's the twenty quid you gave me. I won't let you down; what'll happen to the landlord?"

"Don't worry about him; he'll get what he deserves. I told you, Sandy is a powerful man. My bet is he'll be arrested and sent back to Iraq before you've finished your first week's work."

I arrived home to find my newly named girlfriend had prepared a lunch consisting of tasty sandwiches with some fruit to follow. As we sat out on the balcony enjoying our snack I described the morning's events.

Elena in turn told me she'd worked out how to use the washing machine. So she'd washed and dried my clothes from the Cyprus trip and her own laundry from her short time in the UK. I told her she was turning into a proper little housewife, she liked that.

We got the early train to Kings Cross and after leaving our cases at the left luggage took a taxi to the Foreign Office. Justin's secretary placed Elena in a comfortable lounge where she was able to help herself to tea or coffee and some delicious looking muffins, with a TV and national papers to keep her entertained.

I was shown into a meeting room where Forrester joined me presently. He'd read the detailed report on the operation in Northern Cyprus and was clearly using the events there as a sort of springboard to undertake other assignments against criminal activities that were beginning to have an impact in the UK.

He gave me a dossier to read later but put its executive summary up on the large monitor fixed to the wall.

Some of the residual criminal elements from the crisis in the Balkans were starting to expand their operations to Western Europe and were busy establishing supply chains for drugs from Afghanistan and the Far East.

The INTEL gathered by Forrester's team also suggested that they'd gangs working in various countries on the Indian sub-continent snatching kids off the streets and selling them to paedophile rings.

Cambodia was also well established as a major player in this evil trade. Apparently, impoverished families, sold girls, and occasionally boys, as young as thirteen for around £150 to pimps who spirited them away to brothels in various cities in Cambodia. They'd even been able to establish links with Eastern European agents.

There'd been an operative in post from Justin's team, but he was now the subject of a burn notice as he was found to be passing classified information to a paedophile ring in Holland.

If I wished I could join MI6 after our holiday in Madeira. A six week induction programme would be followed by a placement in the general Balkans area with my handler based in Belgrade.

The terms were acceptable to me and the opportunity to be involved in bringing down peddlers in misery and human suffering was of significant interest.

I discussed with Justin my growing relationship with Elena, her background and that of her father. He was happy with that and understood my wish to discuss matters with her before giving him my final decision. I agreed to come back to see him before we returned to Leeds.

He gave me details of the White House Hotel where he'd made reservations so I left him, feeling quietly pleased with myself following our discussions.

Elena and I went back to Kings Cross, collected our cases then took a taxi to the hotel which was near Regents Park. When we checked in and saw the quality of the place and the rack rates displayed behind the reception desk, I muttered to myself,

"I'm glad Justin's paying for this!!"

We enjoyed our time in the capital, despite the shoving and jostling of the crowds on Oxford street and the regular attention of street beggars.

Elena was thrilled at the superb view from the top of the London Eye, and after our flight we visited the nearby London Aquarium

She was amazed at the size and beauty of the Houses of Parliament and as we walked across the Millennium Bridge she stopped in awe to admire St Paul's Cathedral.

As the hotel was so near to Regent's Park we took a long walk round London's green lung. In the relative quiet, away from the hordes of shoppers and tourists I was able to discuss with Elena the possibility of my joining MI6.

After we'd looked at all the pros and cons, we decided I should take up the offer and see if I could be based in Dubrovnik. As we reached our decision Elena put her arms around my neck, gave me a warm kiss and smiled.

"Then I would be looking after you instead of the other way around!"

I phoned Sandy just to get his view before making a commitment to Forrester. He suggested it was an ideal role for me. Justin was available at 11.00 hours on the morning we planned to return to Leeds.

We paid our hotel bill then checked our luggage in with their concierge before getting a taxi to meet Justin. I made sure I kept the receipted hotel bill and took great delight in handing it in for eventual reimbursement. I could get used to this expenses business!!

I gave Justin the news which put a smile on his face and told him I'd read the dossier he'd given me and the trail of human misery that was portrayed in there was part of the reason why I decided to accept the offer.

He would courier me the necessary documentation in the next couple of days and commence my induction after the holiday.

I'd be introduced to my handler on the first day as he was keen to get me up to speed with the progress they'd made so far.

After having spent most of my adult life in combat, highly visible and being shot at, to now be working under cover and observing, watching and gathering evidence was going to be totally different. But, nevertheless, the thrill I'd experienced in Liverpool and Northern Cyprus in bringing down three evil empires was a major factor in my decision.

There was a high level of excitement in Elena's voice as we chatted on the return journey to Leeds. She said she'd now make plans to set up her legal business and start her search for offices once she arrived home.

Her father had offered her a suite in his building but she wanted to be independent so he said he'd lend her the money to set herself up professionally.

CHAPTER 20

Yomping Outside

As I looked out of the window the ground was coming up at a rapid speed and then the plane's wheels gently bumped down on to the strange but cleverly designed runway at Funchal Airport, Madeira. The runway was built like a short motorway, just sticking out on a promontory. It was high above the road, resembling a flyover, but it did its job very well and in 2009 had handled just under 2.4 million passengers.

An hour later Elena and I parked the rental car in the multi storey car park opposite the hotel in Calheta and we completed the check in procedures at the front desk. We were soon unpacking our luggage in our bright and contemporary suite with vivid colours reflecting the endless sunshine that the island enjoys.

Elena marvelled at the stunning views from the furnished balcony which overlooked the Atlantic Ocean and the hotel's pool. It was a great base for winding down and from which we could look forward to exploring this lovely island together.

We wolfed down a sandwich and glass of coke in the beach bar then went back to the suite to take a private nap and enjoy some sunbathing on the balcony, or at least that was the plan.

I elected to go straight out on the balcony while Elena said she would change out of the clothes she'd worn since leaving England, so took herself off into the bathroom.

Five minutes later I heard a sound behind me and propped myself up on one elbow and squinted to see what it was. Framed in the doorway was a vision of beauty that took my breath away. The slight breeze was caressing Elena's dark hair, causing wisps of it to stray over her face; she'd rubbed suntan lotion on her body which gave it a lustrous glow in the bright Madeiran sunlight.

Her glistening skin was a light golden olive colour, beautifully set off by a tiny cherry coloured bikini. The briefs were tied in a bow at each side and the deep cut top had two cups trimmed in white lace that displayed her perfectly shaped bust to perfection.

I rolled off the lounger and took the couple of steps I needed to take hold of her outstretched hands and bring them up to my lips, whispering in her ear as I did so.

"You look absolutely beautiful."

I slowly kissed one hand then took the fingers of the other and gently put them in my mouth, one by one, leaving the long index finger until last.

As I tenderly sucked that elegant digit she moaned softly and drew me inside the suite, walking slowly backwards until she reached the divan.

She stopped as the back of her legs touched the bed and kissed me fully on the mouth then slowly eased herself down backwards, drawing me on top of her.

We hitched up so we were both fully on the queen size bed and as my legs moved up I kicked off my deck shoes at the end of the bed which landed on the marble floor with a loud plop.

That caused Elena to giggle nervously, so I gently stroked her hair then began to nibble her neck, gently at first then with increasing purpose as my passions were aroused.

Elena pulled my shirt out of my jeans and put both her hands up on to my back then lifted the shirt over my head and flung it on the floor.

My lips searched for new pleasures and I moved my mouth lightly on to her right shoulder and bit her gently just alongside her arm.

She was now kissing away at my forehead, my neck, my shoulder whilst dreamily drawing her nails up and down my spine.

I moved six inches down the bed and rested my lips on Elena's cleavage and gave her a long kiss in the bare area between the cups of her bikini top. Then very slowly started to move her left strap out of the way, kissing her gently as she yielded willingly and with a look of longing in her eyes whilst she continued to caress my back and neck.

As the strap came away and slipped silently off her shoulder I smoothly pulled the bikini cup down, exposing her lovely left bust to my searching lips.

I hungrily kissed all around it then found the central pleasure zone and greedily sucked on her nipple which was now erect and looking for company.

In a second I removed the right cup and lifted my head slightly to admire her lovely form as she lay there looking me straight in the eye and giving me a dazzling smile.

She arched her back and I was able to unhook the top and cast it off.

I rolled on my back while Elena sat astride me and pulled off my jeans while I pressed my head to her bust and stroked her perfectly flat stomach.

We locked in a passionate embrace, kneeling upright and panting hard, then Elena pushed me back on to the bed and with a look that could almost be described as embarrassed, she pulled down my boxer shorts then discarded them.

She kissed me hard on the lips followed by my chest then straightened up and slid off her bikini bottoms in a gesture of triumph; in a second I was inside her.

She moved up and down rhythmically whilst nipping my chest and pulling on my nipples with her lips. I retaliated and softly pulled my teeth over her own nipples then turned us round so I was on top and gently swaying, wondering if I could last the course.

No worries, my delightful new found lover gave out a loud moan and shriek, falling back on to the bed covers as I in turn felt the pain of ecstasy swim over me and I too collapsed in a heap.

After a couple of minutes of whispering in her ear and stroking her tenderly I withdrew and lay beside her, cradling her soothingly in my arms as she slept, totally spent but with a smile on her face.

I was woken by my mobile, its irritating vibration making a pinging noise as it moved about the glass top on the bedside table. I looked at my watch; we had slept for almost two hours.

Our holiday on Madeira was perfect; we used the hotel as a base to explore the island's hidden delights in our hire car.

One day it would be a drive up to Cabo Girão to wonder at the second highest cliff in the world with its 589 metre drop into the Atlantic below, watching the large raptors swirling round to catch the thermals and then lazily gliding in the strong sunlight.

Then, the next day we would take a local bus into the island capital, Funchal, and admire its elegant avenues and belle époque mansions which now housed banks and government offices.

We even followed in the footsteps of Sir Winston Churchill in Câmara de Lobos where the great man made frequent visits from 1949 onwards to paint many of the local landscapes and commit to canvass this quaint fishing village in particular.

I could see why he was attracted to its innate beauty with its gaily painted fishing boats pulled up on the pebble beach and the residents' houses painted in strong primary colours.

Elena was soaking up the history and the beauty of our island paradise and our time spent on the golden sands at Calheta was gradually turning her flawless skin first to light mahogany then gradually to a bronze that stunningly set off her dark hair and dazzling smile.

We'd discussed briefly the phone call that woke me from my post coital slumbers. Justin had called to give me a brief run down on my joining instructions which circumstances had forced him to change.

Instead of the original planned six weeks, I'd now agreed to a week's induction at the SIS HQ at Vauxhall Cross followed by an intensive familiarisation week with my handler, based in Belgrade.

Once I was in post, he was to arrange a four week language course that was intended to give me at least some basic understanding but it was stressed that I should become proficient in the Serbian language ASAP.

Events had moved on since our last discussion and he wanted me out in the field as quickly as possible.

Following our successful break up of the Turkish, Russian and British gangs a vacuum had been created and now there was increased activity from the Far East in abducting children and young women and selling them as sex slaves to fill the void.

Elena and I finished off our holiday with a dinner al fresco in the coastal town of Machico. We chose a small local restaurant on the promenade, with good views of the sea.

It was close to the Forte do Amparo which dated from 1708 and which we explored thoroughly to give us a fine appetite, climbing up and down its ancient steps.

We started with the local delicacy, fresh tomato and onion soup served with a poached egg on top then caldeirada which is a fish stew with potatoes, onions and tomatoes to complement the tasty fish.

As we enjoyed the food and the spectacular views, I thought we should get an accurate fix on our real feelings for each other, so we discussed the last two weeks together and the previous months since our momentous meeting in Liverpool.

We knew we'd found something special and dearly wished to develop our relationship. Elena was still a little nervous about my future role as a spook for the British Intelligence Service. She was beginning to come to terms with it, though, as she'd realised that I could look after myself and would have a good back up team to call on.

So, as our holiday ended, we set off back to the UK and she spent a couple of days with me in Leeds until a suitable flight home was available from Manchester to Dubrovnik.

We had established that Belgrade, where I was to be based, was only 300 km from Dubrovnik, where Elena's father had one of his offices, and just a little further to Kotor where they were living, so travel wasn't going to be too difficult for us to reach each other. We made a solemn promise to do that as often as our respective duties allowed.

Driving towards Manchester airport our demeanour was a little sombre as we knew our life was going back to some sort of reality after the blissful enjoyment of our holiday and our time in Leeds together.

Elena had phoned her father to advise him of her travel plans and Milo arranged to collect her from Dubrovnik airport.

After she checked in, we took what would be a last coffee together for some time and, strangely, our mood was lifted somewhat as we planned our next meeting which would be on Elena's home turf.

By then I'd have finished my training and would be a fully fledged field officer and she'd be the proud owner of a law practice.

"Well Miss Borovic, it's time for you to go through passport control."

"OK, Nathan," she stuttered' then put her arms around my neck and whispered in my ear.

"I love you."

With that she was gone and I was left with a warm glow but also with a sadness creeping over me with the realisation that she was leaving me, albeit for a short while.

I drove back to Leeds and pretty quickly packed my case ready to start my new career.

I'd taken the offer Captain Parker had made for his secretary to arrange to rent out my apartment in Leeds.

Whilst the British economy was in a dire strait, this had, paradoxically, helped the rental market. The banks, the main cause of the problem, were looking after their own interests and even professional people with solid credit ratings were struggling to get a mortgage and were turning to the rental market for quality properties like mine.

Sandy took great delight in telling me that Steve Cooper, the ex soldier who had been kicked out by his landlord, had fitted perfectly into Sandy's organisation.

He was a hard worker, dedicated, and took to his new role very quickly. He'd also now settled into a stable home situation so was making his way quite nicely in Civvy street. The SSAFA Caseworker had sorted out Steve's finances and he was now a very happy bunny.

Parker felt that when his engineer retired the following month Steve would be perfect in that role.

Justin sent me a rail warrant so I caught the first train to Kings Cross the next morning which safely delivered me to London precisely on time at 07.53 hours.

My induction in the SIS HQ at Vauxhall Cross was a relatively easy passage. The building was acquired for its present use and then refurbished prior to its official opening by Her Majesty the Queen in April 1994.

Basically I'd crammed into a week the key elements of the intensive programme that all intelligence officers undergo when they join the Secret Intelligence Service.

This, in my case, centred on comprehensive briefing on the Service and key skills required of an operational officer. I would receive more of the training needed on the job with my handler in Belgrade.

Such was the possible threat of further massive organised crime polluting the UK that my recent experiences and my time in the Corps cut through much of the personal development needs. Clearly the terms of engagement in combat were somewhat different to what we followed In the Royal Marines. So The Service recognised that my training needs were procedural as I was fully up to speed on most modern weaponry and was more than a little skilled and experienced in unarmed combat.

A week later I was on the plane to the capital of Serbia and landed at Nikola Tesla Airport, Belgrade, just after 12 noon.

After a lengthy queue at passport control then a frustrating wait for my luggage, I caught the JAT airport shuttle bus and alighted at Slavija Square, right in the heart of this ancient city, whose past was as tumultuous as any in Europe.

I'd received directions on my mobile of how to find the offices where my base would be, only a short walk from the bus terminus, so by around 14.00 hours I was shaking the hand of my new boss.

He was a man with a strong grip and a steely eye who introduced himself in a pronounced Belfast accent as Paddy Ramsden; he looked to be in his mid forties and was dressed in a smart casual way.

The message on my mobile had advised me not to eat on the plane as Paddy would take me out for lunch so we could have a private chat away from the office.

We sat outside, at a quiet table in a pleasant local restaurant, a couple of rows away from the pavement which was busy with people scurrying about their business.

After the attentive waiter had taken our orders Paddy gave me a quick run down on his background. He'd been married for seventeen years, had two kids in their early teens, who were living here with him in Belgrade, along with his wife.

He'd spent a number of years in the army and had then gone under cover in Belfast at the height of the troubles. He'd been wounded twice, once in Northern Ireland by friendly fire, which was deemed necessary so as not to blow his cover.

Then he'd been recruited by the SIS, this posting in Belgrade being his second appointment. The first was UK based but involved breaking up an international gun smuggling ring.

The streets of London and many of our larger cities were being polluted by criminals with no regard for human life and for whom using a gun came as second nature.

Paddy had headed up the unit that was successful in closing down a major smuggling operation producing guns to order in high volumes to both individuals and organised crime gangs.

The supplies were coming in via Amsterdam from Eastern Europe. The ring leaders and their henchmen, twenty in total, were now doing almost two hundred years in high security prisons. So Mr Ramsden got himself a truck load of brownie points for that.

As Paddy got into his stride, I pointed out there were two men seated at opposite ends of the restaurant, each with a clear view of our table, and both were carrying concealed weapons in a shoulder holster and watching us closely.

"Well spotted Nathan, the man in the dark green suit is our wing man. If any two from the office are out together in a public place such as this, we have a shadow as an added security measure.

The eastern European looking guy with the cheap dark glasses is from the Serbian secret service. We have a reasonable relationship with them but have to be a little careful whom we work with.

In reality we've identified a small group of untouchables and only deal with them. The rest like to keep an eye on us most of the time. Unfortunately some of them believe they're still serving under Slobodan Milosevic, so we have to really know who to trust."

I gave him a summary of my service career and my activities since I left the Royal Marines. I saw an interested smile come over his face when I brought him up to speed with the events in Liverpool and since then.

"Yes, the report I got from the Foreign Office said you could look after yourself and had done a great job in closing down the people smuggling operation in Liverpool and also stopped Northern Cyprus becoming a second front for the bastards."

Paddy gave me some background on the major assignment he wanted me to get into as soon as possible. It had been briefly described in the dossier Justin had given me, but now I'd be given a thorough briefing the next day and meet the other field officer on the case.

We finished our lunch and went back to the office where I was kitted out, ID cards, firearms and ammunition, light body armour, night vision equipment, digital camera, a laptop, heavily encrypted and with a level A password protection and a couple of mobile phones.

The first was a safe phone and could be used to call or to take calls from any number, all calls being untraceable. The second was an emergency phone, simply press the red button and the office would triangulate the call and send in armed back up immediately.

Finally keys to my apartment, plus details of its sophisticated security system and a swipe card to get me into the office building.

The office had set me up with a pool car which was to be kept in our secure car park under the building. Apparently my apartment, owned and furnished by the SIS, didn't have its own parking, as it wasn't deemed safe and was only half a mile's walk away from the office. Also the office car park was under armed guard 24/7 so there was no chance of any of the staff cars being interfered with.

As darkness started to fall I was told to go home and get myself settled in. My luggage and some of my kit had already been taken there for me so I left the office via the car park.

I did a first parade maintenance on the car, all seemed to be in order, full tank of diesel, oil and water OK, tyres all seemed fine, and having been pre-warned, I checked under the wheel arch to see that the tracking device was in place. Yes it was.

I exited the car park and turned right to start my short walk to my new home, walking past the series of CCTV cameras my new employers had deployed on the outside of the building.

I walked at a brisk pace and had covered a couple of hundred metres when an oldish car started coming down the street towards me, on my side of the road. About ten metres away from me it stopped by the kerbside and the front door opened; a man jumped out and stood behind the open door, pointing a hand gun in my direction.

A harsh guttural voice shouted out in a heavy Serbian accent.

"Sawyer, put your hands behind your head and get into the back of the car. My boss wants to speak with you about you fucking up his business."

Being a good boy, I did as I was told, put my hands behind my head and walked slowly the last few metres towards the car.

When I was half a metre feet away, in a flash I raised my right leg to my chin and kicked the sole of my shoe, with as much force as I could muster against the middle of the car door.

This had the effect of trapping his neck and his wrist in the car door, which was only prevented from closing completely by his head being banged against the edge of the car roof.

My assailant screamed in agony and the gun fell from his grasp on to the floor. I kicked it away and reached round the car door and dragged him out. His wrist was broken and blood was pouring from his nose.

I glanced at the driver as I pulled my attacker out he gave me a terrified look and slipped the car into drive, put his foot down and screamed off in a cloud of smoke as his tyres struggled to get a grip.

He had gone no more than twenty metres when he screeched to a halt, having spotted the three SIS men standing in the middle of the road. They were pointing their cocked guns in his direction, a few metres behind the stinger that they'd thoughtfully thrown across the road and which had now shredded all four of his tyres. Oh dear.

I dragged laughing boy to his feet and threw him up against the wall, face first, kicking his ankles to spread his legs apart.

Did a quick search and relieved him of a large knife, a second gun and his wallet to look for some ID. My new best friends hauled the other guy to the same wall and cuffed them both, hands behind their backs then made them lie face down. The first guy was still screaming in agony, we ignored him. For good measure though, I kicked him hard in the groin and whispered in his ear.

"Hey you little shit, the girls send their regards."

One of the three helpers was Paddy who smiled and winked at me.

"Welcome back to Serbia, Nathan. Nothing much has changed since you were away!! Job well done and also it shows that our new CCTV system's up to scratch and the screens are being properly monitored."

"What do we do now, boss?"

"We'll take the two of them inside and interrogate them. One of our guys has already called for a medic to look at the one you tangled with; looks like you broke his wrist.

Serves the fucker right if he's involved in smuggling women and children as sex slaves. After a couple of hours we'll call in our contacts in the local outfit and let the Serbs lock them up. We'll also bring in the car for their forensic team to work on. If you can just give me another hour or so, for a statement to the locals, then you can be on your way. It should be pretty easy to get what we want as we have them on CCTV."

Eventually I set off again towards the apartment, this time I reached it without further incident. It looked like my reputation had preceded me so I needed to keep on constant alert in this strange city.

Once I'd unpacked and put all my stuff away I made myself a cup of strong coffee and a cheese omelette then set about looking at the security in my new abode.

It'd been well chosen by the Service as no windows looked on to the street and it was on the 3rd floor so was well away from prying eyes.

All the windows at the rear overlooked a park and had bullet proof glass and steel bars. There was a PIR detector in each room and a camera to the entrance lobby on the street plus a second one guarding the front door to my apartment.

I took off my firearm holster and put the gun on the coffee table in the lounge then picked up my own mobile to ring Captain Parker to give him an update.

Then I had second thoughts, so I quickly put it down in case it was monitored and phoned him on the firm's phone and covered all my bases with him, including my attempted kidnap right outside the office.

He wasn't best pleased with that as clearly my movements were being monitored. He suggested I hand over my mobile to the IT geek in the office and have him check it out for a monitoring device and also check my clothing for miniature bugs.

Call over, I put the phone back on the table and made another coffee, planning to watch a bit of TV before I turned in. I was just musing to myself that yomping outside could turn out to be as eventful as it was inside, in the Royal Marines. As that thought eased its way into my tired brain, my personal mobile rang. It was Elena.

We chatted for half an hour and she brought me up to speed with things at her end. She'd spent the day filling in all the forms to set up her business.

Milo had sorted out an office for her so she ordered the furniture and whatever equipment she needed and basically got on with establishing her law firm.

I opted not to tell her about my fracas outside the office and we agreed to speak every couple of days. Then I turned in, ready to start my life as a spook in morning.

For the next eight weeks I was kept pretty busy. In the evenings I attended language classes and was by now beginning to understand the basics of the Serbian language. Day time was spent reading files, going out on surveillance and getting to know the local crime lords and their operations.

My team member and partner was Andy Blackburn, a thirty three year old graduate in Eastern European studies who'd lived in the region for five years and was pretty good in the local lingo and had a good knowledge of the city.

He was from Newcastle and was as hard as nails. In fact it was he who'd blown the whistle on my predecessor. He suspected for some time the guy was dirty so, quietly collected the evidence then bang, the man was gone. Good, I could get on with this guy and felt we'd make a good team.

Two months into the job I had a full day of surveillance on two Thai nationals who we believed were looking to establish a local operation for their lord and master who was based in Bangkok.

In their homeland the gangs were buying girls as young as thirteen from their families for £150 or so and then putting them in brothels.

Having proved the model worked they were now looking to replicate this in Europe. It was hard keeping watch on someone, you'd to keep your wits about you and make sure you weren't spotted.

Today, however, we'd amassed a great deal of evidence and had been into several different parts of Belgrade watching our quarry make contact with Serbian crime lords. So by the time I got back to the apartment I was really tired and looking for an early night.

I'd just made myself a sandwich when my personal mobile rang, it was Elena.

"Hi, it's me. Nathan, I'm pregnant."

Glossary and Marine's Slang

AWOL	Absent without leave
CPS	Crown Prosecution Service
Divs	An attractive woman
Green Beret	Royal Marine
HMRC	Tax Office
INTEL	Intelligence reports
Meze	Wide range of Turkish starters
NT	National Trust
Outside	Life after leaving the Corps
R&R	Rest and Recuperation
Rupert	Officer
SSAFA	Soldiers Sailors Airmen Family Association
SIS	Secret Intelligence Service
SITREPS	Situation reports
SOCOS	Scene of Crime Officers
Scran bag	Scruffy individual
Scum bag	Worthless individual
Stripey	Sergeant
Yomping	Forced march with heavy load